BEACH READING

BEACH READING

ACORNPRESS

P.O. Box 22024
Charlottetown, Prince Edward Island
C1A 9J2
acornpresscanada.com

Edited by Richard Lemm
Cover and interior illustrations by Timothy Elliott
Designed by Matt Reid
Printed in Canada by Marquis

Library and Archives Canada Cataloguing in Publication

Elliott, Lorne
    Beach reading / Lorne Elliott.

ISBN 978-1-894838-91-7

    I. Title.

PS8609.L5495B42 2013   C813'.6   C2013-901578-7

Library and Archives Canada Cataloguing in Publication

Elliott, Lorne
    Beach reading [electronic resource] / Lorne Elliott.

Electronic monograph.
Issued also in electronic format.
ISBN 978-1-894838-92-4

    I. Title.

PS8609.L5495B42 2013   C813'.6   C2013-901643-0

 Canada Council Conseil des Arts
for the Arts du Canada

The publisher acknowledges the support of the Government of Canada through the Canada Book Fund of the Department of Canadian Heritage and the Canada Council for the Arts Block Grant Program.

LORNE ELLIOTT

ILLUSTRATIONS BY TIMOTHY ELLIOTT

BEACH READING

THE ACORN PRESS
CHARLOTTETOWN
2013

1

My father died when I was seventeen, and I found myself more free than I would ever be again, suddenly cut loose from the expectations of success which he had held for me. He only wanted me to be happy, and to someone like him who in his youth had known poverty, success was a necessary component of happiness. So he'd worked his whole life to achieve goals which, although they afforded me protection, also insulated me from ever really knowing the sacrifices he had made. I must have seemed to him an alien creature, blissfully ignorant of at least one of the wellsprings of his energy, as well as his demons. But he loved me, and I loved him, even though I didn't weep at his funeral.

It was odd. All I felt was that sense of freedom, and an uncertain guilt about whether I should be feeling worse. I wondered if this was shock, or if it was just that I was a cold-hearted bastard, though I guessed it wasn't that, because I *was* deeply moved by what Mom was going through.

From the time Dad died she acted mechanically, dealing with all the details efficiently, holding everything back. Then the undertaker asked her what clothes she would like him to be wearing in the coffin and without thinking she said, "He likes that blue tie...," then corrected herself. "... Liked," she said, and with that change of tense a string snapped inside her, and she crumpled visibly and sobbed. "I'll be all right," she kept saying, "I'll be all right," not wanting her family to be put out. She looked older than I ever remembered.

A friend of hers took charge, and from then on things were arranged by others. Food was prepared, hushed conferences were held, rituals were observed, and a few days later, in what was undoubtedly a good-hearted attempt to make things easier for everybody, somebody got me a job.

It might have been meant more as a gift for my mom. Although she would never have even thought it, her friends may have sensed that, particularly now, I was perhaps becoming a bit of a burden. Six months before I'd flunked out of my first year of university at Christmas on account of not having done a damn thing the whole time I was there, wandering around the campus with my hands in my pockets and my head in the clouds. I had all the time in the world, so I wasted it. A previous tenant of the dorm had left behind a banjolele which I carried around with me or strummed while sitting in the corner of the Student Union building. No passing girls swooned. In the few classes I attended, the pall of boredom settled on my shoulders like chalk dust. Finally I simply neglected to go at all.

I think that I got away with a lot because of my strangeness. People who would have otherwise demanded that I smarten up tended to give up on the idea once they saw me in person. My dress consisted of plaid pants, a pyjama shirt and a tuxedo vest and when it was cold I would don orange overalls, virtually identical to prison wear, which explained my lack of success when I tried hitch-hiking. For footwear

I went through flip-flops, Chinese slippers, construction boots and tennis shoes before I finally settled on a pair of my father's brogues, which fit perfectly when worn without socks.

Nobody knew quite what to do with me, but because I seemed harmless they let me be. It had been the same at home. Born at the tail end of a large family, by the time they got to me my parents had become tired with meting out any real discipline. It wasn't the worst way to grow up: it all depends on the personalities involved. Now, at the age of fifty-eight, I see how lucky I had been.

I didn't feel lucky then, though, after the funeral, with a job that I didn't really want. Apart from everything else, it would interrupt my development as a banjolelist.

Near the end of July my mother saw me off at the train like she was sending a four-year-old into heavy traffic. I rode into Windsor Station where I caught the overnight connection to Moncton, then took a bus to the ferry at Cape Tormentine, crossed Northumberland Strait in the rain, and remounted the bus on the other side to ride through countryside sharp and green, with wrecked cars in farm yards and wet soil the colour of liver. Work began in two days and I had three hundred dollars to last me to my first pay-cheque. I had turned eighteen a week before and I felt as free as oxygen.

In Charlottetown I walked from the bus station down to the waterfront by the oil tanks, past three scowling men who stood deep in conversation, then stopped talking as I came near. Low secrets, I supposed, about unions and management, power and corruption, who was doing what to whom and how to get even. One of the personae I was quite willing to act out was of a revolutionary and friend of the working man, although that might have been hard to pull off if I kept using words like "personae." I might also have found it difficult to adopt with any sincerity their attitude that the world sucked. On the other hand I wasn't looking forward to my job, so maybe there was still hope for me. As I walked I practiced saying to myself, "I hate this goddamn job" and "This goddamn job sucks." I found if I spat that it helped with my characterization.

I picked up this year's tide charts at the Coast Guard Station, then walked up Queen Street and around town, passing government buildings, boarding houses and private homes, a plywood taxi-stand and a dance studio, an upstairs tae-kwon-do gym and a pool hall. There was no sense to any of it. The architecture was either nondescript or beat-up. The Department of Ugliness had apparently passed a mandate that all new buildings would be hard to look at, while the old ones continued to rot. A poster at the Arts Centre showed *Anne Of Green Gables* brimming over with unbridled phony ecstasy in a suspiciously pristine landscape, but it didn't represent anything I'd seen here so far and so could probably not help me with any real information. Rather it was meant to manipulate my emotions and sell me something, so as a result I felt no need to see the show. Instead I walked along Grafton and into a slummier area, where things looked more hard up. A woman leaned out of a second story wooden balcony and said exactly this: "Eugene? Get the fuck in here right now Eugene! Are you listening? I don't want any fucking problems with you, you little fucker. Now! I said *Now*! Fuck!" Then she added, "And don't swear." She probably wouldn't be auditioning for the role of Anne.

I saw a junk shop on a corner and went in. It was chock-a-block full of what nowadays would be sold in trendy retro shops, but back then was just crap. There was a broken washing machine, a broken porcelain lamp and a broken blender. A sign on the wall said, "If You Break It, You Buy It". But how could they tell?

A radio wrapped in scotch tape sat on a shelf, and from it a voice was singing over a jangly guitar, "Crimson effervescent stardust, universal rainbows of your mind..." I looked towards the back of the shop and saw a massively obese man sitting in a chair beside the counter. He lifted his eyes at me heavily as I approached, and sighed with the very thought of having to deal with someone. I asked how much for the bike leaning against the wall, and he said it was his nephew's and wasn't for sale. He added that he had another out back, then immediately regretted that he'd said that.

"Could I see it?" I asked.

"Are you gonna buy it?"

"I'd have to see it first."

He'd been afraid of that. He sighed again mightily and looked at me like I had ruined his week. He grunted and wriggled forward to the front of his seat with roughly the same effort as it takes to push a mountain up from the earth's crust. Leaning forward as far as he could go, he grabbed the corner of the counter, pulled and straightened, found the tipping point and rocked onto his feet. He looked at me accusingly and tilted his weight till one foot reflexed forward, then the other, and he was walking, negotiating the narrow path between a rusted metal cooler and a push lawnmower.

I started to say, "I can help you with that..." and made like I was coming around, but he held up his hand like a traffic cop and said, "Stay on your side of the counter please," and left through the back door. I waited, looked around and read some of the advertisements taped to the front of the counter. I heard swearing in the yard and noises like a combine harvester being demolished by a gang of navvies.

As though in counterpoint, the radio was now playing the heartfelt song of a young swain who, having spent the night with a woman, was explaining to her how he was the wandrin' ramblin' kind of guy who couldn't be tied down, that the open road was a-callin' and that there were just too many other women out there for him to love. It must've made her feel great. The song came to an end, and the DJ said that next up was The Barley Boys, who would be playing at the Towers Mall tomorrow night. It reminded me of something, I didn't know what, but then my eye fell on the front of the counter again where, sure enough, an 8x10 black and white handbill advertised the date and time of their show. It was printed over the xeroxed photograph of the boys themselves standing in the rain in front of what looked like the wall of the prison they had just been released from, a group mug shot, all three of them furtively looking from under their brows, large, bearded, Irish and scowly. In direct contrast to the *Anne of Green Gables* poster, they gave the impression that they didn't care whether you showed up or not. No phoney ecstasy here. Life was grim, and human beings were mainly bastards. I wondered what their show was like.

And, as though to inform me, from the radio they started into a song in jig-time, a high-speed ballad with harmonies. It was rough-edged and rowdy, but during the instrumental break the guitar was taken over by the banjo and suddenly there was something new in the world, fluid and mercurial, intricate and heavenly...

From out back came a particularly long drawn orchestration of swearing, gasping and industrial percussion, like tin sheds being ripped apart as wild boar were slowly slaughtered. The shopkeeper appeared at the back door, glaring murderously at me and drenched in sweat. He wrestled the bicycle in, then wheeled it forward. "There," he said. "You gonna buy it or what?"

It was a faded pink CCM. I took it from him, rolled the chain back onto the sprocket and spun the front wheel. It seemed true. I squeezed the tires. They were taut. But...

"It's a girl's bike," I said.

"So?" he glowered. I'd better not push it.

"How much?"

"Two hundred bucks," he said.

He had to be kidding. "I was only planning to spend five," I said without thinking.

He sighed, then sat down heavily and felt for his pack of cigarettes. "OK," he said. I thought of asking for a receipt but that would have been too cruel.

Outside the shop I hummed that banjo solo I'd heard on the radio and strapped my small pack and banjolele onto the frame behind the bicycle seat. I hopped on and started pedaling towards the North Shore.

I stopped at a gas station and picked up a road-map of the Island, looked where I wanted to go, and saw how I could do that and how long it would take, about six hours, I figured. University Avenue looked hot, so I took a side road through leafy streets with small neat family houses on quarter-acre town lots, toward Brackley Beach Road. One pedal on the bike jerked a bit with every revolution, but I didn't mind: it was a beautiful day. I came out onto a street with welding shops and garages, crossed a railway track and pedaled up a hill halfway, walked the bike to the top and coasted down the other side. A breeze was blowing from the south behind me, and no dogs ran out and chased me. I walked the bike up another long hill to the airport, and looked back at Charlottetown below, church steeples like inverted carpet tacks, the Hillsborough River at full tide under perfect clouds like a Dutch painting.

Past the airport I took a road to the right, until it bent around to the north again and I was biking through farm country, red lines of soil between potato rows, and three shades of green on the fields: pale oats, dark corn, and silvery barley which the wind brushed back like a cat licking its fur.

Since I had heard that banjo lick at the junk shop I must've been turning it over in my subconscious, because I suddenly realized how I could break up a chord to create that sound. I stopped beside the road, unstrapped the banjolele off the rack, tuned it differently and rolled my fingers across the strings. I placed my left hand in different positions until I could play a repeating major scale, an uncomfortable stretch for my little finger, but pleasant to my ear. When I moved the second note in the chord down a half tone, running my fingers over the strings produced the first few bars of "*La fille aux cheveux de lin*" by Claude Debussy. I re-packed the banjolele and hopped back onto the bike. Coasting down the hill I thought how I could play the rest of that piece, and, distracted, I almost drove into the ditch.

I came over another hill and saw the ocean off the North Shore, cobalt blue against the red soil in front, the colours vibrating against each other, and I turned east and biked along back roads, some of them red dirt, some paved, finally crossing into King's County. A merlin left his perch on the single telephone wire, performed a little circuit of flashy flying, and returned back to his perch behind me after I passed. I crossed another railway track, my bum a bit sore from the seat already, but I didn't care. Two turtle doves looked at me from the wire. They'd better watch it or that merlin would get them. One time I heard heat bugs trill then go silent as I passed and at the bottom of a hill three geezers with trout gear stood on a bridge and smiled at me and said hello. And so, all that summer day, I bicycled the back roads of Prince Edward Island, heading for the North Shore.

***

Near my destination I came to a T in the road with a potato stand that operated on the honour system: take potatoes, leave the money. I left the suggested amount and took a five pound bag, strapped it on top of my packsack and coasted down a hill and past a sea-marsh to come out through a spruce wood where the dunes started. A park gate stood beside a newly built park office where I was due to report the day after tomorrow. There was an advertised fee to enter the park, but nobody was around so I continued straight through. This was different than the potato stand, this was government, and for a moment I imagined myself again in the role of a revolutionary.

I turned left behind the dunes with the sea sounding out of sight, and the bike suddenly swerved as I pedalled over a tongue of sand which had drifted across the pavement. I came down onto a natural causeway with a shallow bay on my left, and now I could feel the breeze strengthening into a steady wind. The sky was bluer than anything I'd ever seen and a great blue heron flew across it with his legs dragging behind. Double-crested cormorants were grouped on a sandbar, noses in the air pointing windward, one ring-billed gull just off to its side, an alien. And over on the right on a dead spruce was an immature bald eagle. White-throated sparrows flitted about in the spruce trees. Ipswich sparrows were also a possibility here.

I knew about birds because when I was twelve my father, seeing my interest in this direction, had given me *A Field Guide To The Birds*, which I picked up and didn't put down again for a month. It was printed on heavy duty waterproof stock and designed to survive arduous expeditions to remote parts of the globe, but by the end of the summer my copy was worn out. If you had a bird identification question I was the guy in the family you went to.

All of my siblings had attempted at some point in their youth to become experts in one thing or another. I thought all families acted this way. Around the dinner table my father would instigate debates on everything from the Warsaw Uprising to *The Bhagavad Gita,* then sit back and watch as impossible positions were defended vigorously on subjects we initially knew very little about, but by this very process would soon become familiar with. Books were hauled out and consulted, arguments adopted and adapted. If it was an escape, I think it was a healthy one. It encouraged a curiosity about the world outside ourselves.

Here for instance, by a path which led across a low spot in the dunes I recognized Wild carrot, also called Queen Anne's Lace after Anne of Denmark. I don't even remember how I had learned this, but I must have taken it in with everything else from the family, by osmosis.

I stopped the bike and, partly pushing, partly carrying it along with my packsack, banjolele and the sack of potatoes, I walked over and down through the marram grass, around the side of a quarter-acre field of driftwood, then onto a sand beach, rock-strewn, with waves lapping on the shore. It was empty and beautiful.

I was hot and sweaty from pedaling, so I took off everything but the swim shorts I wore under my pants and walked down to the ocean. The smell of salt air made me feel about fifty percent more alive. I watched two sanderlings chase the lip of the waves like kids near cold water. You could almost hear them say eek! as they narrowly escaped another drenching, then on some sudden signal they took off together and flew shakily around the point to the west. What were they eating which only existed that close to the wave edge?

A wave washed over my ankles and back again, dragging the sand from under my feet. I stepped in further. It was almost too cold, but the longer I stayed the more lovely it felt. I walked out up to my knees and stopped. There were a few jellyfish floating around which I avoided and walked out further, to my waist, stopped again, and turned. If I pointed my face just right I could hear the wind equally in both ears, and knew I was facing right into it. I washed my body with sea water, then to get it over with, crossed my arms over my nipples and fell backwards into the sea, dunking my head and immediately resurfacing.

A new man.

Or only a boy, really. I remembered, for the twelve-hundredth time that day, that I had never been with a woman, and I contemplated this woeful truth as I floated there, bobbing in the waves which made little slapping noises around my ears.

Perhaps my lack of success in this area was one result of my unusual upbringing, or some innate strangeness I'd been born with. Undoubtedly I had been a very odd child. When I was nine, for instance, I latched onto the belief that my parents were not really mine, but that my real parents were these incredibly wealthy and cool people who had loaned me to "Dad" and "Mom" to make sure that I wouldn't grow up spoiled. By the time I was eleven it occurred to me that if I was right, my real parents had better show up quick. They didn't, so I was forced to accept the obvious: that I was the heir to the throne of a foreign country, switched in the cradle to protect me from a rebel group who was trying to overthrow my real parents' kingdom, and awaiting my triumphant return to assume my place as their legitimate monarch. No letters to any existing royalty exploring my suspicions were ever answered, and Mom, when she heard about it, took me aside for a talk.

"I don't remember you being switched, Christian," she told me. "And anyhow, you've always behaved like one of us."

"How can you say that?"

"Every one of you children, at one time or another, has thought they weren't ours."

"No way!"

"Afraid so. And I must say, it's very complimentary."

"You're saying that we might be related?"

"There's a slim chance, as repugnant as that might seem."

"Are you secretly wealthy and cool?"

"Not terrifically wealthy. I like to think I'm pretty cool."

"You're not royalty by any chance?"

"Sometimes I'd like to believe that."

"Why don't you?"

She thought for a bit, then answered. "Because it's un-*likely*. Or at least, not as likely as the idea that we are all here, on this earth, as we are, now."

The way she said it, irrefutable, shook the foundations of my universe. This was serious. It was all real, it was all happening now, and, with the implication that it would not last forever, it was all a bit terrifying. That night I had nightmares where it was up to me, child genius, to find The Cure for Death.

"I think you should spend some time with Christian," I heard Mom say to Dad next morning. So, when next he had time off work, that's how we ended up taking a trip together to L'Isle-aux-Coudres, where he used to go when he was a boy. We pitched two tents and camped under spruce by the sea. It rained that night, and at first I didn't quite know what I was supposed to be doing there. Then, with his work behind him, Dad loosened up, and I guess so did I. We played chess, and at first he just went through the motions, making the effort to stay engaged. He used a sober and conservative attack strategy while I harried his flanks with my cavalry, and imagined bold and artistic flashes of military brilliance. When he castled, I accused him of making up rules, and later, since he was apparently allowed to do that, I suggested that under certain conditions my bishop could move across the squares and not just diagonally. He challenged this, finally allowed it, and then added that in that case, he could jump with his queen, and also enlist the men he had captured as turncoat mercenaries. We played a few times more, with the rules becoming steadily more fun until the game finally fell apart by the sheer weight of its own complexity.

The first clear night he pointed out the stars to me. There was the big dipper, upside down so that it would be spilling down its handle, and on the other side of the North Star, Cassiopeia.

"You won't be able to see Orion, this time of year," said Dad. And he told me about the Hunter and the Dog Star, the hunter's dog, at his heels.

"What's he hunting?"

"Taurus the Bull and Aries the Ram."

"Pretty easy hunting. Farm Animals."

We picked berries and he showed me some edible plants. We tried fishing but caught nothing. We rented a boat and he let me row, the tide pulling us down river then back again as he explained it to me. He said it would be at its highest on the night of a full moon. Something bothered me about that, and a day later I asked him about it.

"It's not any more 'full' than when it's a half-moon," I said.

"There's no more *moon*, just more light on it. So why is the tide higher?"

"You've been thinking," he said. "That's dangerous."

"Come on. Tell me."

"What are the gravitational conditions that would make the tide higher?"

"More mass."

"And..?"

"If it's closer?"

"Proximity. Yes. Also?"

"Also nothing."

"Don't get frustrated. So..?"

"I dunno."

"Maybe it's not just the moon that's creating the tides."

"What? The sun?"

"And the other planets and stars, to a very minor extent. But apart from the moon, yes, mainly the sun."

"So then...?"

"Figure it out yourself. You can do it."

I placed rocks on the sand in different configurations of the earth, moon and the sun. I figured it out.

At the end of a week, we went back to Montreal. I fell asleep south of Quebec City, and woke up as we were entering our driveway. But though I couldn't articulate it then, I had made a discovery: The cure for not going camping with your father and boating and stargazing and making up rules for chess and figuring out how the tides worked, was to do all those things. The cure for death is life.

***

Back on the beach on Prince Edward Island, I got out of the water and walked back to my belongings. All fatigue was completely washed away, but I was hungry now, so I took a potato out of the bag, washed it in the surf, scrubbed it on a red rock and ate it like an apple. It was tastier than you'd think. On a day like that, boiled cotton would be tasty.

I saw a gannet pumping along the coast and, over the dunes, Bonaparte gulls with their military bearing and hangman's hoods. Maybe this goddamned job was not going to entirely suck. I spread out my poncho, sat down, took out my notebook and listed the birds I'd seen in the park so far. Besides the ones I'd spotted while riding my bike I wrote, "crows, black-bellied plover, semi-palmated sand-pipers, kingfisher, osprey, and sanderlings." Next to this last entry I made a note: "What are the sanderlings eating?"

The tide slipped notch by notch down the foreshore. The sun sank and reddened. The air turned cooler and I stood up and walked the quarter-mile up the beach and back, then picked a place near where I'd swum to pitch my pup tent. Because the sand wouldn't hold the pegs, I tied the guy lines to large pieces of driftwood which I dragged from the quarter-acre field in the dunes. That would also provide my firewood, but I'd have to carry in drinking water.

The wind was veering toward the town of Barrisway, which I could just see across the inlet, past the end of the point to the west. I took my binoculars and looked at a fishing boat returning to harbour. I crawled into the tent, ate another potato, and examined my thoughts to see whether I was ready to feel sad about my father. I felt a sudden twinge when it occurred to me that he would never have begrudged me for how happy I was feeling.

2

The next day, I woke up to the sound of a long swell on a smooth sea that rose and fell like something breathing, under an unruffled surface. It snapped and thudded on the shore, then a long wait till the next one. The sky was overcast, but the clouds were breaking up to the north and the wind had veered a few points towards Newfoundland.

I crawled out of the tent and waded into the ocean, swam for a while, dried myself with my shirt, and crawled back into my tent. I pulled out my banjolele, tuned up, and went over my new scales in G, D and C.

"Anybody in there?" said a voice outside, and I poked my head out the tent flap. A big girl in a red checked shirt too small for her was standing beside a twelve-year-old boy wearing the same make and size of shirt, but for him too big.

"Hello," I said.

"You owe us money," said the girl.

"What?"

"You're camped on our land, so you owe us money." She sighed like she was saying it solely out of a sense of duty.

"Oh."

"Yeah. Twenty bucks." She sighed again. "We're suppose to kick anybody off our land unless they pay us. And we *do* need the money, so I kinda see the point, but I told Wallace already there's probably a more civilized way than just, like, demanding cash from strangers. I mean, God, what are we, highwaymen? But when I tell him that he just starts singing some song he knows about 'The Bold Deceiver.' So like I say, we *could* use some cash and you *did* sleep here, so if you got thirty bucks..."

"You said twenty."

"No I didn't." Her eyes darted around and her mask of authority, anyway not too firmly affixed, slipped a bit further.

"Yes you did. Twenty bucks."

"OK. Twenty bucks, then. Or we have to steal your stuff. At least that's what Wallace told me." But she seemed less and less committed.

I was sitting in the doorway of the tent now and I hadn't let go of my banjolele.

"Not a lot to steal," I said.

"There's your bike," she suggested, but with almost no conviction now. She peered at it more closely, then at me. "You a *girl*?"

"No."

"It's a girl's bike."

"I know. But it works."

She was looking at me with more interest.

The boy started to say something. "D-d-d-d......"

"Go ahead, Brucie," she said, looking at me like I'd better not make fun of him.

"D-d-d-do you play that thing?"

"Not really," I said, ignoring the stutter, and seeing out of the corner of my eye the big girl relax slightly. I put my fingers into position and did a G scale three times, then a transition into the relative minor, resolving on the highest note of the D. I looked up and they were looking at me wide-eyed, like I was an angel. "Do that again," said the girl. So I did, with a little fillip in the middle.

"Let me try," said the little guy with the stutter, and I held it out to him. It briefly occurred to me that that might be the last time I saw my banjolele, but I didn't think so. They were music lovers.

He strummed the open chord and started to sing.

"Like seeds in spring, beneath the snows, Love stirs deep in my heart..."

And right through the whole song without a stutter. He strummed only the open chord, but I could hear in my head the accompaniment as he sang, a cycle of three chords, fifth, relative minor and a first. He had a beautiful singing voice, and the song itself was heartbreaking. Women were the only thing worth living for, it said, and as he sang he acted the part of somebody who believed just that, helpless in their presence.

He finished the song and the big girl applauded. "Good job, Brucie." Then to me: "He's good with music."

"Want a potato?" I asked. We'd forgotten about the money. I dragged the bag out and we sat on the beach together in the beautiful morning.

"How long you been playing?" said the girl.

"A couple of months."

"You s-s-sound good."

"You too."

The girl's name was Roberta, or Robbie. "We were both named after Robert the Bruce," she told me.

"Who's that?" I said.

"Robert the Bruce. You know, and the spider?"

"Sorry."

She looked at me in growing disbelief. "You never heard of Robert the Bruce?"

"No."

She kept looking at me like I hadn't heard about the existence of gravity. "We'll get Wallace to tell you." She jumped to her feet. "Come on..." she said. "And bring that banjo thing."

They started walking away and I followed them down the beach and up onto the land. The path went around a pile of driftwood like broken statues, then past wild rose and bayberry and into the spruce forest, plastered by the wind on the seaward side into a thick mat, but once behind, a protected grove, reddish brown and dappled. We came out by the side of a sea-pond with water the colour of whisky and we rounded the end where there were more wild rose bushes and labrador tea. We walked around the back of a dune, down through another smaller spruce wood, and into a clearing where there was a farmhouse and a barn. Scattered about the yard were junked cars overgrown with weeds, and in the middle of the lawn an old spindly tractor. The remains of what once was a dock stuck out from the shore and a small heavy skiff lay half-sunk by the water's edge.

The house, with its porch that went right around, was well-built but had seen better days, and a blue plastic tarp covered part of the roof, inexpertly tacked on with nailed planks. In the yard was a big linden, a row of balm-of-Gilead trees lining the dirt road in, and behind, the dune which had ringed this side of the sea-pond was moving in and had half-buried some of the spruce. Soon it would be engulfing the porch where it wrapped around the back of the house, but it was happening so slowly that marram grass had taken root on the crest.

Just as we came around the front the screen door exploded open and a large man burst out. "Robbie! Brucie! You!.." He stopped, looked at me and then remembered he had things to do and did not want to be distracted. "...Whoever the hell you are. Get over here. We gotta move that tractor into the barn. Get the damn thing outta sight once and for all. And put something overtop of that oil patch, or cut the grass. No! Damn! The mower doesn't work. Scythe! That's it, there's a scythe in the shed. Shit! No, its handle's broken. But we had a what-do-you-call it? Swipe, there's a *swipe*. Where the fuck did I put that? Robbie, you see that swipe? Brucie? No? You? Whoever the hell you are... Who the hell are you anyway?"

"He was camping on the beach," said Robbie. "I wanted to charge him for it like you said we should, though I still think that's horseshit, but he played a song, then said he didn't know who Robert the Bruce was so I said you'd tell him."

"You don't know who Robert the Bruce is?" he said. He looked as astounded as they had. All other plans could wait. This was a problem that demanded immediate attention.

"Or the s-s-spider," said Brucie.

"Jesus Christ," he snorted, with disbelief that anyone should be so uneducated.

"So, who was he?"

"Robert the Bruce was one of the ancient Kings of Scotland."

"A-a-actually only a g-g-g-general."

"Yeah well that's the way *you* tell it."

"H-h-h-he was!"

"OK! General, then. Doesn't make a difference. The point

is, he was sitting in a cave after a battle, all bloody and scarred. Some English bastard had stabbed him from behind, and he had already killed about a thousand of those sons-of-bitches, so he was bleeding, and his ear was ripped off nearly, and he sewed it back on with twine. Must've hurt like a bastard. So he's lying there, bleeding, wounded, his whole army wiped out..."

"He r-r-ran away."

"He didn't run *away*, Brucie. Christ! He was hit over the head."

"From behind."

"Right. From behind. Which was against all the rules of war in Bannockburn or Glencoe, or wherever the fuck it was. Doesn't matter. Point is, he was feeling pretty out of it. And he was lying there."

"Wounded."

"Pouring blood. One eye all swole up."

"V-v-vomiting. "

"What?"

"You said they'd p-poisoned him."

"Who said?"

"You said. Last t-t-time."

"Oh yeah. They'd poisoned him, that's right, that's why he was wounded in the first place. They'd invited him over to a dinner the night before the battle, I remember now, and there were all these hoity-toity stick-out-your-little-pinky tea-drinking English bastards sitting around, and he only went over because though he was their sworn enemy, he was a trusting Catholic soul who always believed that his enemies had a chance at mending their ways, but they poisoned him, thinking, 'He'll be dead now for sure.' But he had a noble constitution..."

"And he drank oil."

"What? Oh yeah. Although he was a trusting soul he still suspected those English pricks were up to no good, so he took the precaution, the *wise* precaution when you're dealing with backstabbing pricks like the English, to drink some olive oil before, which coats the inside of your stomach so you can't be poisoned. And they were all "how come he didn't die? He must be superhuman, some sort of a God," as he marched away straight as an arrow after the truce, but it didn't completely stop the poison from working and that's why next day when they ambushed him he didn't just wipe them out entirely, 'cause he was feeling poorly 'cause of the poison."

"Where'd he get the olive oil?" said Robbie.

"G-g-good point."

"What?"

"The olive oil. It's like thirteenth century Scotland. Lot of olive groves around, were there?"

"Look, Scotland in the middle ages was the most civilized place on earth. They had universities when the rest of Europe were living in mud huts."

"And the sun was in a different place in the sky?"

"What are you talking about?"

"Well, olive trees don't grow farther north than the Mediterranean."

"So what? They traded for it."

"From where?"

"Italy or France or wherever the fuck they make olive oil."

"Thought you said they were living in mud huts there."

"Mud huts with olive trees outside, then!"

"Just trying to get the facts straight."

"*Facts!*" Wallace snorted. "Where was I, Brucie?"

"He was w-w-wounded."

"Yeah, 'cause he'd been poisoned. Otherwise they could

never a-laid a hand on him."

"Though he did p-p-pretty good though."

"Well, yeah, he did pretty *good*, no doubt about that. I mean, Robert the Bruce, even half-poisoned with a dose that would leave the average man writhing around on the ground or dead, could still kick the bejeezus out of anything they could bring onto the field of battle, let me tell you..."

"The cave," reminded Robbie.

"Right! Anyhow, the cave. So he's lying there, and a spider's making a web and he figures, if that spider can do that, I can beat the British, so he got better and he did. Now where's that fucking lawn mower?"

"That's not how it goes," said Robbie.

"Look. You telling the story or am I?"

"Well, tell it right."

"It's my story."

"No it's not. Dad used to tell it."

"Well, *you* tell it, then."

"The spider. That's the important part. He was watching the spider make a web. And he'd been beaten six times."

"Robert the Bruce?" said Wallace.

"Yeah. But then he watched the spider make his web *seven* times."

"Why would he do that?" said Wallace.

"I dunno!" said Robbie. "Because he had fuck-all else to do."

"Robert the Bruce had fuck-all else to do? How about saving Scotland from the English?" said Wallace.

"Yeah, but he was wounded, after he lost six times..."

"Not *my* Robert the Bruce."

"Yes your Robert the Bruce. That's the way you used to tell it!"

"Well....how the hell am I supposed to remember what I

tell you? And who gives a shit? The point is he rallied and beat the crap out of the English. Got it, Whoever-The-Hell-You-Are?"

I nodded.

"OK. *Now* can we cut the grass and move the tractor?

"You said the l-l-lawn mower was broken."

"It is."

"And you also said the t-tractor won't start."

"It won't ."

"So how we g-gonna move it?"

"Push it." We followed Wallace over to the tractor. "Get behind, there. And Brucie, get up in the seat."

"How come he gets to drive?"

"You're too heavy to push."

"Well, what about you?" said Robbie. "You're no sylph."

"What's a 'Silf'?"

"A skinny little scrawny fuck."

"Don't swear. OK. Now, Whoever-The-Hell-You-Are get behind here. One, two... and *push*." We heaved. Nothing happened. "Is it out of gear, Brucie?"

Brucie rattled the gear shift in neutral. "Yeah."

"Is the brake on?"

"I g-g-guess."

"Well take the brake *off*."

"H-h-how?"

"One of those foot pedals."

"Which one?"

"I dunno. Just start kicking things."

Brucie stood up on the tractor and stepped on pedals until the tractor unclenched and rocked.

"There! OK. Ready? One. Two. *HEAVE*!" And we pushed and the tractor moved. Wallace grabbed the tread of the wheel and leant into it, and the tractor proceeded across the yard with Brucie steering, and when it was rolling, Robbie ran ahead and opened the barn door, and we rolled it right inside, where it was quiet and strange and the light came through the gaps in the boards and streaked everybody like zebras.

"Right," Wallace announced. "Lunch!"

We traipsed back out and across the yard to the house, onto the porch and through a door on the side to enter the kitchen.

The house was built on Rural Canadian pre-electricity standards, and the kitchen had a table and big shelves, a huge woodstove, an electric stove as well, and beat-up linoleum on a sagging floor.

Over near the corner where a lawnmower was stripped down and lying about in parts something rustled in the walls and the fridge was humming with a dangerous electrical sound. Wallace flung open its door to reveal not very much.

"No bread, no milk, no eggs," he listed. "What's this? Cheese Whiz?" He opened the jar and sniffed. "Smells OK, and...What else?.... Oreos. That'll have to do." He threw the package of cookies onto the table. I ate one. The filling tasted like chemically sweetened paper and the chocolate biscuit was like sugar and soot.

"OK," said Wallace when he'd finished. "I'm going to Barrisway to get some nails. You, Robbie?"

"I gotta read up on something."

"Brucie?"

"N-nothing."

"O.K. Then I suppose I'll have to buy something for supper. You want supper, Whoever-The-Hell-You-Are?"

"Sure," I said. "I can bring some potatoes."

Wallace looked at me. "Oh good. They're hard to find on

PEI."

"That was pretty sarcastic," said Robbie.

"It was supposed to be funny." And because Robbie was still looking at him accusingly he added, "What? I'm inviting him to supper."

"Yeah, and all he's got to do is bring his own food, and oh yeah, food for us. What does he get out of it?"

Wallace looked around at the sagging floor, the worn linoleum, and the rodent-infested walls. "Atmosphere," he said.

"That's OK," I said. "I'll go get what I got."

"And you can stay here overnight if you want," said Robbie.

If this was the kitchen, I thought, the upstairs was probably not spotless. I thought of my fresh bed in my tent, aired by sea breezes. "That's OK. I'm set up pretty good on the beach."

"Suit yourself."

We walked out onto the porch. Down by the remains of the dock, the twinkling inlet had swollen up on the shore. A quarter moon stood in the daytime sky.

"High tide," said Wallace, taking a deep breath and drumming his fingers on his chest.

Shit, I thought. "Shit," I said.

"What?"

"I gotta get back..." I leapt off the porch and ran around the corner of the house.

"Where's he going so fast...?" I heard Wallace say as I scrambled over the dune and sprinted down the path. I ran around the sea-pond and through the spruce wood and jogged out onto the beach and toward my tent.

The tide hadn't swamped it yet, but it was a near thing. I dragged everything above where a line of eel grass marked high water. It wouldn't have been disastrous, even if the tide had washed everything away. I could always warm some stones in a fire and sleep on them or wrap myself in kelp and let the mermaids sing me to sleep. Anything was possible on a day like today.

I ate a potato to take the lingering taste of Oreo out of my mouth, and went back to the path to MacAkerns' where I'd seen a raspberry patch which I ate my way through. When I'd had enough for myself, I went to the shore and found a plastic bottle bumping in the waves and with my penknife sawed off the heel for a berry basket, then went back and filled it. I didn't know how long the season would last and thought I'd better pick as many as possible while I still could.

Then, walking back to camp, I saw under the spruce a small patch of chanterelle mushrooms, picked them all then saw another patch a few feet away. One patch led to another. A squirrel sat on a limb and chattered at me, calling me names at high volume and velocity until I walked off. I went back to the beach, left the food in the tent, then walked to the road and picked some thyme. I could also make raspberry leaf tea, or labrador tea. I could try for trout where I had seen the geezers by the bridge, and over by the rocks, if I dove down, I might find lobster or crab. I went for a walk up the beach in the other direction to see what else I could forage.

The dunes to the east cut up sharply above jumbled piles of flat red rock like terracotta, but in one spot the cliff had eroded under and toppled a weathered spruce, its roots in the air, making a ladder which I scaled. I dropped over the lip into a bowl of marram grass, and the sound of the sea passed over my head in the wind. I walked out of this bowl around a small dried marsh, and stopped when I saw a rabbit crouched motionless ten yards ahead of me. He waited, then hopped tentatively toward the undergrowth, took three quick zig-zag hops and disappeared. I could always snare rabbits too, I thought, but I didn't know if I'd like to do that. I didn't have any qualms about killing fish, which was odd, come to think of it.

In the distance somebody was honking a horn.

I had to remember, though, that not everything was edible here. Growing around the driftwood there was a beach pea which looked delicious but contained a neuro-toxin, and I must never mistake wild carrot for wild parsley, the same plant as the hemlock used to poison Socrates.

The honking in the distance became more insistent.

I looked up and saw a truck parked on the road and standing beside the truck was a man in a brown uniform looking right at me. I couldn't make out his face, but even at this distance, I could see his whole body scowling. I heard him yell something like "Get over here," I guessed, judging from the way he pointed at me then jabbed at the ground at his feet. I could easily have dodged away and escaped back in the direction I'd come from, but I'd never felt more innocent in my life. And his anger was reaching out across the beautiful day and made me want to retaliate. Why should I be bullied? What had *I* done wrong?

So, innocent no more, I purposely took my time picking my way towards him, which made him angrier. He was so concerned with glaring at me that he didn't notice Brucie, a hundred yards behind him, wandering up the road towards us. The man stomped, put his hands on his hips and glowered, reminding me of the squirrel. As I got closer, he started nodding his head faster and when I was within earshot I could see his red face and a vein in his forehead pulsing. What *was* his problem?

"Do you have a permit?"

"No."

"Well, you need one."

"What for?"

"To walk in the dunes."

Brucie arrived. "Hi, C-C-Christian," he said to me.

"Hi," I said.

The man in uniform looked at Brucie. "Well, if it isn't the MacAkern brat." Then he turned back to me. "C-C-Christian is it? Is that your name?"

"Hi, R-R-Rattray," said Brucie.

"My name's not R-R-Ratrray. It's Rattray."

"Sorry R-R-Rat-face."

"You mean Ratface."

"So you admit that's your name?" snapped back Brucie without a hint of a stutter, looking right at him.

Rattray's face dropped. "I don't admit anything. I don't have to. *I'm* in charge here, and I was just arresting your friend for walking in the dunes without a permit."

But I didn't like the way he'd mocked Robbie's stutter. "Where does it say I need a permit to walk in the dunes?"

"Never you mind where it says. You just come with me."

"Where to?"

"That's none of your business."

"Excuse me," I said. "But it is so my business." He stopped, surprised at my new tone. "First we have to establish where I am going and whether you have any authority to take me there."

"Who says?"

"Every citizen of Canada has the right to liberty, as defined in the Canadian Bill of Rights."

It was a game I used to play with my older brother Benjamin, who was studying to be a lawyer. One day, bored, I had come up to him as he was reading. "Why do you want to be a lawyer, Benny?"

"Why *don't* you want me to be a lawyer?"

So I fell right into it. "I'm not asking whether or not I want you to be a lawyer, I'm asking you why it is that you, personally, want to *be* a lawyer."

He looked up from his books. "And on whose authority are you asking this?"

"Mere idle curiosity," I said, a phrase I had read somewhere.

"Well, I'm sorry," he said. "But I do not choose to indulge it."

"And who gives you the right to withold that information?" I said.

"The privacy section in the Canadian Bill of Rights."

"Oh to hell with it. I don't want to know anyway," I said and started to walk away.

"That is of course your right," he said, turning back to his work and smiling. I was thirteen at the time and he was in his second year at McGill. I went off and memorized the damn Bill so that I could argue with him better. My next encounter I was more informed, and a few arguments later, it ended, I remember, in an imaginary Supreme Court case.

Back here on the beach, Rattray was looking at me narrowly. "What do *you* know about the Canadian Bill of Rights?"

"'No law of Canada" I said, "shall be construed or applied so as to (a) authorize or effect the arbitrary detention, imprisonment or exile of any person; or' (jumping down to (c)) '...deprive a person of the right to be informed promptly of the reason for his arrest or detention.'"

Both Brucie and Rattray looked at me with surprise, but it was really nothing special. Once memorized it was like *A Field Guide To The Birds*, where you sifted out what was pertinent from what was not, until you had identified the animal in question, or in this case, the relevant right or freedom.

"Exile?" said Rattray. "Who said anything about exile? Nobody's going to send you off to a...goddamn island somewhere."

"We're a-a-already on an Island, Rat-face," said Brucie, grinning widely.

"Shut up!" said Rattray, turning and pointing a finger at him.

But I broke in and he turned back. "'Arbitrary detention' is the relevant phrase in the Bill. On what authority are you threatening arbitrary detention?"

"On what *authority*?" and pointed with his thumb at his shoulder badge. "You see this?"

"I do. But by my interpretation, you seem to be over-reaching that authority." I said it in a tone of voice which was undoubtebly very annoying. "Perhaps we should talk to your supervisor. Who's the head park ranger?"

Strangely, this allowed him to find some solid ground. "*Provincial* parks have rangers," he sneered with contempt for anyone who would not know something this basic. "This is a *national* park and we have wardens."

"Then who's the head warden?"

"We don't have a head warden. We have a *chief* warden," said Rattray, flying high now.

"Who's the chief warden?"

"Fergie Monroe, not that it's any concern of yours."

"Let's go see him, then."

"Now you *want* to go?"

"Sure."

"So what's the difference?"

"Consent," I said.

"Jesus! It's the same *thing*. I mean, you either come with

me or you don't!"

"It's a question of principle," I said.

"What principle?"

"My mother told me never to take rides from strange men," I said. "You might be a pervert."

"*What?*"

"A p-pervert," said Brucie. "That's what he said. You might be a p-p-pervert."

"Fuck off!" Rattray said, stomping over to his truck, getting in and slamming the door. Fumbling for his keys, his face was beet red.

"On second thought, I won't go with you right now, thanks all the same. I'll be over tomorrow morning anyway."

He didn't even want to know what this meant. He was livid.

And to tell you the truth, it shook me. It's taken until my age now to be able to push that sort of behaviour behind me as soon as I see it. But at eighteen it was disturbing. It was an argument, but it wasn't for fun. I looked past him across the inner bay. There might be clams there at low tide, which I could dig and eat, though I didn't know much about shellfish...

"Is there a library near here?" I asked Rattray, I suppose to try to change the subject. His face was red and murderous.

"A *what?*"

"A library?"

"Do you see any big fucking buildings with, like, fucking *librarians* in them?" he said, then added, "You can both go fuck yourselves," and roared off, spinning his tires and spitting up gravel.

We watched the truck disappear down the causeway.

"Poor old Ratface, has no c-c-clue, what to say, or what to

do," said Brucie like a schoolyard rhyme, though I don't know whether he had composed it on the spot or if it was something he had just picked up.

We went back to my tent and retrieved the food I'd collected. I left a few potatoes and some raspberries for myself, and Brucie said I should bring along the banjolele. On the way to MacAkerns' I told Brucie how I was hired at the park and how I would start work tomorrow.

"R-r-r-really?" And he didn't say another thing until we entered the kitchen when he blurted out, "We got a m-m-man on the inside!"

"What? Who?" said Wallace, looking up. He was seated at the kitchen table drinking instant coffee from the jar that held the last of it, filled with hot tap water.

"Him," said Brucie, pointing at me. He had particular difficulty with the letter C and I think my name was hard for him to say.

"Whoever-The-Hell-You-Are," said Wallace, who on the other hand simply didn't know my name.

"He's going to work at the p-park office."

"No shit."

"I start tomorrow."

"You sly bastard!" Wallace said with admiration. "You can be our spy!"

And it seemed to me there could not be any complications arising as a result. Whoever-The-Hell-You-Are: The Spy With No Name.

"And he knows about l-l-law, and r-r-rights and things."

"What are you talking about?"

"R-R-Rat-face stopped us, and he just s-s-snowed him under. You should have seen it."

"Really?" Wallace looked at me. "Well, tell me now. I'm pretty sure they can't just kick us off our land, but where does it *say* they can't."

"Who?"

"The government. They want to kick us off our land."

"Exp-p-propriate us."

"I don't know much about the law," I said. "I just memorized the Canadian Bill of Rights is all."

"OK. In the Bill of Rights then, where does it say that they can't kick us off our land?

"I'm not really..."

"C-come on, you told Rattray that he couldn't move you. How'd it g-g-go? That bit about 'no law of C-C-Canada...'

I repeated the part of the Bill of Rights about detention, imprisonment or exile.

"That's it," said Wallace. "Exile...They want to *exile* us!" He turned to me. "And you're saying they can't."

"Yeah. Well I guess not...But like I said, I'm not a lawyer..."

"Exile! Just like they exiled the proud clan MacAkern before. And exiled Bonnie Prince Charlie." Then he started to sing:

"Speed Bonny Boat,

like a bird on the wing,

something the sea to Skye.

Born to be something the something the king

Why God oh why tell me why...."

"That's not how it goes," said Robbie. We all turned to look. She was standing in the doorway to the parlour with a large mouldy reference book in her arms.

"Well *you* sing it, then."

"I don't sing."

"Well then?"

"Just 'cause you sing a song doesn't give you the right to change the words."

"Oh?" said Wallace grandly, and with a sweeping arm

gesture indicated me. "Talk to my lawyer about it".

"Well?" said Robbie.

"There is the right to freedom of expression, I suppose," I said.

"There. See!" said Wallace.

"OK. Maybe. But it doesn't make you *sound* any smarter."

"What's smart got to do with it?"

"Nothing, in your case," said Robbie. Wallace punched Robbie on the shoulder. "Ow, that hurt."

"It was meant to. The point is, they want to *exile* us. Like Bonny Prince Charlie was exiled."

"Yeah," she snorted and sat down. "To France, where he lived high off the hog in the lap of luxury, thank you very much, while his own people were dying for his sake at home."

"A pack of lies!"

"From some bog in Scotland, to a court in France? That's not exile, that's social climbing."

"G-g-good one," said Brucie.

"Watch it," said Wallace to Robbie, "You are dangerously close to defaming the name and reputation of the rightful heir to the line of James."

"He was gay."

"He! Was! *Not*..!"

Robbie waited with a raised eyebrow, and Wallace looked at Robbie, and backed out of a trap he sensed was being set for him. "Not that it matters, of course, and even if it did, which it doesn't, so *what*? You some sort of a gay-bashin' red neck arsehole?" A neatly turned accusation, I thought.

"On the contrary," said Robbie, as though from a prepared text, "I think homosexuality is both a natural part of the human heritage, and, as can be seen by the innumerable important advancements which can be traced to their involvement in the arts and sciences, that the gay community is, if anything, more creative than the majority of dough-head heterosexuals..."

"There you are, then."

"...But for all that, it's not a community which has ever been known to be good breeding stock."

"So?"

"Pretty hard to preserve the line, then, wouldn't you say?"

"G-g-got 'im again, Robbie."

"What about artificial insemination?" said Wallace.

"Yes, that was very popular back then. But have it your way," said Robbie. "If you prefer the image of Bonnie Prince Charlie lying in a bed with his makeup and manservant, and some big hairy bastard in a kilt sneaking up on him with a circa 1750 model artificial insemination syringe to jab into his testicle ...well, fine, believe *that* then. Might explain why he *did* bugger off to France, with that waiting for him back home."

Wallace saw a chink in her argument. "But I am confused," he said like an overly-polite barrister. "Why would they jab his nut with a needle?"

"To extract the semen."

"There are methods which are simpler," said Wallace. "And a tad more pleasurable, I should imagine."

Robbie's eyes darted around quickly. She obviously didn't know much about this topic. "What? You're saying that they don't use a needle in artificial insemination?"

"They do not."

"Well then...I mean, how do you get the cow to..."

"You don't get the cow to do anything," said Wallace. "You get a bull." He was smiling and dominant now.

"All right smartass. How do you get a bull to, you know..."

"*I* know *some*thing *you* don't know," sing-songed Wallace.

"Oh for God's sake! How?"

"That's for me to know and you to find out."

"Tell me."

"I'm not sure that you're ready for it."

"Do not condescend to me."

"I'm not condescending to you. I'm patronising you."

"What's the difference?"

"When you're old enough to understand, I'll tell you."

Robbie flung an arm around Wallace's neck and hauled him back in a choke-hold so that the chair was leaning on its hind legs.

"Ow! Stop it!"

"How.Do.You.Get.A.Bull..."

"OK OK OK I'll tell you!"

She let the chair rock back forward. "Now," said Robbie. "How do you get a bull to, you know..."

"Donate?"

"Yes."

"Knock on his door and sell him some girl-guide cookies," said Wallace, and he mimed a rim-shot on the table and said, "Badum-bum *chhh*!"

Robbie snorted a laugh.

"The point is," said Wallace from his new lofty perch on top of the argument, "Bonnie Prince Charlie was a great Scottish Hero..."

"Aha!" said Robbie, seeing an opening. "He was *Italian*."

"He...? Oh...bullshit!" And they were back into it.

"'Fraid so. Born and raised in Rome."

"You're just making that up."

And she opened the book she had carried in and flipped through it. "Charles Edward Louis John Casimir Silvester Severino Maria Stuart."

"No need to swear," said Wallace.

"Born In Rome, in 1720..."

"O.K. OK. I get your point. It's just a fucking *song*. And where did you pick up all this garbage, anyway?"

"All my life I have been listening to you spout your BS and it occurred to me that maybe I should start checking up for myself."

"I should charge you for the education."

"I should fine you for the mental abuse."

"Let me see that book," said Wallace. Robbie handed it to him. Wallace read the section, then flipped to the front page and snorted.

"What?"

"Read *that*."

"*The Oxford Encyclopedia of History*. Yeah? So?"

"It's *English*. What do you *think* they're going to say?"

I realized right then why I liked them. They were as different from my own family as it was possible to be, but they reminded me of home in the way they used argument as play.

Robbie boiled the potatoes I'd brought, and after they cooled we sliced and stirred them up with a little water and thyme along with the chanterelles in the frying pan. While we cooked, everybody ate the raspberries, an hour of picking gobbled down in minutes. The cook's life. I thought of Mom, and reminded myself that I should phone her.

"Excellent," said Wallace, finishing off the last handful. "Where'd you buy these?"

"They're wild."

"Really? In our woods?"

"Around the edges."

"Hunh! Those mushrooms too?"

"Yep. Chanterelles."

"Aren't wild mushrooms poisonous?"

"Not these kind."

"Didn't by chance find any wild beer, did you?"

Wallace cleaned off the table and put the dishes in the sink to "soak", then he turned to me, where I was fiddling with the banjolele.

"Give us a tune on that thing, Whoever-The-Hell-You-Are. Know any songs?"

"Not many."

"How about 'The Lass of Glencoe'?"

"Don't know it."

"'The Green Fields of Montague'?"

"No."

"'Farewell to Peter Head'?"

"Hum a few bars."

"Dum diddy dum dum...Ah, fuck it, I hate that tune anyway. Well, you gotta know 'MacAleese's Lament' or 'The Lament of the Bartons'?"

"No."

"Any laments at all?"

"Not really."

"How about 'Vanderburgh's Fusiliers'?"

"Never heard it."

"(Jesus!) 'My Love Has To The Lowlands Gone'?"

"Sorry."

"Christ! Well, play something you do know."

I put my fingers in the position of a C minor chord and rolled the chord backwards and forwards twice.

Wallace waited. "That's all?"

"So far."

"What's it called?"

"'La fille aux cheveux de lin' by Claude Debussy."

"Jeez. Title's longer than the piece."

"I told you I didn't know much."

"Right, well, we'll obviously have to teach you some." And

he looked up suddenly. "I've got it! The Barley Boys are playing at the mall tonight." Robbie and Brucie looked up at him, then Wallace had a depressing thought. "But what about money?" The Old Problem. "How much we got in the jar?"

"Nothing," said Robbie. "We never have anything in the jar."

"Brucie? You wouldn't have any money, would you?"

"G-g-good one, Wallace."

They sat thinking. I coughed. They looked up. "I got some," I said.

"How much?" said Wallace.

"Almost three hundred bucks."

Wallace smiled at me. "What's you're name again?"

***

"Now Brucie. You're obviously underage so you can stay here and hold down the fort."

"OK."

"You're gonna be all right?"

"Sure."

"Good man."

Wallace got into the driver's seat, I got in the middle and Robbie opened the passenger's window, saying, "Oh my. What ever will become of us?"

We spun out of the driveway, scooted down the causeway, and in less than an hour drove the distance to Charlottetown that I had taken six hours to pedal by bike. We took the more direct Town Road and not the back roads I had biked, passing abandoned farms and gas stations, churches and tamarack swamps, lone houses with woodpiles outside and monogrammed aluminum doors. With the windows open, wind buffeting us like a gale at sea, Wallace played an eight track of The Barley Boys and turned the volume up so loud the cab was shaking with the high notes. They played a variety of stringed instruments and sang stirring songs of violent insurrection and cruel betrayal. Manly harmonies retold the heroisms of betrayed soldiers of bygone revolts. Happy ditties celebrating the joys of intoxication were interspersed with grim ballads narrated by soon-to-be executed prisoners. Thievery and rebellion were celebrated. Wallace and Robbie sang along with everything and I joined in where I could.

As we approached town, we drove through a small new subdivision and suddenly onto a road through an empty field, around the back of a large store, past dumpsters, and out front onto the parking lot of the mall. The gold and pink sunset cast a light which came very close to making even the mall beautiful.

There were people standing around the entrance beneath a billboard which announced the upcoming movie, *Jungle Justice,* a poster of a body-builder in camouflage holding a machine gun to his hip and protecting a girl from a motor-cycle gang swooping down on them. "Sometimes you have to make a stand..." ran the byline.

Inside the mall, the stores were all closed and shuttered around the atrium that acted as the lobby for both theatre and bar. A drunk was retching into a potted plant and a young security guard was saying, "Eric? You can't do this here...Ah, Eric, why did you have to do that, Eric?" We went to the entrance of the Shamrock Lounge in the corner. From inside, I could hear thumping of microphones and the babble and hum of a large crowd. Entering, we approached a lady set up with a cash box, and I paid the two dollar cover charge for everybody. Nobody asked me for an ID.

Once inside I could see and hear a full house in the dark, and standing on a brightly lit stage against the back wall were three large Celts, recognizable from their poster, but in real life, uglier. A bearded man with a twelve string guitar, another with an eight-string mandolin, and a dour gnome with the shifty eyes of a terrorist and a five-string banjo. That made a total of twenty-seven strings, all of which they were in the process of tuning. "Ping ping thump ping babble hum *ping*!" went the room. The guy in the middle of the trio was probably the hardest to look at, but they all had a fair shot at that title, and in wildly individual ways. It said something about the marvellous variety of life on earth that three of God's creatures could all be individually that ugly yet so different in their ugliness. Their foreheads were either low and Neanderthal or high and boxy. Their eyebrows were thick and bushy or matted as if they had been applied with road-working tools. Their noses were the shape of potatoes and the colour of beets, or veiny and snubbed. Their eyes were squinty and piggish or staring and thyroid. Their hair was everywhere. Two of them had thickets of red straw, kinky, curly and profuse, climbing up to their eyes from their beards, down their neck, and out of their ear holes and nostrils. The third sported a page-boy haircut which did not in any way lend innocence to his seemingly oft-punched face.

They wore identical thick cable-knitted turtleneck sweaters, perfectly suited to the deck of a dory in the North Atlantic, but under a bank of spotlights in a crowded bar it must have been like wearing parkas in a sauna. Sweat was pouring off their faces and they must have lost pounds every night, though what remained was still substantial.

"There's a table over there," said Wallace, and we followed him to the back corner through the close press of the crowd.

"Move over, make a space...Now, introductions..." He looked at the crowd around the table, realized he'd never be able to recall anyone's name and said, "Everybody, this is everybody. Introduce yourselves. I'll go get myself a chair." He left and Robbie and I sat down next to a man with a face like an axe.

"How you doin' Robbie?" said the man.

"Fine, Sid."

"What are you having?

"Nothing, thanks. I'm driving."

"No. Really. What are you having?"

"Nothing. Honestly."

"You gotta have something."

"OK. An orange juice."

"With vodka?"

"No. I told you. I'm driving."

"Christ! I'm not buying just juice!" said Sid, as if it was an insult.

"Look, Sid," Robbie said with perfect seriousness. "I lied to you about driving. I've sworn off alcohol because I've just recently taken Jesus as my personal saviour."

"Oh," said Sid, and he nodded for a while then started talking to the person on the other side of him.

"I've found that usually works," said Robbie to me.

"Are you a lesbian?" I asked.

"Moot point," she said. "I haven't been laid in a dog's age."

"That's all right," I offered. "I'm a virgin."

"I figured."

"Oh shit. Does it show?"

She laughed.

"It doesn't bother me," I said. "I'll find something."

"Better start thinking about her as some*one*, is my advice. Assuming it's a her you're interested in."

43

"It is."

"So you're the competition, then."

"Oh..."

"Only kidding. I'll keep an eye out for you."

"Thanks."

By this time, the band was tuned up and ready to go. They nodded at each other, and the guy in the middle came to the microphone and said in a thick Belfast accent, "Good evening. We're The Barley Boys, and this is a song I'm sure you all know. One! Two! Three..." And they hit a chord and started to bellow their first number with gusto. Their voices were powerful and raw with the timbre of heavy machinery. They grinned and shouted with a verve and brio which belied the lyric's tragic narrative, a tale of the miseries of alcoholism in a northern industrial town. Within the song they interspersed shouted demands to participate. "Sing along!" "Come on!" "*You* know it!" "*Every*body!"

As soon as the music started the audience welded into one organism with a common purpose. Not only did they sing along with all the words, there was even some choreography. At a given place in the chorus of that first song, for instance, everybody pounded the table three times. There was a small dance floor in front of the stage, but who needed it?

A large mug of beer appeared in front of me, and when I went for my wallet, Sid reached across Robbie and stopped my hand, then gestured that he was buying this round. I raised my glass to him, put the mug to my lips and sipped my first beer ever.

It tasted awful, like licking brass. What was all the fuss about? Robbie smiled at my puzzled face. Sid reached in front again and chinked his glass against mine. I sipped again unwillingly, but the second taste was better than the first, more like old pennies with a hint of dandelion. I might be able to finish this glass and not embarrass myself by revealing that I was not a hard-drinking man. I saw Robbie move her lips, but I couldn't hear her over the music.

"What?" I yelled.

She had to lean in and yell into my ear. "Wallace!" She pointed, "Look!"

Over by the dance floor on the far side of the room I could see him, picking his way slowly towards us through the seated crowd, smiling apologetically to the people around him while holding upside down over his head a chair he had discovered in the back corner. His path was impeded by having to time his progress to the movements of the drinkers who were swaying in rhythm to the song they were singing, but he had made it this far without incident, to where the bank of lights spilled out, shining on him like he was part of the act. Now though he found himself having to go beneath a rustic chandelier, a wagon-wheel affair with red glass mock candle holders, held by chains to the ceiling. He couldn't lower the chair because of the heads around him, and he couldn't hold it up much longer because his arms were tiring. Disaster loomed. And just as he elected to turn around and get out from under this trap, he attracted the notice of the Barley Boys, who all saw him at the same time, smiled broadly, then nodded to each other. Those of the audience who were watching the band now had their attention drawn to Wallace who crouched there, twisted and panting, holding a shaking chair above his head like antlers, a stag at bay. And just then the Barley Boys, with devilish looks in their eyes, switched into their next song without a break, and as the first verse headed inevitably toward the chorus the audience saw what was about to happen, and nudged each other in anticipation.

The song was "Stand Up!", a stirring political shanty which

inhabited a place in the culture somewhere between a political call-to-action and a soccer chant. In the course of its
performance history it had accumulated its own set of moves:
during the chorus, at "Stand up!" everybody would leap to
their feet, and then, at "sit down," they would likewise obey.
Newcomers to the song were quickly recruited into these
moves because if they didn't, they'd be crushed. Waitress-
es had learned to stay clear whenever the song started lest
they be pummeled by the sudden press of upward-shooting
bodies and displaced chairs.

The Barley Boys started slowly, punctuating the words
with a simple root chord.

"The rich live off the poor while the poor are left to rot
The bastards just get richer and the meek inherit squat..."

The chorus was approaching. Anxiously, Wallace glanced
around.

"Now I'm a peaceful man, but sometimes you must fight
When the only way to stop it is to stand up for what's
right..."

And then the chorus.

"Stand up! (Stand Up!) For the right to fight for Freedom.
Sit Down (Sit down!) for everything that's wrong.
Hooray! (Hooray!) for our rights, by God we need 'em.
Stand up, sit down and sing out loud this song."

At the first *stand up!* the crowd leapt to their feet, and
two chairs and a patron bumped Wallace, who lost his
balance and started to teeter backwards onto and across
the dance floor. If he had just allowed himself to fall he
would have put an end to it then and there, but he chose
instead to make a heroic fight to stay upright, and so
managed to turn a harmless case of clumsiness into a sprawl-
ing catastrophe. Trying to get his feet back under him, he
took three rapid steps backwards across the dance floor

towards the stage, but the chair he was holding smacked another chandelier overhead and he slipped. It clattered to the floor, he hung in the air for a second, then fell like a tree, smacking the back of his head against the edge of the stage, and instantly going limp as a rag doll.

The music stopped. Robbie shrieked. The room was suddenly very quiet.

And from where he lay motionless, like a voice from the grave, singing the same tune but with new words, his voice warbled,

"Fall down (Fall down!) for everything that's wrong...."

And the room erupted in a huge explosion of laughter and relief.

"Hit it!" said the head Barley Boy, and the band went into a fiddle tune as Wallace pulled himself to his feet, picked up the chair and carried it towards us. Patrons cleared the way for him now, slapping their congratulations on his leg as he passed.

Without thinking, I took another gulp of beer. It seemed to be quite drinkable now. I giggled at the thought of what I had just seen, started choking, and to clear my throat, took a good large swallow. I don't know what I had been thinking, it didn't taste bad at all. You just had to get used to it.

Soon there was a break in the music between sets and we could talk. Two men who had to be brothers, dressed in jeans and Canadiens hockey jerseys, came over and sat down in some temporarily vacated seats.

"Hey Christian," said Robbie. "This is Toe and Gump Blake. They run the stand where you got those potatoes."

They were built close to the ground, squarely, as wide as they were tall, and Gump may even have been wider. If he was a goalie he would have fit almost perfectly into the opening of the net.

"Are you a goalie?" I asked.

"Yep," he said. "Heard of me?"

"Can't say I have. But your name, of course."

"Yep. That's who they called me after. It's not my real name though. My real name's William."

"Like the poet."

"Yeah. Mom's an English Professor."

"What's your brother's real name?"

"What do you mean?"

"Well, Toe? I mean..."

"No. That's how they christened him. Mom fought it, but Dad said if she could name me after some fag poet then he could name Toe after the finest coach ever to lead the low-flyin' Frenchmen to victory."

I had a brief shocking glimpse of what life in the Blake household must've been like.

"I didn't know William Blake was gay," I said.

"He was a *poet*, wasn't he?" said Gump. "Name me one poet who wasn't a fag?"

"Wilson MacDonald," I said, and his eyes lit up.

"Boston she 'ave good hockey team," he recited. "De Maple leafs is nice, But Les Canadiens is bes' Dat hever skate de ice!" He clicked his tongue and winked at me. I was all right. "Got me there," he allowed. We chinked mugs.

"I met Maurice Richard once," I said, not knowing why I said it, except that it was true. But the effect was sudden and extreme. They both looked at me in awe, their eyes wide as pie-plates.

"Where?" said Toe.

"My father was doing some sort of a fundraiser with the Molsons, and there he was. I was only, eight, though. It's not like I had a long conversation with him or anything.

Just said hello. And he said, 'How you doing, little fellow?'"

" 'How you doing, little fellow'?"

"Yep."

"How'd he say it?"

"Sort of 'Ow' ya doin' little fella.'"

"What did *you* say?"

"I said, 'Fine'."

"Shoulda asked him about his fifty goals in fifty games."

"No time. He'd left."

"Wow. Maurice Richard!"

"The Rocket!"

"Yep."

"Let me shake your hand," said Toe.

"Me too," said Gump. "I'm buying you a beer!"

"Me too," said Toe. And they left to do so. Robbie came over.

"They seem to like hockey," I said. She nodded. "They don't seem to like gays, though."

She nodded again. "That pretty well sums up Gump and Toe."

The Barley Boys got onstage again and launched into their second set and my beer arrived. I could feel my forehead giving off heat from the sun I had caught that day, and the skin there was stiff and tight when I wrinkled my brow. The beer was tasting better and better.

More songs, and everybody linked arms and swayed. Like in a jostling crowd, you were forced to follow. I watched one patron, his arms hopelessly linked with his neighbours, trying to sip from his beer as he passed and repassed in front of it. Sweeping close, in a doomed drunken effort, his jaw hit the mug, knocking it over. Next time he passed, he tried to lick this spilled drink off the table.

It seemed to me that the music of The Barley Boys was

both thunderous and wondrous. That rhymed. I tried to tell Robbie that I'd thought of a rhyme, clever me, but she couldn't hear what I was saying. She told me this by yelling into my ear, which hurt my ear-drum, and rendered me more deaf. So, next time I had to yell harder just to hear myself.

Another beer appeared, this time from the man to the far side of Sid. "Oh! Thank! You!" I bellowed, astonished at the goodwill and generosity of the human race. This was the way the world should be. It was all so simple. Not that I had ever found anything particularly wrong with the world before, but I knew it wasn't that easy for everybody, and this buying of each other beer was one way we could all improve things, by welding together more firmly the Brotherhood of Man. I caught the chorus of the next song, which as it happened was a celebration of alcohol. I couldn't agree more. This stuff was great. More songs followed, and more great cool refreshing tankards appeared, which I now slurped down not just with sips but large sloppy gulps. The rounds were being bought by these lovely strangers whom I'd only just met, and who were now firm friends for life, whatever their names were. One after another around the table they bought beer for the whole table, till it was Wallace's turn, who looked at me. My round? I was honoured. Besides, I was in no condition to deny. The world was free. You just had to share. Everything so-called wiser heads had told me about propriety, sobriety and piety was utter horseshit. "Propriety, sobriety and piety" rhymed too. As it turned out, I was quite the poet. And contrary to Gump's opinion on the subject, I wasn't gay, either. Not that it mattered if I was. Nothing mattered. I had discovered my place in the scheme of things. Poet and buyer of beer. I pulled out my wad of bills and peeled off what was needed. Other people saw me from neighbouring tables and started to nudge slyly closer. I sent down towards the waitress the cost of the round plus a huge tip, which arrived in Sid's hand, half of which he passed along, the other half kept to help for future rounds. The waitress scowled at Sid.

The music was unending and visceral. It shook you with its force and plain good sense. No woozy-poozy "Crimson effervescent stardust, universal rainbows of your mind" lyrics here. Hangings, thievery and military insurrections mixed with paeans to God's Golden Gift To Us All: Beer! Which kept coming. I looked around, smiling hugely. Wallace was walking from table to table with a sheet of paper which people were signing, for some reason...

The next thing I remember clearly was hitting the fresh air outside the mall as though I was coming awake, and walking across the parking lot toward the truck.

"Here's the truck! The truck, everybody! It's here! I found the truck!"

"You don't have to shout," said Robbie. "We're outside now."

"What? Oh," I shouted. "Wait!" and I ran in a stagger around the corner of the mall, unzipped, faced the wall, and pissed like a horse. I was at it for ages, the whole time bellowing a deep maniacal laugh I didn't know I possessed. I felt much lighter when I finished, making it easier to walk back, nearly floating in fact, my legs, oddly enough, filled with helium. I refused to get into the cab, arguing that it was cramped in there and that the fresh air would do me good, and Robbie got me into the box of the pickup truck after only three tries. Maybe I should forget it, I said, once I was in. Why go home at all? I could go back to the bar to live. I could sleep under the stage. I had money.

"Well, actually..." she started, then stopped, waiting for a more opportune time. "Now stay down," she said, but as soon as she started the truck and got it rolling, I stood up in the box with my hands on the top of the hood, thumping the remembered rhythm of their last song, their fifth encore. The Barley Boys were the most sublime musicians ever to tread this great green earth. By comparison, Claude Debussy was garbage.

I maintained my balance as the truck picked up speed, but the air wasn't sobering me up at all. Maybe it would help if I opened my mouth wide to absorb more oxygen, I thought, but it didn't seem to, possibly because it roared into my lungs and pounded the alcohol more firmly into my bloodstream, making me actually drunker. I faced straight ahead and let bugs bounce off my face. One large insect the size of a June-bug zoomed right into my windpipe, causing me to sit down and try to cough it out. It wouldn't dislodge, so I flung myself onto my back in the bed of the truck again and again until it spat out, bounced off the side of the truck and thrummed away dizzily. I knew how he felt.

But I was lying on my back now, and suddenly very sleepy. We turned onto a bumpy dirt road shortcut and the back of my head bounced up and down against the floor of the pickup box for a good ten minutes, but it didn't bother me at all, in fact it felt rather pleasant. I might even have slept for a while. Eventually we halted.

"You're home," said Robbie. "Unless you want to come to our place."

"What! No! *Home!* Here!"

"You don't have to shout," she said.

I leapt to my feet. It suddenly seemed very important that nobody should think that I couldn't hold my liquor. I took two quick swaggering steps to the back of the truck and the tailgate caught me on both shins and flipped me face-first into the ball hitch, then continued to flip me, and deposited me on my back half onto the pavement and half onto the gravel shoulder. Robbie shrieked.

"It's all right!" I shouted, quite relaxed. "I *meant* to do that."

Robbie, still terrified, laughed in spite of herself, "You really don't have to shout," she said. She helped me to my feet. "Are you all right?"

"Perfectly."

Wallace in the cab was leaning his head against the side window, asleep. What a wimp.

"Well, go to bed," said Robbie. "I'll wait till you're on the beach."

I walked down the path and to the top of the dune, Robbie watching.

"OK?" she yelled in the distance.

"Yes."

"What?"

"Yes."

"You *do* have to shout *now*!"

"O! K!" I yelled back.

She waved and got back into the truck.

A fine lass, I thought. Too bad she was a lesbian, though I'm fairly sure that I could at any time entice her to switch. I had detected a definite note of concern for my well-being after that flawlessly executed tailgate flip.

I giggled, turned and slid down the other side of the dune, cutting my ankle at the bottom on a broken beer bottle. I faintly heard behind me the truck pulling away, the sound almost lost in the music of the darling surf. I saw my tent in the starlight and tacked toward it like a crippled warship. It was the poor footing of the sand that caused me to stagger.

I fell to my knees in front of my tent and unzipped the door and crawled inside. Life was good. I flopped down, the tent started spinning like a fair-ground ride, and I pushed myself up to crawling position and raised my head until it slowed somewhat. But what the hell, it was *fun*, so I flopped back down, and the tent revolved faster and faster until I was flung off into sleep, where I kept falling, falling, falling...

3

...And hit the ground next morning head first.

Outside, some industrial raking noise, like metal on concrete, was repeating incessantly: the sound of waves crashing on the shore, and crashing in my head as well, like rocks dropping on both temples. It was not a calming rhythmic massage now, it was random grating booms and slaps. Inside their rumble I could hear the squeaks of chalk and crushing shells. Sand was grinding down to squealing powder and depositing itself under my eyelids. Sharper pieces of driftwood had been crowbarred into my sinuses along with rusting jagged bits of metal.

"Oh, sh..." I started but then stopped, the violence of the thought alone too painful to finish.

My face was bruised. My lip was swollen, one eye was partly closed, and bile rose to the back corners of my mouth, causing my face to distort into an awful sneer. I wanted a big soft cool pillow to bury my head into, but all I had was my packsack of hard canvas. My shoes, which somehow had climbed up and lodged themselves next to my nostrils, were radiating a pong that would have knocked me over if I hadn't been lying down already. I pulled myself out of the tent and stood up, then immediately sat down on the sand again. The sky was green and sickly. I shivered with what felt like the flu. A wave thudded on the shore and I said with feeling, "Oh, *shut up*," but immediately and maliciously another larger wave thudded again, on purpose. I got to my knees, and then to my feet, decided it was possible to move, and tentatively put one foot in front of the other. I felt something awful lurch inside me and quickly ran three steps in four different directions. I stopped in dumb shock at how utterly painful life could be, and bending over as far as I could, grabbed both knees and made a face like a Chinese Dragon. I retched my guts out onto the sand, and kept retching, again and again, even though after the second retch there was nothing left to throw up. The smallest outlay of energy was causing massive unimaginable pain, so what was possessing me to expend immense agonizing effort for no reason whatsoever? The irony of this was not lost on me, which was maybe why I kept whimpering: Why? Why? *Why?*

I craned forward and down, and emitted a long keening sound like a two-hundred-pound bat giving birth to a three-hundred pound porcupine. I distorted my face until I nearly dislocated my jaw.

When I had finished, I wasn't much better. The world was an aching bruise, and I was in it.

So I went to bathe in the ocean, which helped, in the sense that a man thrown off a moving train is helped by a half dose of Children's Chewable Aspirin. I lay back in the water and wished that it was colder, the better to numb the pain. My face felt puffy and swollen, there were bruises on my lip, nose, and forehead, and my shoulder was scraped, as well as one knee. Both shins were dented and hurting. Also my hip. And neck. And a tooth was loose. I had an ear-ache, too. And a wound on my ankle, which I had twisted. "Oh, oh, oh," I said.

But I was slowly evolving from a retching animal into something that resembled a human. I limped ashore and back to the tent. I caught a whiff of my own sick on the sand and nearly vomited again, caught myself, then looked up the beach, where wind was blowing salt spray in from the waves.

Today was to be my first day of work and I wondered if I could legitimately phone in and tell them that I wouldn't be able to make it. The nearest telephone was at the park office itself, so showing up there to call in sick might raise some eyebrows, but I could say that I fell off my bike, and that's why I was so beaten up. They might even take me to the hospital, where they would probably have a cure for hangovers, wouldn't they?

I checked to see if I had any money left. Nothing. I had a brief memory of giving the last few bills to the waitress who had served us. If I did call in sick I might get fired, and then I would have no other money coming in, but maybe I could just live off the land here forever.

I strapped on my watch like I was clamping on handcuffs. It was eight-forty and I had to be at the park office by nine. A different type of pain assailed me when I thought that this was my last few minutes of freedom. I snarled and spat on the ground like the men on the wharf in Charlottetown, then got onto my bike and, sensitive as an exposed nerve, bicycled back across the causeway. Wincing as I bumped onto the gravel in front of the Park Office, I dismounted and leant my bike against the side of the building. I looked at my watch. Five to nine.

The building was a prefab construction the size of a small town post office, and not yet quite finished or landscaped, set into the low spruce forest which had been cut out to accommodate it. The Department of Failed Trendiness had designed it in a manner which just managed to fall beneath the standard of nice-to-look-at. You got the sense that although it may have looked fine in the planning stage, at the last minute some department mucky-muck had swept in to justify his position, added a line here, a line there, and *voila!* made it worse. It looked like one of the smaller pavilions I'd seen at Expo 67 from one of the cash-strapped Baltic countries. The gate across the road, like an Eastern European border crossing, didn't help either.

I sat in the sun by the corner of the building, and right at nine o'clock I heard a truck approach and saw Rattray roar in the driveway, the tires making a sound on the gravel like a clash cymbal, fanning the embers of my headache. He hopped out angrily and slammed the door, the son of a bitch. I was sitting almost around the corner of the building and he didn't see me as I watched him check in his side mirror to see if his shave was close enough, his shirt collar buttons bore a high enough gloss, and his jaw was the regulation squareness.

He turned, saw me and stopped, altered his display of obsessive grooming to appear as if it had been merely the kind of natural tic every sane person indulged in, then came toward me, looking at my face and wondering where he recognized me from. Halfway there he recalled, glared, spat once to get back into character, and marched the rest of the distance to me.

"What are *you* doing here?"

"I've come to see Mr. Monroe."

"What for?"

"I was told I should." I was about to say that I was told I should report to him, but that would have given it away. I still had that headache, and it made me want to spread my pain around to him and somehow diffuse it.

"By who?"

"I'll tell him that."

"You can tell me anything that you'd tell him."

"I'd rather not."

"It would be better for you if you did…" he started, but just then another truck rolled in the driveway. The sound as it hit the gravel made my head hurt again, but the man inside was older, and smiling at nothing in particular. He was wearing the same uniform as Rattray, but not so ferocious-ly. He stopped the truck and got out. "Hello!" he said to me with a big wave, then to Rattray, "Good morning, Barry."

"I caught this guy on the dunes yesterday without a permit," said Rattray immediately.

"I see. Well. Wait till we get inside, anyway." He took out his keys from a briefcase and jumbled through them, while Rattray looked at me as if to say, "you're in for it now".

I don't know what I could have been in for. Fergie Monroe looked as harmless as cotton, and was fumbling with his keys, which somewhat deflated the tension Rattray was trying to create.

"Dammit," said Fergie gently, "I know it's *one* of these." He looked at them more closely, then counted. "Nope. They're all here." Then in another voice, as if to himself: "It all comes down to that, though, doesn't it? Just *finding* the right *key*. You got all these plans, what you're going to do, how you're going to organize things, and then, *no key..* Wait!" He tried one more and the door opened. "And just when I had almost discovered the fundamental problem of the universe," he said to us.

Once my eyes had adjusted to the light inside, I found myself in an unfurnished lobby with the drywall in place but the seams still visible, awaiting a few coats of paint. There was a fountain over in the corner next to the bathroom door, a counter out from the back wall, and boxes stacked around. Everything smelled of newly dried plaster, fresh paint and cement dust. There were four doors in the back wall and Monroe went into one of the offices, said, "Come on in," and when we entered, "Sit down. Please. Now. What's up?"

"Like I said," started Rattray. "I caught him in the dunes without a permit yesterday."

"So, why did you bring him here just today?"

"I didn't. He was here when I arrived this morning."

"When was this?"

"This morning."

"I mean when did you catch him in the dunes."

"Yesterday. I let him off with a warning."

"I see. Well, of course, there wasn't much you *could* do, was there? We haven't started to issue permits yet."

"No, but since we're about to, I thought I'd get a jump on things."

"Took the initiative?"

"Yessir," said Rattray. He nearly saluted.

"Relax, Barry," said Monroe. "And where exactly was this?"

"Sector four on the other side of the causeway."

"MacAkerns' land?"

"Sector four."

Monroe sucked his lower lip. "I don't see a problem," he said, then turned to me. "What Barry is saying here is that he's worried that since the dunes are a delicate ecosystem, the more people we can keep off them the better it is for the flora and fauna we're mandated to preserve."

"Me too," I said.

"What?"

"I'm mandated to preserve them too."

"Well, that's nice. Exactly the type of visitor we hope to attract to the park."

"Actually," I said, "It's more than that. I'm supposed to be starting to work here today."

"What?"

"I'm the guy sent down by Project Ecology." That was the office that the friend of my mom had organized this job through.

"Oh!" said Monroe. "That's great. And yes, it *is* today, isn't it? And right on time. Well, well...But, I'm confused. Why didn't you just tell Barry that yesterday?"

"Didn't get a chance to," I said innocently. I glanced at Rattray and saw that he was looking from me to Monroe quickly, trying to catch up, which was all extremely satisfying to see. Then, when he saw me looking at him, he started to seethe, as if I had somehow betrayed him, which I had, in a way. But I still had that headache.

"Oh," said Monroe. "Just a little misunderstanding, then."

"Yep."

"And how much of life's trouble can be attributed to *those*..." he said, then caught himself from going off into the same dreamy generalizations that his problems with the keys had set off. "So. In that case...well...What do we do now?"

"I made some notes," I suggested.

"Oh yeah? Notes are good," he said. "What do you got?"

"Well...from where I'm camped..."

"Wait!" said Rattray, jumping on it. "*Camped?*"

"Let him finish, Barry..."

"You're not allowed to *camp*..."

"Strictly speaking," said Monroe, "until we're officially open as a park you can camp wherever you want. As long as you have the landowners' permission."

"That's OK then," I said.

"He was with that MacAkern brat," said Rattray, like he was giving evidence of a conspiracy.

"Thank you, Barry," said Monroe. "You got those crates out back to sort, don't forget."

"Yes. Some of us have *real* work," he said and left.

Monroe waited till he was gone. "Don't worry," he said. "Barry...Well, he's *like* that." He looked at me closely. "Christ! You look like shit. Did he..?"

"What? No. *Him?* Nope."

"I wonder every now and then how fucked-up he really is. Sorry. You probably don't need to know that. Anyhow, do you want an aspirin?"

"Yes please," I said quickly.

· He went out to the lobby, found a safety kit, broke it open and removed a small plastic bottle. "There," he said, handing it over. "You can keep that." I took two and chewed them raw so that their pain-killing qualities would not be diluted.

"Christ, you *are* in pain." We went back into his office and sat down. "Now, you were saying?"

I took out my notebook and read him my list of birds. He nodded and said, "Very good, I guess. Can't say that I know birds too well myself," and then he told me that although I would be receiving my paycheck through Parks Canada, my job was mandated by a different agency, Project Ecology, and funded by a Youth Opportunity grant. "Also," he said, "I've just received word that the guy who was supposed to be your supervisor won't be coming down, just yet, anyway. He had a nervous breakdown (probably bullshit-induced, if he worked with *this* Department...). Sorry, you don't need to know that either (but God almighty, it just seems every now and then to be so *meaning*less, although I guess it's not...). Sorry again. I'm ranting I see. The point is, you'll be more or less on your own for the first week or so until they re-assign somebody. And they told me to tell you that your duties are..." He picked up a slip of paper and read from it. "'...to study, observe and collate environmental information pertaining to the Park and write a report which should be handed in at the job's termination.' (Which seems kind of a broad mandate, if you ask me. Still, ours is not to reason why...)"

Monroe rambled on for a bit, then rallied his attention, leant forward, and in a confidential tone added that the main thing in his experience was to act like you knew what you were doing, make the report look official, and that maybe I should read some of the other reports to see how that was done. He added that I seemed to have something of a clue about the subject, so it shouldn't be much of a problem, and apart from that, I should just show up on time, look like I'm working, and generally help out. "It should be simple (though God knows it isn't... And the MacAckerns, God bless 'em, but why they have to be so difficult is *anybody's* guess)." He looked up. "Still, well, that's not your concern."

"Actually, I know them."

"Really. From where?"

"We had a meal together last night." I didn't mention going out drinking.

"Well well. Maybe we could use you as a liaison."

"Sure."

"In fact. I have a letter for them here. When do you plan to see them next?"

"Probably tonight."

"OK then. Here it is. Save on postage. (Not that I'll get any thanks for that from the department. Nossir. Spend like a drunken sailor, otherwise they'll cut back on funding next year, is *their* logic. It makes no sense whatsoever...) Sorry. You'll have to excuse my babbling. Bad habit." He handed me an envelope.

"What is it?"

"Another offer on their house and land. Wallace rejected the first one, so I relayed that to the boys upstairs and they instructed me to tell Wallace that this was their final offer, so you might want to pass that along to him as well. Also you might want to tell them that apparently somebody in Ottawa might be getting money from Heritage to preserve their house. I wish I wasn't in the middle of all this. I *like* Wallace... Anyhow!" He slapped the desk-top and stood up, looked off in the distance for a minute, then turned suddenly back to me. "Nice to have you aboard!" he said, holding out his hand to shake. "Call me Fergie." I shook his hand and folded the letter into my vest pocket.

***

Next door to Fergie's was the office I would be using for the summer, a clean new room with a window in the back wall that looked straight out into spruce undergrowth, dark branches with lichens on the trunks and old man's beard hanging like rotting cloth from the branches. There was a desk in the middle of the room, empty shelves along one wall, and a stack of boxes containing books and scientific papers in the corner. I looked around and didn't have a clue what to do next.

I unpacked the boxes and arranged them onto the shelves, one for flora and another for fauna. Some publications fell between the cracks, or covered aspects of both, and I put those on a third shelf. There was one box which contained fifty copies of the same booklet, *Birds, Plants and Animals of Barrisway National Park*, a spanking-new volume put together specially for our office to hand out to interested visitors. I sat down behind the desk, flipped though it and noticed right away that although many of the drawings were stiff and childish, some were brilliant. The beach pea for instance, showed just enough of the surroundings where it was most likely to grow to help identify it. But the jellyfish looked as if it was walking across the ocean floor, and the gannets in flight seemed to be mechanically operated. I couldn't explain it. They were both just ink-lines on paper, but some sketches were drawn by someone who understood the subject's nature, and the others were lifeless. I looked at the title page: "Text by Andrew Solomon, illustrations by Claire Duschesne and Andrew Solomon." I immediately concluded that Claire Duschene was responsible for the good drawings, on the grounds that it simply had to be a woman, the life-giver, who wielded that feeling for the natural world and eye for the distinguishing detail which made these sketches flowing, organic and whole.

Then I remembered that Andrew Solomon was the name of the man who was supposed to be my supervisor, and I looked at the bad drawings more closely to see if I could detect signs of his impending nervous problems. I thought I saw possible lunatic symbolism in the ham-fisted drawing of the beach hopper, which seemed to be struggling up an impossibly steep dune ripple, its path in the sand tortuous and erratic. I took one copy of the book from the stack and put it in my pocket.

"Stealing stuff?" said Rattray behind me. The bastard had snuck in.

"Don't worry, I'll tell Fergie I'm taking one."

"Oh , it's Fergie now, is it? That's *Mr.* Monroe to you, or Chief Warden Monroe."

"And what do I call you?" I asked, thinking "Rat-face" perhaps? But he'd been practising.

"Assistant Chief Warden Rattray is my official title."

But I still had the remnants of that headache. "Jesus Christ," I said.

And just then Fergie walked in. "Yeah, that'd work too." He'd heard everything, but he wasn't a sneaky bastard. "Look, you two, you're going to have to get along. Now shake hands, and then, for Chrissakes, just stay out of each other's way."

"Fine with me," I said, holding out my hand.

"He didn't mean it literally," said Rattray.

"Actually, I did," said Fergie, "but it doesn't matter. Barry, this might be a good time to go pick up that crate at the bus station in Charlottetown."

Rattray looked at me meaningfully, turned and left.

I took the booklet out of my pocket. "Can I take one of these?" I asked Fergie.

"Yeah. Sure. Take a few. The authors will be pleased they're starting to move."

"OK."

"They'll be down here Friday...No. Just one of them will. The other guy....I told you about the nervous breakdown? Yeah? Anyhow. That's two days from now. No it's not, either. It's tomorrow. Fuck! Excuse my French."

"Seal," I said.

"What?"

"French for seal. *Phoque.*"

"Yeah. That's it." He smiled, and left me to my work.

But I didn't have much else to do. I unpacked and set up

a stereo microscope on my desk and looked at one of the demonstration slides that came with it. I read parts of some other books and pamphlets. The morning ticked by and my headache started to dissipate, leaving behind an empty howling space, like Warsaw after the bombing. I took more aspirin, which made me feel fuzzy and cocooned. Fergie popped his head in again at lunch time, said he was going to get something to eat and asked would I like to come along. But I had no money and didn't know whether I wanted to bounce around in a vehicle for I didn't know how long, or whether I could hold down anything more challenging than the potato I had brought with me, so I said no thanks.

He left and I walked out and crossed the shore road to an area that was different than the rest of the park, wind-blown stunted spruce smeared up in a thick mat by the weather. According to one of the publications I had seen that morning it was a feature known as a "Krumholtz" or "Tuckamore." It was all run through with a network of winding paths like a rabbit warren, beat down to the red soil underneath, then sand as I came to the shore. I thought of taking a short dip in the ocean but the water's edge was knee deep in seaweed. I looked at my watch. Forty-four minutes until I was due back. It wouldn't be so bad if I knew what I should be doing. I supposed I could continue making bird lists or maybe I should explore all of the beaches in the park and write a paper. "An Evaluation of the Suitability of the Beaches of Barrisway Park, PEI, in Respect to Tourism, Natural Resources and..." I couldn't think of a third. I sat on a rock and took another aspirin while I ate my potato. They didn't taste bad together. *Pomme de terre à la mode Aspirine.* Maybe I could add beach recipes as an addendum to my report.

I timed my arrival at the park office just as the second

hand on my watch touched one o'clock. I went to my room and sat down behind my desk. The problem now was how to fill the rest of the day. A work-sheet Fergie had given me informed me that there would be a half-hour coffee break at three-fifteen, which meant I had almost two hours of solid time-wasting till I could officially waste time for fifteen minutes. I opened a book at a chapter on the life cycle of the jellyfish, and read that some species were an edible delicacy in Japan. I made a vaguely oriental face and said Ah So! which as far as I know means nothing in any Asian language, then I delivered an imaginary karate chop to the imaginary neck of Rattray.

I started sketching a chart to break down the work-day into component parts. It wasn't a bad job, really. It certainly hadn't been difficult so far, and was as interesting as I could make it, but outside the office the day was passing, and on the beach the tide would be going out again, never to come back in quite the same way, and I was missing it. I looked at my watch and started to count the hours until Quitting Time, that holy grail at the end of the work-day, receding further out of your reach the more you focussed on it. And, after that, it was home and sleep and back to work tomorrow. And tomorrow and tomorrow, as the man said. I found myself thinking, for the first time in my life, the word "fuck," mildly shocking myself that I had said it, if only in my mind. But it felt cathartic as well. I tried saying it again, out loud this time. "Fuck." The heavens did not fall. In fact, it made me feel grown-up. Just a word, I thought, subject to the same grammatical rules as any other word. "Fuck you" was directed. "Fuck off" was dismissive. "What the fuck?" was the interrogatory form. "Un-fucking-believable" was comic in its steadfast dedication to inserting the word at every fucking opportunity. "For fuck's sakes!" was the appeal to some mythological being (either the Great God Fuck, or that mischievous woodland sprite out of *Midsummer Night's Dream*, Robin Goodfellow, also known as "Fuck"). There were a fuck of a lot of fucking ways to use the fucking word, that's the fucking truth.

I picked my teeth with a piece of cardboard and took another aspirin.

There was, of course, another way to get through the day: Concentrate on this moment, the slippery Now, and fill the time with satisfying achievement. So I flipped through more pamphlets and tried to concentrate. I read. I sighed. I looked at the clock and read some more.

One publication was on the diet and behaviour of shorebirds by Andrew Solomon, so I scanned it, on the lookout for more signs of incipient madness. "We observed fourteen migratory flocks of sanderlings in Fundy National Park over a period of two weeks," it started. There was a footnote which said, "See chart 1A." I found three columns there which listed the approximate numbers in the flocks sighted, the weather, and the time of each sighting. 3:35...3:07... 2:49... 2:26... And it seemed to me there was a pattern. The sightings were roughly twenty minutes earlier every day. I felt my interest in the subject stirring. I looked for and quickly found a navigational guide in the books I had put on the shelves and while I was checking this, I heard a truck arrive. I turned back to the guide and read some more, and then Fergie came into the office.

"How's it going?" he said.

"Good. There may be a connection between feeding times and tidal height amongst sanderlings."

"Whoa boy! Slow down. No need to blow a gasket. Take it easy."

"Some of the data is all in this paper by Andrew Solomon,

but I don't think he's made the conclusion."

"Really? Hunh! Well, best follow that up then," he said, and left quickly.

I had something to occupy me now so the afternoon no longer dragged. At three-thirty, workers appeared in the lobby where they opened large boxes, extracted and carried fixtures and mirrors into the bathroom. I sat in my office and listened to the whirring of power tools and hammer-blows on metal and cement. At twenty to five I was pacing around in front of my desk, and at five exactly I was out the door. Fergie met me there, locked up and got into his truck.

"See you tomorrow," he said, and spun out of the driveway. But I had an interesting project to pursue now, so tomorrow did not seem such a dreary prospect. High tide was in three hours. I filled my water jug from an outside tap and biked over the causeway to my campsite.

I swam, lay down and slept for a while, then woke up just as high tide was starting to ebb. I went down to the water's edge and noticed the line of detritus marking where it had reached its high point on the shore. I crouched and looked at this detritus closely, took a handful as a sample, and thought about that. I was still thinking about it as I cooked my supper of potatoes fried in saltwater. I also thought about how I probably could do with some variety in my diet. Maybe I could go to MacAkerns' for stale Oreos and Cheeze Whiz.

It was getting dark now, and the air was becoming chilly and clear. A sea breeze sprang up and immediately settled down. I got on my bike and pedaled back across the cause-way to the phone booth at the park office and put a collect call through.

"Hi Mom."

"Christian! How *are* you? Is anything wrong?"

"No. Just phoning."

"You sure?"

"Yep."

"Oh...good. So! How are things?"

"Great. I'm camping on the beach, and I met this family, and I went to work this morning and met everybody and just finished my first day working, though they told me that I wouldn't get paid till Friday..."

"You're out of money."

"No...Well, at least I don't *think* so. Maybe. I mean, I *might* be able to hold out till then, but, no. I *should* be all right..."

"You want me to send you some?"

"Well, I don't think you have to, like I say, Mom. But, well, maybe..."

"Will a hundred do?"

"Yeah, but like I say, I don't really need it. There's a lot of berries around here which I'm picking...and, oh yeah, I found some chanterelles..."

"You're living off berries and mushrooms?"

"No. Not entirely. That family I told you about..."

"You're begging from a family you just met?"

"Mom. I'm not. Really..."

"OK. Listen. You know that shirt I gave you?"

I didn't know why she was bringing that up now. It was a white shirt which she insisted I take in case I needed to attend some formal event. I didn't see the point. A few times during the trip down I wanted to throw the shirt away or leave it behind accidentally-on-purpose, but Mom told me that it had been Dad's, and that he had always wanted to give it to me, though it didn't look like anything he'd ever worn. It had a stiff wide collar, and short sleeves, and looked cheap.

"Dad's shirt?" I said.

"Well, no," said Mom. "It wasn't really. I just told you that because I didn't want you to throw it away."

"Mom? Why?"

"I've sewed a hundred-dollar bill into the collar."

"Really?"

"For emergencies."

"Why didn't you just give me the money?"

"Because you would have spent that too." Which was fair enough. To be angry with her would have been hypocritical. In truth, having someone care about me enough to lie to me for my own good gave me a warm and secure feeling. "It's been how long since you left?" she asked.

"Three days."

"So that's a hundred dollars a day you've spent. For six weeks, that'll be four thousand two hundred expenses, and you'll be paid how much? Eighteen hundred?"

"Yeah, about that."

"So at this rate you'll come out of the job two thousand four hundred dollars poorer."

I suddenly realized what that meant. "Fuck," I said, almost to myself.

"Christian?"

"What?.. Oh. Sorry Mom. People down here seem to swear a lot."

"Well, don't around *me*."

"Sorry."

"Fine. Now. How did you manage to spend so much?"

"There's been some unforeseen expenses."

"Initial start-up cost overruns?"

"Exactly."

"Spare me. I've heard them all."

"OK. Well, thanks anyway, Mom."

"Now. How's everything else going?"

And we talked about other things. What responsibilities I had at work. The rumour of my supervisor's nervous breakdown. The necessity of changing my socks, brushing my teeth and wearing clean underwear. I told her I had heard about a guy down here who was wheeled into the hospital to undergo a lung, liver and heart transplant, but his mom was OK with it, because he had on clean underwear. She laughed.

I told her about the beach, and the birds, and the park. I did not inform her about my first experience with beer and the injuries to my face. And as we came to the end of the call we didn't assure each other that we loved each other. We didn't say those things, not because we didn't love one another, but rather, I like to think, because we believed that Love was sacred, even the word, only to be said at special times, and casting it around indiscriminately diminished its value. So when I said that I'd better get going, she said, instead, "Yes. Don't want to bankrupt me too. Have fun. Work hard."

"OK. Bye, Mom."

"Bye Christian."

I hung up and immediately felt the thick dark night surround me more closely. It was silent and chilly and I shivered. I biked back to my tent and it was even colder out there, the stars snapping brightly way out in space, with only the thin skin of atmosphere down here to keep us warm and alive, and outside of that an infinity of absolute zero. Everything felt fragile. I needed a woman.

Or a beer.

Like the first time in my mind I had said "fuck," I surprised myself with that thought too, and I wondered if I was now an alcoholic. I shook the thought out of my head, and started to walk to MacAkerns', making a serious and firm commitment then and there to never, ever, even if forced at gun-point, so much as look at that vile product, beer.

***

"Want some scotch?" said Wallace.

"OK," I said, and sat down.

"You look like shit."

"Lay off him, Wallace," said Robbie. They were sitting around the table and Robbie had a forty-ounce bottle in front of her. "Are you in pain?"

"Not really."

She poured some scotch and passed the glass across to me.

"Better keep a close eye on him," said Wallace. "I mean to say, I like the occasional tipple, but he's a maniac." He looked at me warily, as though I might pounce on the drink. "Patience," he said. "I know you're dying to get hammered as soon as possible, but wait for it."

I took the glass. "It was my first time."

"That bodes well."

"Nobody told me to slow down."

"Drinking is like any other sport," said Wallace. "You gotta pace yourself."

"Now you tell me." I looked at the glass of scotch and decided I would not drink it immediately, but would take my time. I believe the verb was to "nurse" it. And one scotch surely could do no harm, particularly if I thought of it as an experiment. The only way to find if I was on the verge of becoming a teenage alcoholic was if I monitored myself under strict laboratory conditions, like here in MacAkerns' kitchen. I tilted the glass to my lip and took a gentlemanly sip.

I stopped and made a face like a leaf-nosed bat.

The scotch tasted very, very bad, both aggressive and medicinal, like gasoline and orange peel. It gave off fumes that caused my nose to wrinkle up and my eyes to water. It was completely undrinkable. When my face relaxed I said, "Is it supposed to taste like this?"

"Like what? I'll have you know this is a thirty-year-old single malt," said Wallace.

"It's awful."

"Oh? You've found that, have you? In your long experience as a connoisseur of fine Scotch whisky?"

"No. This is my first. But it's, like... *awful*."

"Well, you have to get used to it," said Wallace.

I sipped again to see if, like the beer, the second sip was better than the first. It wasn't, although by anticipating its awfulness I was not as cruelly surprised. Then I had an idea.

The trick to avoiding becoming a raving teenage alcoholic was to stay away from alcohol altogether, and nothing would help me do that better than this vile concoction, of which I clearly would never be able to drink enough to get drunk. Any worries I had on this front could therefore be put to rest with one simple move, the logic of which seemed to me absolutely iron-clad. To confirm the vileness of alcohol, as well as teach myself a lesson I would never forget, I put the glass to my lips and downed the contents in one gulp.

Wallace, Robbie and Brucie all looked at me, then looked at each other, then looked back at me again. I shuddered horribly and made another more extreme grimace, squeezing the muscles in my face to cause a pain large enough to drown out the taste. I moved the sides of my lips like I was trying to worm a gag out of my mouth. I worked the cords of my neck while I frantically cleaned the insides of my pallet with my tongue, and swallowed the saliva out of the way of my taste buds. Blinded by tears, I coughed, stood up, marched the two steps to the sink, turned the faucet on full blast and stuck my mouth under it, washing it out and coughing extensively afterwards. When I finished I returned to my seat and sat down again.

"Are you OK?" said Robbie.

I took time to consider the question, because now something else was happening. The scotch, hitting the floor of my stomach, seemed to be spreading in a slow explosion of delicious warmth, soothing and healing like a Balm of Gilead, right unto my fingertips. It not only healed the pain of drinking it, but added something extra. "Could I have another?"

"No way," said Robbie, and she took the bottle, stood up and put it on the counter.

"Just one..."

"No!" And she meant it. She poured me a glass of water and set it down in front of me. "Now, drink this."

I obeyed.

"If we had any aspirin I'd give you a few, but we don't," said Robbie. "Lots of water and aspirin prevent a hangover."

Hangover! Even in a universe as benevolent as the one I was now inhabiting, I remembered that a hangover was a very bad thing indeed.

"I have aspirin," I said.

"Well, take a few."

I obeyed again, took the aspirin bottle out of my vest pocket and popped two into my mouth.

"Can I have a w-w-whisky?" said Brucie.

"No," said Robbie.

"Why not?

"You're too young,"

"Wallace said he had a d-d-drink when he was my age."

"Yeah. And look how he turned out."

"C-c-come on."

"Do you want to wake up one morning with a face like *him?*" said Wallace, and he pointed at me.

"G-g-got a point there," said Brucie, backing off.

"Or *be* like him, God forbid," said Wallace with a massive shudder. "No, Boyo-Me-Lad Brucie. Whatever path you take in life, abide by this one simple principle: Don't Be Like Whoever-The-Hell-He-Is. I mean, first he swans into our house and tries to poison us with wild mushrooms, then forces us to go on his drunken debauchery in town, and doesn't even tell us his *name*, for Chrissakes. Consider him an unacceptable role model. Much better to fashion yourself after your older brother, me."

"You really want to screw him up that bad?" said Robbie.

I was sitting comfortably now inside a marvelous warm cocoon. Even the fact that I had to go to work tomorrow wasn't that bad when you thought about it. If I was able to sustain the mood I was feeling now, the wastes of time I had to endure there would be quite manageable. I should bring a bottle to the office and drink my way through the workday. I smiled, and then for some reason remembered Fergie wearing that same smile. So that's how he did it.

"Fergie," I said to no one in particular. "He's a drunk."

"He sure is," said Wallace. "I like him though."

"Me too," I said. "Rattray's a pain in the ass, though."

"Got that right."

I felt expansive and willing to inform. "Did you know that there used to be walruses on the beach here?"

"What a load of crap," said Wallace.

"Well, that's what it says in one of the pamphlets I was reading, anyway. And there was an Indian settlement over by where the Ultramar station is now in Barrisway."

"Horseshit," said Wallace. "That place has *always* been an Ultramar station."

"Don't listen to him," said Robbie, sitting down. "Tell me what the office is like."

"Hard to say. It's not finished yet."

"Does the roof leak?" She looked pointedly at Wallace.

"Of *course* their roof doesn't leak!" said Wallace. "And who *paid* for it not to leak, eh? Us taxpayers, that's who!"

"When have you ever paid taxes?" said Robbie.

Wallace ignored her and sucked down some more scotch. "John Q Average-Canadian, forking over more of our hard-earned cash so the government can steal land from people who've built it up with their blood sweat and tears. And where does that money go? Into the padded swivel chairs that cushion the fat arses of an already overblown government bureaucracy which the Liberals are enlarging even as we speak, though they swore they wouldn't."

"The Conservatives are in power."

"Same thing."

"Well, you got a point there," said Robbie.

I remembered something. "Oh" I said, and I drew from my pocket and placed on the table the envelope Fergie had given me to deliver. "It's an offer on your house and land. They told me to tell you that it was final."

Wallace picked up the corner of the envelope between his thumb and forefinger like he was handling a dead rat, and, wrinkling up his nose, he squinted at the address.

"'MacAckern is spelled wrong," he said. "Typical."

"Oh, what's the *diff*erence?" said Robbie.

"M-*A*-C is how we spell it," said Wallace. "'M-C' means you're a Protestant bastard prick-faced pretender."

"Garbage," said Robbie. "None of our family could spell

worth shit. And since when are you a Catholic, anyway?"

"Since always."

"Really? And when did you last actually *go* to church?"

"It is true that I have successfully maintained my oath of non-attendance, in protest of certain so-called reforms by the Second Vatican Council."

"You're just too lazy to get up on Sunday morning."

"That too." Wallace turned to me and gestured with the envelope. "Now, Whoever-The-Hell-You-Are. What have you heard around the office? What's the scuttlebutt?"

"Well," I said. "Apparently somebody in Ottawa might be getting money from the Department of Heritage to preserve your house."

"Heritage..." said Wallace looking up. "I hadn't thought of that angle. This house is *heritage*..."

"It's shit," said Robbie.

"Whoa whoa whoa!" Wallace turned to Robbie, took another stiff belt of scotch, breathed in sharply through clenched teeth and straightened in his seat like a man with something to say. "I will be the first to admit that this building has seen better days..."

"Yeah. Like the Pleistocene Era."

"...But I'll have you know it was Red Rory Angus MacAkern himself who laid the foundation, with stone he cut and brought from the quarry at Salvage Head down east of here..."

"Here we go..." said Robbie, putting her elbows on the table and sighing.

"...With a tripod crane he invented and fitted onto the deck of the boat he built with his own two hands, a boat with a shallow enough draft to come right into shore at high tide, but large enough to float the rocks he carried back. And after mooring down by where that Buick is now, he towed by windlass those rocks up to just under where you're sitting."

"And a truly crappy job he did, too," said Robbie.

"And the porch was added by Little Johnny MacAckern and his wife Monique Taillefer..."

"You paint a fascinating historical tableau."

"For little did we know that when the proud clan MacAckern left from Arisaig, Scotland..."

"Oh Christ. We've started him..." said Robbie.

"...that cold February morning, to cross the frigid north Atlantic with their borns in their arms..."

"Borns?"

"Wee ones. Children."

"Do you perhaps mean bairns?"

"I was using the family pronounciation."

"Oh *great*. Can't spell, and don't know how to speak, either."

"...To cross the frigid North Atlantic, boat tossing in no less than three of the mightiest gales ever to blow, forced into exile from their ancestral home by those heartless English Protestant pricks, and commanded at gunpoint to leave their humble bothy..."

"W-w-what's a bothy?" said Brucie.

"Gaelic for shithole," said Robbie.

"...Where we were living the simple life of the happy peasantry."

"Last time you told this story you said we were forced to leave the proud Castle MacAkern."

"We'd come down in the world since then, Robbie girl. Unfairly driven as we were from our ancestral seat where the great mountain Ben Nevis looks out on the Western Isles from the Highlands of Fife."

"Fife is in the Lowlands. And it's on the *east* coast."

"Don't interrupt. 'Twas after the brave Scots fought to a standstill the English at the Battle of Boyne..."

"The Battle of *Boyne* was in Ireland."

"Whatever. Some fucking battle somewhere... And where we were unfairly outmanned ten to one by the English, not to mention the thousands of foreign mercenaries, like the Swiss. (*Those* bastards got a *lot* to answer for...) Where was I?"

"We were leaving our non-existant homeland with a crew of kilted leprechauns on the Good Ship Lollipop with Captain Scaramouche and his Seven Dwarfs."

"Fuck off... On the good ship The Mary, named after Mary, Queen of Scots..."

"Who was French. "

"Don't start... And it was a leaky scow with ship's rats the only food."

"I thought you said it was a good ship."

"Manner of speaking...Tossing and turning, headed for Cape Breton..."

"Which we missed."

"...Where we had family, a branch of MacAkerns who live there to this very day."

"*Those* bunch of inbreds".

"...but south of Newfoundland, lost in a fog as thick as soup, a storm came up. We were headed ashore, but the good skipper Sir Patrick Spens of the Clan Macrimmon took us straight out to sea directly into the teeth of it."

"Well, that wasn't very bright of him, now, was it?"

"You'd think so, wouldn't you? But that's because you obviously are not aware that in a sailing vessel in a storm, Robbie, it's safer to get out to *sea*. Didn't think of *that* now did you, Smart-ass?... And so we were blown to the North Shore of Prince Edward Island, or as we called it, New

Arisaig. And the clan all said we must get back to Cape Breton, for there our family abides, and the head of the clan, Colin Ray The Dhu…"

"I thought you said…

"…Who was also y-clept Red Rory Angus MacAkern the Great…"

"OK, then…"

"…crouched down and took a handful of soil and said, 'We will no longer roam. This land is good.'"

"Didn't know much about farming either then, did he? 'Cause that beach is nothing but sand and rocks."

"And yet we built up the soil with seaweed and…and… manure, and worked it heroically by the sweat of our brows with our own hands, and sowed and reaped until it bore fruit. And so we came to this land and built the house whose walls have sheltered five generations of MacAkerns."

"Well, the roof sure hasn't. It leaks like a sieve."

"And that is the tale of the Great Clan MacAkern and how we came to the new world. A noble tale. A tale of heroes. A tale of a giant race of men who though bloody were unbowed. And that is why I must reject this offer of the government. And if you have a problem with the roof, then *fix* it."

"*You* fix it. Or get Martin the Sore or one of your fictitious relatives. The eaves-troughs are full of leaves, and my room is right under the V, so it actually collects rain. A roof should keep you drier, not make you wetter. We should move, Wallace."

"I refuse."

"Are you even gonna *look* at that offer?"

"No need to."

"I will, then."

"No you won't. It was addressed to me."

"But…"

"Don't *worry* about it, Robbie. I'm just playing with their heads, tenderizing them up before I sweep in for the kill. Last offer I gave them a list of demands which they cannot possibly meet."

"What good will that do?"

Wallace started shaking his head slowly from side to side and clucking his tongue. "Robbie Robbie Robbie. Poor, innocent, sweet, dim Robbie. What I am doing is establishing a negotiating position."

"Why don't you just ask Fergie for what you want?"

"Oh RobbieRobbieRobbie*RobbieROBBIE*. This is why we have to go on living here. If we sent you out into the world as you are now you'd be pulled apart limb from limb." He sighed heavily. "I'll try to explain."

"Oh, please do. And remember, no big words."

"If I just went and asked what I wanted, they might give us half, if we're lucky."

"Still better than nothing."

"Not good enough. I'm asking for at least twice as much so I *can* get what I *do* want. Also I'm throwing in some rejectables amongst the deal-breakers."

"What amongst the what?"

"In every negotiation, Robbie, you have items which you don't care about which you throw in to let them drag out of you at the last moment amidst great gnashing of teeth and rending of garments."

"Why?"

"I don't know really. That's just the way it's done."

"Amongst movers and shakers and world leaders such as yourself?"

"Exactly."

"You might get fuck-all."

"Never."

"Look, Wallace. They make the rules."

"Only if you believe they do."

"Whether you believe it or not."

"I, for one, refuse to believe that."

"Then you, for one, are delusional."

"Ah then, lass. 'Tis a fine madness."

"What?"

"It was in a movie I saw. Look! I'm not asking for the moon!"

"I thought you just said you were."

"Well, yes, those rejectables, but what we *really* want, it's no sweat off their balls."

"What did you ask for?"

"First, a salary of a hundred thousand a year until I die, and the same for you and Brucie, of course. Also, it goes without saying, alternate permanent accommodation within the province on comparable coastal acreage, and transportation of goods and possessions from here to our new place of residence, aforesaid acreage to be provided with enough arable land to feed our poor starveling family..."

"'Starveling'?"

"...Who our sainted father left penniless (thanks to those pricks in Ottawa) to fend for ourselves, with only the soil beneath our feet to till."

"When have you ever tilled anything?"

"Poetic license."

"Anyway, you don't have a hope in hell of getting even half of that."

Wallace put the fingers of one hand to his heart and adopted an expression like I once saw on a frontispiece to a volume of poems by Shelley. "My only wish is to live in my beloved home with my beloved family, until my demise, when such time comes that I am, (as well as you, sweet child, when comes *your* time) to be buried in the family graveyard of Glen Mochrie."

"Where's that?"

"Out this side of the point."

"The dump?"

"The same."

"Why would I want to be buried in a dump, and since when is that dump Glen Anything."

"Glen Mochrie. It's what our family have always called it."

"No we haven't. We've always called it the dump."

"Yes well, best not to bring that up now, is it? With negotiations already in progress, and them all afire about heritage? We're trying to talk it up, Robbie, not down. So it's Glen Mochrie from now on, and right next to that is the Vale of Bethmeer..."

"That bog with the Pontiac in it?"

"Once again, best to soft-pedal all this bog chat. It is henceforth the Vale of Bethmeer named after our Aunt Beth, the old bat, just on the other side of the wee fen..."

"The swamp?"

"Correct. But call it the wee fen."

"And that's where you want to be buried?"

"When comes my time," said Wallace, tilting his head up and gazing off heroically at the wallpaper. "There I shall be laid to rest with the scent of wild thyme wafting through the air and the music of the surf in my ears, accompanied by a hundred pipers playing 'As Softening Shades of Evening Fall.'"

"It'll have to be a hell of a surf to be heard over *that* racket. Why would you want *that* at your funeral?" said Robbie.

"It'll give the mourners something to cry about. And I won't have to hear it, because I'll be dead." He seemed quite pleased at his cleverness.

"So you agree!"

"Of course I do."

"Then why...?"

"That's one of my rejectables. And since there is no way they'll guarantee to that condition, it should hold up things handily."

"Oh yeah. You got *every* angle covered."

"I like to think so."

"But what's all this about the second offer? You never told us you got a first."

"Oh. That. Well. You'd just try and stop me from doing what I was going to do anyway, which would be very frustrating for you. That sort of pressure could be very unhealthy for you, Robbie, what with the stress of sleeping under a leaky roof and all."

"What did you do with the first offer?"

"Don't worry. I showed it to Bernie Panting at the bank, who loaned me a thousand bucks on the strength of it."

Robbie absorbed this information. "So....why then did you make like you didn't have any money for that big blowout last night?"

"A penny saved is a penny earned. You should make a note of that, Whoever-The-Hell-You-Are."

"So you got Christian here to finance your drunk?"

"Amongst other things," said Wallace mysteriously.

Robbie stopped again and thought for a bit. "So *that's* why you were acting so strange at the bar. With those signatures..."

When she said that, a dim memory swam out of the blur of last night and through the blur of tonight's aspirin and scotch, a memory of Wallace walking from table to table in the bar, getting people to sign something, then signaling to me with a big questioning smile while pointing to the person who was signing. I had signaled back Yes to whatever it was, happy to be in agreement with everybody. Then, after signing, the waitress would arrive and deliver beer to that person, Wallace would slap their backs and move on to the next.

"Well, I was fairly drunk at the time..." said Wallace, but you could see he was waffling.

"And when I asked what you were doing getting everybody to sign something," said Robbie, "you said it was some sort of drinking game. And when I asked later who won the game, you pretended you were too drunk to know what I was talking about."

"Like I say, I *was* a bit tipsy..."

"What were the signatures for, Wallace?"

"A petition to let us stay on our land."

"You *used* him," said Robbie, pointing to me.

"How?"

"*He* was paying for it."

"So."

"*So?*"

"Oh...I see. You're accusing me of tricking him into bankrolling the alcohol I had to buy to procure the signatures I needed?"

"No. I'm accusing you of being a lying dickhead."

"Well, that's a given. But Whoever-The-Hell-He-Is doesn't mind, do you, Whoever-The-Hell-You-Are?"

The warmth I was feeling had settled into a humming and vibrant bonhomie. "No problem," I said.

"See? And isn't he, right now, enjoying the scotch I took the initiative to buy from the bartender there?"

"Yeah. And put on his tab."

"Certainly."

"What would he do without you?"

4

Next day, I fell in love.

In the morning I woke up suddenly, walked down to the ocean, shaved, and just in case there might be any lingering effects of the scotch, I drank a lot of sea water and stuck my fingers down my throat to vomit, making up a new word which I uttered as I spewed: "Aueackh!" It sounded Gaelic. But the rear-guard treatment of water and aspirin administered by Robbie had worked. I did not have a hangover, and I thought: You should always listen to women. There are of course a few Lady MacBeths, but all else being equal, they know best.

I spent most of the day at the park office, avoiding Rattray and looking up everything I could about tides, sanderlings and shoreline micro-fauna. I was starting to see how it all might be connected. At mid-afternoon coffee break I asked Fergie if I could take the rest of the day off to bike to Barrisway and do some banking. He said, "Fine."

I went outside to get my bike, and there, across the road, I saw her.

Silhouetted in front of the sparkling inlet, moving like a

fawn along the shore towards a grove of birch trees, she was a colleen, a dryad, a silkie. Keep your eye fixed on her forever, I said to myself as I approached, lest in a twinkling she transform herself into one of those slim birches in that sacred grove, or a seal who would slip away under the darling waves. I moved toward her because, like the tide before the moon, I was powerless to resist. I approached her as you would a goddess, trembling before her beauty. With a movement like falling silk she turned and saw me, accompanied by tempered harps in harmony. The dome of her brow was perfect, her ears were newly coined seashells, her cheeks were fresh apples. Her hair was spun bronze mink, her skin ivory, and at the cusp of one divine eyebrow, a rising Venus of the tiniest of beauty spots, to highlight the surrounding glory, a perfect imperfection. I could live with that.

She slapped her forehead. "Goddamn mosquitoes," she said. "Nature sucks!"

"They're an important part of the ecosystem," my mouth said, while my heart cried out to wash with my tears of joy the dearest dead bug from off her alabaster brow.

"Who *cares*?" Even when complaining, her voice was like a thousand rising larks. "Goddamn it. Do you have a Kleenex?"

To do your bidding, my lady, I thought, I would crawl to Barrisway, run to Charlottetown, or work all my days in some corporate hellhole in Toronto to finally corner the Kleenex market, but a handkerchief woven from the

finest silks of the Indies and embroidered by all the artists of Cathay was not too fine for her.

. "Never mind, I've found one," she said, then took a balled Kleenex out of the pocket of her dress and spat on it. O lucky ball of Kleenex, to be so spat upon by those lips!

"You missed it," I said and I actually touched her face. Angels trilled a perfect fifth in both my ears and an electric shock ran through my finger and to my heart.

"Godamn bugs," she said, "Why don't they use DDT?"

"It kills birds," I said, softly, meaning to impart in my tone the ineffable sadness of a falling sparrow.

"Who *gives* a shit?" But I knew that her cruelty was like the cruelty of nature, and who said DDT was all that bad anyway? Its dangers were probably over-rated. All previous conclusions I had made about the world were up for grabs. She was beautiful, and so could not be wrong. I was a goner.

Then she looked at me straight in the face for the first time. I hoped she had been hit by the same thunderbolt as me, but she seemed only to be examining my features with curiosity, not adoration. I was aware that my face was damaged somewhat from my fall two nights ago, and I felt a certain tightness and swelling, but there was no real pain. I assumed that it was minor damage, that it might even *add* to my appeal, like the saber-scar on the cheek of an action hero that women were reported to find attractive. I raised an eyebrow and adopted what I imagined was a roguish curl to my lips. I felt the swollen side spring off the tooth, which, if the sunlight caught it, might even glint. It didn't hurt to smile, exactly, but it did make my lips tighter.

"What's wrong with your face?"

"Three guys jumped me down at the wharf in Charlottetown and we had a fight."

"Looks like they won," she said, taking out a cigarette and

lighting it.

I wished I smoked, and then I would have been carrying matches to light it for her. Why hadn't I learned to smoke? My parents had neglected my education horribly.

"What's that?" She peered closely where I had shaved that morning with my dull razor and no mirror. I had nicked myself, and to stop the bleeding, I had found a spiderweb to ball up and put on the wound.

"Spiderweb," I said. "It's a coagulant." I hoped she would recognize the effort as well as be impressed with the extent of my woodland lore.

"It looks dirty."

"I nicked myself shaving this morning. I always do when I shave. Twice a day. Like I do." Being a full-grown shaving adult male, was what I meant. "My name is Christian." I held out my hand.

"I'm Claire."

I took it that the reason she did not take my hand was because both of hers were occupied with the lighter or the cigarette. Then something occurred to me.

"Claire Duchesne?" I said. But then I thought, of course, it *had* to be her. "The artist?"

"Well, I don't know about that. I drew some pictures for that book..."

And modest as well. "Pictures?" I said. "They are Works of Art! Those drawings are yours?"

"Some of them."

"The best ones," I said. "Who's the

other loser?"

"Andrew Solomon? Total jerk."

"You can tell by his drawings. Yours are much better."

"You think so?"

"Of course! It's obvious."

"I'm glad you like them." She looked me in the eyes for the first time.

"They're wonderful. Brilliant. Beautiful," I said. "Much better than that other guy's. *His* drawings are garbage."

"That's what I said," she pouted, and a line appeared between her eyebrows as my heart back-flipped. "He said that mine weren't any good."

"What does he know?" I said. Give me the word and I'll have him killed. Then I realized I still had a copy of the pamphlet in my pocket. Perfect. "Here," I said "Could you sign a copy for me?"

"What? Like an autograph?"

"Exactly."

You could see she was pleased. I gave her my pencil, and in a moment of inspiration I presented my back for her as a desk. She placed the open pamphlet on my back and I could feel the pencil point scribbling through the paper, and her other hand holding it flat, touching my wing-bone, sending scorching ice needles into my heart, which was pounding so fast I wondered how she could write: the pencil must be bouncing off the paper. In the spruce thicket behind the park office a warbler sang the first two notes of "*La fille aux cheveux de lin*".

"I have to tell them at the office that I've arrived," she said.

"OK. I gotta get to Barrisway, change some money at the bank," I said, sounding just like a real grown-up. "See you tomorrow."

"I don't start work till the day after." She discarded her

cigarette onto the ground like, it seemed to me, any other suitors she might have been considering before she had met me, then turned and walked off.

I hopped on my bike like all three Musketeers and pedaled at high speed toward Barrisway. There was a slight grade down on the way to the first hill and in case she was still watching I pedaled with my hands off the handlebars and my arms folded on my chest, nonchalantly. But this was not as dramatic as was called for, so I grabbed the handlebars again, leant forward, shot my right leg out back and knelt on the seat and coasted, got back into my seat, straightened up and hauled the handlebars up in a wheelie, using a bump to attain front wheel lift-off. I came to the first hill, up which I expended twice as much energy as was necessary, swinging the bike from side to side like a trick cyclist, the no-bar girl's-bike feature helping me to swing it way over either side with every pump of the pedal, asking myself but when? but when? and hearing the tires on the pavement reply, *soon Soon SOON*.

The horned lark which sometimes nests along this coast is famous for its courtship displays where he rises suddenly up into the air to twinkle his wings, whistle and sing. I twinkled, whistled and sang. At the crest of the hill I looked behind, but there was nobody watching. It didn't matter. It was good exercise and made me stronger, and so improved me for her, although with the effort my face was now beating with something resembling pain. For

the first time I wondered how bad I looked. A school bus passed, twenty kids inside hooted and one threw a milk carton out the window at me. I waved, smiling. I was once like them, young and stupid. Now I was on my way to losing my innocence, and to the most beautiful girl in the world.

At normal speed it would have taken twenty minutes to get to Barrisway but that day it took me fifteen. Main Street turned out to look like a western town in a cowboy movie, with facades of old stores and clapboard walls. Except for the presence of the telephone poles, you could see a gunfight happening there. With a burst of speed, I arrived at the bank downtown. If there'd been a hitching post, I would have flipped my reins around it. I leapt up the bank stairs but it was closed. I looked down Main Street. A grocery store, hardware store, post office and a few boarded-up shops. I was probably in no danger of being swept away by the glitter. I imagined myself saying that to Claire and making her laugh. I practiced a wide winning smile and felt my face hurt again. Once more I wondered what it looked like. I touched my face as I crossed the street to the hardware store.

"What's wrong with your face, kid?" said the guy behind the counter.

"I fell."

"Yeah, well the way you were riding that bike no wonder." He looked at me with an accusing eye that said, "We don't like your kind in this town."

I thought of saying, "It's nice to have an audience," but chose instead to ignore the comment and not sink to his level. Love raised me above such petty sparring.

"Can you change a one-hundred-dollar bill?"

"No."

"The bank's closed."

"Come back tomorrow."

"I'll try at the grocery."

"It's closed too."

His problem was that he was not in love. I left his store and hopped on the bike and rode to the far end of town where the houses petered out, and then turned in a wide loop and rode at high velocity back past the store, standing on the opposite pedal like a cowboy using his horse as a shield from gunfire. I was doing it to amuse him, but I could see his face through the window looking back at me sourly. I know what you're up to, it said, I was young once too. But his face lied. He had never been young, and had never been in love, the poor bastard.

On the way back to the park office I stopped at the vegetable stand to buy more potatoes. It made me feel excellent that such an establishment existed, running on the goodwill and trust of one's neighbours. As a result there was no bitter shopkeeper feeling his life tick away and taking it out on his customers, throwing rocks at horned larks.

There was one problem though. I couldn't make change for the hundred here either and even as generous as I was feeling, I couldn't very well leave the whole amount, so I sat down cross-legged on the grass beside the road, took out my notebook and pencil and composed a note, making three drafts before I was satisfied. I knew it was Gump and Toe who ran the stand but I adopted an impersonal tone, which seemed to fit the loftiness of the

thoughts I was expressing.

"To whom it may concern:

First of all let me say how impressed I am by the trusting nature of your enterprise, and let me offer my congratulations to the noble souls who have constructed and filled with the fruit of their labours this unique and friendly establishment, the excellent edibles for which I have already paid and enjoyed once. The simple act of trusting your fellow man is one small way that we can knit together the community, strengthen the social fabric and enrich ourselves in an honourable and (I hope in your case) profitable fashion. Its existence encourages other such enterprises, and so, with luck, shall goodness spread, even to the ends of the earth. Hear hear.

Having said that, I nevertheless regrettably find myself temporarily embarrassed on the financial front, and so, although I do in fact have the cash with me, it is in too large a denomination to reasonably leave here now. I am ashamed that I am not as trusting as you in this regard, but perhaps due to my upbringing in an economic philosophy which you do not obviously share, I balk at the thought.

So what I am proposing is that I take what I need now, and hereby promise to pay you with a more convenient and manageable sum when next I am passing this way. If there are any questions, you can find me at the park office. Thank you."

I tore the page out of my notebook, folded it and inserted it through the slot of the money box. I was pedalling across the causeway before I remembered that I hadn't signed my name. Not to worry, though, the very nature of Gump and Toe's business showed that they would be okay with that. And I found myself smiling when I considered how, apart from everything else, trust simplified things.

When I got back to my campground it struck me that it wasn't a very fit place to invite Claire, so I tightened up the tent and straightened the driftwood around it, then picked some beach-pea and hung it from the peak like a pagan charm. I walked the length of the beach, carried back the largest shells I could find and lined both sides of a walkway up to the tent door, grading them by size towards the entrance, to draw her in. Then I crossed the dunes to the meadow where I cut an armful of sweetgrass to lay inside. It smelled like heaven. I collected flatter stones to ring the fire-pit and make level surfaces for my pots and pans, and straightened up the sitting log.

It would also be nice to impress Claire with some sort of professional triumph at work, preferably some sudden blinding coup which would establish my standing in the scientific community as a boy genius, accompanied by global media attention as I humbly accepted the wonderment of my colleagues at the enormity of my achievement. That would be perfect. So I re-read my notes about the relationship between the detritus left at high tide, the isopods that feed off it, and the sanderlings which in turn feed off these isopods. My hypothesis was that all three groups comprised a feeding cycle which was put into motion by the high tide.

But I could do with some more observations, so I looked at my tidal chart, which told me that the next high tide in Barrisway would be 6:27 tomorrow

morning. It would be slightly later here, and by checking the reading further east and judging my position between it and Barrisway, I approximated the high tide where I was, and wrote in my notebook, "MacAkerns' Beach, August 2nd, high tide: 6:30 PM." But that number looked rounded-off and unprofessional, so I changed it to "6:29."

Then, suddenly, my father's voice in my head said something that I couldn't quite understand, and I caught myself. Desiring to appear more scientific, I had sullied the spirit of science. I erased what I had written and wrote "6:30" again, feeling noble and serious. My mind was working clearly now, and it occurred to me that the numbers on tide charts at best could only ever be close approximations, and in general were probably posing as more specific than they ever could truly be, so I made another note: "Query: How to predict local tides more accurately and honestly?"

That was as much as I could do for now, so I walked out to the road and down toward MacAkerns', composing in my head a rough draft of my Nobel Prize acceptance speech. "I could never have conceived of the work for which you are honouring me without the unwavering love of my dear wife, Claire Duchesne…"

I was healthy and alert, my lungs cleansed with sea air, blissfully tired from the exercise I was getting and probably also starting a nicely bronzed tan. My face still felt a bit puffy, but the swelling might only fill out my jaw and make me more attractive. I was young, fit, and with no bad habits, although smoking cigarettes was a possibility I might explore. Claire smoked, so it must be all right.

***

I entered the kitchen wanting to tell everybody how I had

just met a girl, but Robbie and Wallace were deep into some discussion, sitting across the table from each other. "Out with it," Robbie was saying to Wallace. "Why did Constable Marjorie come by this afternoon?"

"I already told you."

"No you didn't."

"I thought I did."

"Why was she here, Wallace?"

"Just checking up."

"That's all?"

Wallace paused. "Oh, yeah," as if he'd suddenly remembered. "Also to tell us that if we didn't respond to the government's last offer, she'd been given the authority to kick us off our land."

"I thought it was something like that."

"Well, there you are then. No reason I *should* have told you if you already knew."

"So now what?"

"Don't worry. Things are progressing exactly as I predicted."

"You predicted that the cops would come to kick us off?"

"It was bound to happen. The honourable Member from Barrisway Riding, What's-His-Face, is on the warpath."

"Robert Logan Head."

"That's the one. The election's coming up and he wants to announce the park opening so he can go into his big smelly look-at-me-all-great-and-mighty routine. Ap-

parently we're threatening his chance for a photo op."

"You mean *you* are."

"I have no wish to take all the credit."

"So what do you plan to do about it?"

"Get our side of the story out."

"Using your vast network of media contacts?"

"I know lots of people. Lots of people know me."

"Yeah. That's the problem."

"Don't worry, Robbie. I got it covered."

"How?"

"I intend to ask for equal media time."

"And why would they give it to you?"

"Because they are legally obliged to."

"Who says?"

"The Elections Act of Canada."

Robbie looked narrowly at Wallace. "Elections Act?"

"All candidates are insured equal media time in an election."

"What's that got to do with *you*?"

"I have registered myself as Independent Candidate for Barrisway riding," said Wallace. "I am running for office".

Robbie put her hand over her eyes and shook her head slowly. "For fuck's sakes..."

"What do I got to lose?" said Wallace.

"The last shreds of your dignity?"

"Too late."

"You got a point there."

"Come on Robbie! We can *do* it."

"We?"

"You can be my chief of staff."

"Thanks a lot."

"Remember, power is the greatest aphrodisiac."

"So?"

"It'll get you laid."

Robbie looked at her wrist where she would have worn a watch if she'd owned one. "Fifteen seconds since you've announced your political intentions, and you're already pimping out your own sister."

"And that's exactly the type of up-front dressing-down I need from an astute chief of staff."

"In that case, you're also an idiot."

"And the humour! Great for building morale in the troops."

"What troops?"

"Brucie? How about it?"

"Sounds like f-f-fun."

"And don't forget Whoever-The-Hell-He-Is. He can be director in charge of communications."

"What's that mean?" I said.

"Don't ask me. We're making this up as we go along."

"There's that 'we' again," said Robbie.

"Come on, Robbie. What do you say?"

"You've actually done this? For real? Signed on?"

"That's what I'm telling you."

"But...what? I mean, you just say you're the Independent wally-wook from Barrisway and you magically become one?"

"No. You have to get fifty signatures."

Robbie paused, thought, then her eyes opened wide. "At the bar!"

"Yep."

"You lied!"

"When?"

"About that paper you were handing around. You said it was a petition to keep us on the

land."

"And so it was. In a way. If you look at it from a certain angle."

"You were getting people to approve your nomination! In exchange for beer!"

"A longstanding Island tradition."

"Beer which you bought with Christian's money."

"Whoever-The-Hell-He-Is doesn't mind, do you, Whoever-The-Hell-You-Are?"

The money was gone anyway, and besides, I was in love. "I am honoured," I said.

"See?" said Wallace. "He's honoured."

"And that's it? Fifty signatures and you get to run in an election?"

"No. I also had to pay five hundred bucks."

Robbie thought a bit, then snapped her fingers. "From the loan!"

"*Voilà.*"

"You lied again."

"Can't expect the truth from me, Robbie. I'm a politician now."

Robbie shook her head slowly. "I can't believe it. Independent Candidate for Barrisway riding."

"It's a free country, isn't it? Have we not the inalienable right to life, liberty and the pursuit of happiness?"

"No," said Robbie. "That's the American Constitution."

"Bullshit. The American Constitution is "Truth, Justice and the American Way...""

"That's Superman, Wallace. You might want to bone up on some of this stuff if you're running for office."

"I'll be relying on my staff to take care of those sorts of details. I'll be front man, leading our victorious sweep through Barrisway riding fueled solely by my charisma."

"That should get you about as far as the park gate."

"And that's the first thing we're gonna do when we get into power: Stop the park. Stop! The! Park!... Stop! The! Park!..." He tried to get a chant started around the table but saw it was going nowhere.

"There's a little matter of getting enough *votes*, Wallace."

"Well, I imagine I can count on yours..."

"Not necessarily."

"Stop screwing around. I can count on your vote, so that's one. Then there's my vote. That's two. Brucie is underage, but Whoever-The-Hell-You-Are, you'll vote for me, won't you?"

"He has to be a resident," said Robbie.

"Fuck. How many's that, then?"

"One, yours, unless you can convince me," said Robbie. She shook her head again. "The Right Honourable Wallace MacAkern."

"There's no need to act so astounded. I come by it honestly."

"You're talking about Smooth Lennie?"

"Yep."

"Hardly honestly, then."

"Who's Smooth L-L-Lennie?" said Brucie.

"He was your uncle in the Provincial Legislature, Brucie," said Wallace. "And the less we say about him the better."

"Nobody ever t-t-told me about him."

"Well, he wasn't exactly the shining pride of the family,"

said Robbie. "And you never knew him personally. You were too young."

"You were too young too, Robbie," said Wallace. "I'm the only one who remembers him in the flesh."

"Maybe," said Robbie, "But I've heard all the stories."

"What s-stories?"

"Scandals, mostly…"

"What ab-b-bout?"

"The usual. Patronage. Cronyism…."

"Corruption. Absconded funds…" added Robbie.

"Then there was that perjury charge."

"Before *that* though there was avoiding arrest, wasn't there?"

"And resisting arrest."

"And bribery."

"Don't forget blackmail…"

"What h-h-happened to him?"

"He was hounded out of the province."

"Where'd he g-g-go?"

"Monte Carlo, I heard," said Wallace.

"I heard Tangier," said Robbie. "And now it's best to forget about Smooth Lennie. Don't want *his* memory brought up during the campaign."

Wallace looked at her. "So you will be my chief of staff?"

"Only if I don't have to vote for you."

"You make no sense."

"Neither does this campaign."

It seemed to me both possible and natural that what Wallace was attempting would come about, and brilliantly. I was in love, and it seemed that the most realistic way of looking at the world was with wide-eyed optimism. I was just about to tell everybody about my meeting Claire, but just then we heard the sounds of an approaching vehicle.

"Probably the cops coming to kick us off," said Robbie as she and Wallace stood up.

Brucie and I followed them onto the porch, and I thought that with my knowledge of the Canadian Bill of Rights I should probably act as an advocate for this lovely family by explaining to the police their lack of legal footing for expropriation, but it wasn't the police, or anything like it.

A battered but elaborately painted van was clattering across the yard, wobbling on its chassis like its suspension was made from elastic bands. It backfired and rolled down to the shore where it came to a halt and backfired again. Its entire outside was covered in an intricate and undisciplined mural of green and orange depicting a jumble of serpents and Ethiopian royalty, all tied together with a peace symbol and a seven-pointed leaf. The license plate was from New Hampshire, and declared, "Live Free Or Die," a motto, it occurred to me, which must have seemed unbearably ironic for the people who manufactured them, in prisons.

The door of the van opened, a billow of smoke gushed out, and from the driver's seat slid a heavy-lidded young man wearing a rainbow tam o'shanter. I heard the door on the other side of the van shut, and from around the back came another young man in a sarong, with blond dreadlocks and camera gear festooned around his neck. He raised one camera to his eye and sighted the surroundings, then focused on the driver and snapped a few pictures. The smell of smoke like burning socks reached me.

"Aha! " said Wallace. "They've arrived."

"Who the hell are they?" said Robbie.

Wallace indicated the driver. "You remember Bailey. He used to come to Barrisway for a few summers with his family, back about ten years ago."

"That's Bailey Hendershott?"

"He does look different, doesn't he?"

"Christ. What's he been up to?"

"Political advisor now."

"You...invited him to help out with your campaign?"

"Correct."

"How you gonna pay him?"

"He doesn't want any money. Said he'd gladly be our chief of staff free of charge."

"You just said I was going to be chief of staff."

"That's before I knew he'd actually show up."

"Well, what am I gonna be, then?"

"What do you want to be?"

"Leader of the Opposition," said Robbie.

The duo at the van had oriented themselves, looked around and saw us on the porch.

"Hallo Wallace!" yelled Bailey, flashing a beautiful smile and waving.

"You made it!" yelled back Wallace.

"Why yes, mon, we did!" He gestured at the man with the camera. "This be Aiden. And Melissa, she still be sleeping in the van. One second while we get our things!" He flashed that smile again and he and Aiden went around to the other side of the van.

"I thought he was from Boston or somewhere," said Robbie to Wallace.

"New Hampshire."

"Then why the accent?"

"No idea," said Wallace. "He seems to have gotten weirder."

Bailey came back carrying a briefcase and Aiden appeared with a small packsack. They walked up to us and Bailey shook hands with Wallace.

"We heard your cry like da wounded stag , and came a-runnin'. High time to leave Babylon, anyway."

"I'm glad you're here," said Wallace.

Robbie was looking at the van. "No difficulty crossing the border?"

"Bailey's, like, a genius?" said Aiden. "It was getting late? And we'd already thought about going across at maybe four different border crossings that day? But they didn't look right? And I was getting tired, I gotta admit, thinking, what's he doing? And Melissa was being bitchy?" All his statements sounded like questions, with the last word on the up-beat. "But then, Bailey? We come to the fifth border crossing, way the hell back in the woods somewhere? A booth, like, with one guy in it? And it's, like, two minutes to five when we pull in? And the customs man takes, like, one look at us in the truck, then looks at the clock on the wall, and you can see he thinks there's two days of paper work here at least? So he says, 'Go. Just go.' And he waves us through!" Aiden started to giggle, holding his camera gear to stop it from bouncing against his chest. "Genius!"

Bailey struck a pose and de-claimed:

"The trick for all who want to stay free is paint it so big they cannot see."

"Break it down!"

said Aiden.

"What's with the accent, Bailey?" said Robbie.

"From my point of view, you de one wit de accent." Then he started reciting again:

"The point of view,

The point of view

Who has the right one?

Me or you?"

He put the fingers of his right hand to his chest and bowed deeply.

"He just makes this stuff up? Like that?" said Aiden.

"Is that how you're going to win the election?" said Robbie. "With poetry? 'Cause I don't know..." She shook her head. "I just don't know..."

There were noises from the van, the back door opened, and a girl with beaded hair backed out, stretched, and came toward us. "Are we here?" she said, rubbing her eyes and yawning.

"We are indeed, " said Bailey. "Everybody. This be my sister Melissa."

We all said "Hi," but Robbie said, "Hello," in a way that was so different from her tone just a few seconds before that we all looked at her. She was staring directly into the eyes of the newcomer.

"Oh. Hi," said Melissa, gazing back directly into Robbie's eyes.

"Roberta," said Robbie, holding out her hand.

"I'm Melissa."

They didn't continue holding hands, but they might as well have. And neither did they take their eyes off each other, which, I couldn't help but think, was the way Claire should have behaved when we had met. It worried me a little when I remembered that she hadn't and my sunny optimism wobbled slightly.

"Come on in," said Robbie.

"OK," said Melissa.

And the rest of us watched them go inside.

"Might as well come in too," said Wallace. "Got any food?"

***

An hour later everybody was sitting around the kitchen table with the remains of the meal jumbled in front of us, a chickpea and flat-bread concoction with Caribbean sauce and limes. It was nice to have eaten a meal without potato, but I was still a bit worried about where I stood with Claire. I wanted both to know and to put off knowing.

"I'm sorry the place is such a mess," said Robbie to Melissa. "I don't know how it got this bad."

"I've been living in a van for two days. This is fine."

"Well you can stay here as long as you want. It's OK with us."

"Thanks."

That's the way people in love talked, although maybe with some people it just took longer to get there.

Bailey pushed back his chair from the table and declaimed:

"For every hospi-tality,

Returns in multi-ples of three."

"I don't know how he does it?" said Aiden.

"Easy," said Bailey. "A com-bin-a-tion of de willing-ness to adopt a

character..." he pointed at his tam. "Plus, what's in here."
He tapped it. I thought he meant his brain, but he extracted from under the brim what looked like a badly rolled
cigarette.

"Time to refuel," he said. "Anybody?"

"Right on," said Aiden.

"Yes indeed," said Melissa. "Robbie?"

"I will if you will," said Robbie. "But, Brucie..?"

"Yeah yeah," said Brucie. "I know. T-too young," and he
left the room.

"Well, none for me, thanks," said Wallace. "I'll just finish
whatever scotch has been left by Whoever-The-Hell-He-Is.
Watch out for that one. He's a hound for the booze."

"Do you partake?" Bailey asked me, indicating his cigarette.

"I was thinking I'd take it up." Claire smoked, and I might
need all the sympathetic behaviour with her that I could
muster.

"It can teach you God," said Bailey, which was a claim I'd
never heard before about tobacco. Bailey lit it, drew deep
and passed it to Aiden. I supposed that they didn't have
much money and were sharing what few meager resources
they had, and I will be the first to admit that for all the
books I'd read, in many ways I wasn't a terrifically bright
lad, for only then did it occur to me that what they might
be smoking was marijuana, which I had heard about. How
interesting, I thought.

"Is that marijuana?" I asked. Bailey nodded. Then, because
I thought they should know, I added, "It's illegal."

"Maybe in the eyes of man," said Bailey. "But not in the
eyes of God."

It was the first time I'd heard such an argument, and I was
impressed. "That's a neat way of putting it."

Bailey looked at me. "What's your name?"

"Christian."

"Then I'm Rastaman." He laughed, and, still sitting in his chair, he performed a little cha-cha with his feet.

"I met a boy named Chris-chin

And he nearly blew my mind

with no hair yet upon *his* chin

He gave me wisdom of his kind."

"You flyin' high, now, Bailey!" said Aiden. He drew in a lungful and the ember roared a quarter way down the joint. He held his breath and passed it back.

Wallace poured the last of the scotch into a glass, looked at the empty bottle and said, "There's another one the English won't get."

"Music!" said Bailey, and stood up. "We must have music!"

We followed him outside and down to the van and when we got there Aiden passed the joint to Melissa, opened up the back, climbed in and put a reggae tape in the machine. One-and Two-and Koo-koo-kachoo-and...Music boomed over the lawn and out onto the still water of the bay as we stood around and watched the reflection of the sunset in the eastern sky. It was spectacular, robin's egg and crimson, with a black line between. Bailey drew another joint from under his tam, lit it and toked. He gestured at all of Nature.

"These are the Things of God, Christian, but we must take a vacation from them soon, into the Things of Man." And there was that idea again.

"I like that," I said.

Bailey held out the joint. "Here, but only if you want."

If a cigarette would make me look cool to Claire, how much more would a joint?

"Live Free or Die," I said, and Bailey flashed his lovely smile. I felt pretty cool already as I put it to my lips and inhaled deeply.

The smoke caught in my throat and I started to cough, then continued without stopping for a good two minutes. While I was doubled over hacking, Bailey took the joint out of my hand and passed it to Aiden. "Next time it comes around, hold the smoke in your mouth to cool it."

When it came back I tried that, puffing out my cheeks like a blowfish.

"Now," said Bailey, "inhale *slowly,*" and I did, and only caught my breath once near the end. I exhaled and waited for whatever would happen. Perhaps there would be swirly colours like television depictions of the marijuana experience, though my mind could not possibly produce more vivid colours than that sunset we were under. It made even the van look drab.

I waited but didn't feel any different.

The music was good, though, bass-heavy with a stress on every third beat. One two THREE four, One two THREE four. The fifth song on the tape was a pleasant surprise as well, a version of "Deep, Deep In My Heart," which they had laid over a different rhythm, and they'd added a little talky section in the middle that rattled on in double-time.

"De Jah voice come, de mighty run like salmon always upstream,

But down dey go, one two and fro and shine de light eternal."

Although English, I found it incomprehensible. It was like

the van painting put into words.

"I don't get it," I said.

"You have to listen a few times," said Bailey. He handed me the cassette case and I looked at the cover. "I'll make you a copy."

"You can make copies?" said Wallace.

"We got all de gear," he said, gesturing into the van.

"Maybe you can dub 'As Softening Shades of Evening Fall.'"

"What is it?"

"You *gotta* hear it," said Wallace, and positively ran inside to get the tape.

The joint came around and Bailey offered it to me again.

"No thanks," I said. "It doesn't make me feel any different."

"First time, sometimes it's like that," said Bailey.

"Oh."

"Then it gets better," and he nodded his head in the direction of Melissa and Robbie, who were dancing, held together as though by little magnets on the tips of their fingers, circling like planets locked in orbit, in odd slow motion moves, purple in the shadows against the sunset above the dunes. I had certainly felt like they must be feeling, but had Claire?

The Mighty Voice of Jah tape came to an end and Melissa and Robbie stepped apart.

Wallace reap-
peared out of the
kitchen door with
Brucie holding onto
his leg, trying to re-
strain him. "No!
G-G-God! Not "S-S-

Softening Shades!"

Wallace broke loose laughing, and came toward us as Brucie on the ground mimed ripping both his ears off then squirmed around, covering his head with his arms.

"What's "Softening Shades"? said Melissa.

"Wallace thinks it's funny," said Robbie.

"Men!" said Melissa, raising her eyebrows and shaking her head. The beads on her braids clacking together said "typical!"

Bailey took the tape from Wallace and put it in the machine. Aiden took pictures.

"Smile," he said.

"Click!" said the camera.

"I was telling Robbie that this is the song I want at my funeral," said Wallace. He straightened up and adopted the Scottish Bard voice he had used to recount the MacAkern Saga. "...For truly the skirl of the pipes are the sweetest sounds to ever touch the ears of man."

"Not if they're playing 'Softening Shades,' they're not," said Robbie.

"Whist, girl!" said Wallace. "I'll have you know that that tune was commissioned by our uncle, Lennie 'The Smooth' MacKay, to be written by Island composer Gilbert Arsenault, 'Piper Gil'..."

"...That tone-deaf sonovabitch..."

"...for the opening of the Provincial Assembly in 1958, because Smooth Lennie knew that one man and one man only could rise to the occasion and create a work of art worthy of such an august body."

"Which he hated with a passion and who he wanted to get even with by making them sit through it," said Robbie.

Wallace turned to us and dropped his heightened tone. This story was too good not to be told straight. "Lennie hated those pricks in the Legislature, see, so he put Gil on salary for a year, composing for their grand opening *the* vilest, most difficult piece of shit-on-a-stick ever written. He pried some funding from Culture and Heritage to use against them, because he had it in for them too, and sure enough, getting a hundred pipers together just to learn the damn thing pretty well blew their budget and finished them off. Now, who would like to hear a recording of it?" he asked innocently.

"Not me!" said Robbie.

"No!" yelled Brucie.

Wallace was well pleased. "I'd hate to have lost it. I was thinking of using it for our campaign song. Maestro?" he handed the tape to Aiden who inserted it into the machine and punched the play button.

"Christ," said Robbie. "Here it comes."

Out of the speaker came the crackling sounds of an old recording and then a noise like the tape recorder wasn't working right. This proved merely to be the rising wheeze of the bagpipes equalizing the pressure in their plumbing as one hundred creatively-tuned and badly-maintained instruments came to life as if they preferred to be left for dead. "Leave me al*one*," they seemed to snarl. After this came a short silence, broken by the thin wavering whine of one piper who couldn't shut off his instrument completely. Then a sharp tap of a baton, followed by another real silence, into which Wallace said in a

phoney whisper, "You are about to hear the live recorded performance of the world premier of the composition performed by the 1954 All Island Pipe Band under the musical directorship of Michael Beaton."

"Mad Mike," said Robbie.

And with a great squeal like a hundred slaughtered hogs, the pipes sprang into the body of the "melody," a disjointed pile of rank offal with no point to the composition other than to annoy. It was like a swarm of giant aggressive gnats, or the collective teeth-gnashing of a talentless mob of Philistines who got their way simply by being so obnoxious they were left to do whatever they wanted. And what they wanted was to inflict pain. Pure, twisted, wrenching, annoyance. As the "tune" rose in volume, it worsened in tone. It split into two, then three, then eleven-and-a-half factions in violent argument with each other as to who could be the most irritating. They fought, they whined, and finally when even they couldn't take any more, they collapsed into themselves, spitting and cursing vilely. Eventually, it all came to a disjointed halt, though not in any definite enough fashion to be considered resolved. It left you feeling What's The Point Of Anything, along with an empty sense of mercy that at least it seemed to be over. Wallace said, "Again?" and Brucie punched him in the leg and yelled, "No!"

"I've *got* to hear dat once more," said Bailey.

But the mosquitoes were getting fierce and I had a high tide to meet tomorrow morning early.

"I should get home now," I said.

"Are you OK?" said Robbie.

"Yeah. Sure," I said. "See you."

"Play it again," said Bailey, and as I walked away I could hear the first strains of the piece once more, followed by great bouts of booming laughter.

The air was getting cool, but the cracked pavement on the road was still warm on my bare feet. The sunset had faded but a half-moon had risen. Off to either side of me the spiky spruce skyline showed against the bright night sky and everything smelled of spruce and salt water. I felt no effect whatsoever from the marijuana and wondered what all the fuss was about.

Where the woods gave way to the dunes, I crossed to the camp where moonlight washed the beach in silver, casting shadows on the sand.

I noticed footprints which weren't mine. They came up the beach from the east, right to the tent where the person who'd made them had shuffled around, then gone back by the same way. I examined them up close, the mark of a quite heavy boot with a tread like a zig zag. The moonlight was bright enough to see all this.

Oh that moonlight, I thought as I crawled into the heavenly-smelling tent and arranged my sleeping bag, thinking of Claire. Everything would be all right, and if not, so what?

And then I surprised myself by finding that my thoughts about her had become quite rude, which shocked me. It made me less worthy of her. She was a flaxen divinity, her brow a dome of heaven, her eyes dark pools, and a bosom on her that would give a gay monk a hard-on. A *dead* gay monk...

Stop it.

Christ her bosom was lovely, though, proof that God not only exists but that He is benevolent. On one side of the equation of life was

all the evil that had befallen humanity since the birth of time, but to balance all that out, on the other side was Claire's bosom. I could imagine what it must be like unconfined by her brassiere. Oh, I could imagine *that* all right.

One of the things I must do was introduce her to Melissa, who wore no bra at all, a style of dress which Claire could definitely think about imitating. Claire's bra, in evidence under her shirt, looked to be the steel-belted official Russian Army model, constructed with suspension bridge technology from fabric of the kind used in bullet-proof police gear. It created a tragic flaw in the line of her divinity, an unnatural assault on all that was holy. One of the Things of Man, goddamn it, confining the Things which were definitely of God. Melissa, in this regard, was much more sensible and progressive, her bra-lessness, as well, supporting one plank in the platform of the Woman's Liberation Movement of which I, for one, heartily approved. Perhaps when I introduced them to each other, Melissa could convince Claire of the oppressive male-dominated power structure which was confining her womanhood, and Claire, now liberated and grateful to me, would show me her tits...

Stop it, I thought. Now go to sleep.

5

I awoke on time, crawled out of my tent, and scanned down the beach where small waves lapped against and stirred up the sea-wrack left by the departing high tide. As though on cue, better than I ever could have planned, a thin flock of sanderlings wobbled down, braked on shaky wings, alighted and started picking, running excitedly up and down the shore. I was amazed and pleased that my hypothesis seemed so easily confirmed. I noted the time and described the phenomenon briefly in my notebook. I would tell Claire first, but she wouldn't be in today. How long, oh Lord how long?

I hopped on my bike and pedalled to the park office in record time, said hello to Fergie, avoided saying hello to Rattray, then buried myself

in my work all day for Claire's sake, to present perhaps the preliminary paper to her tomorrow. The book that would result would be dedicated to her, and all that morning and afternoon I wrote and rewrote my notes, the workday passing quickly until it was time to leave.

Back at my camp, I swam, ate a potato, practiced some banjolele and wrote a song about her, then played it all the way out to the road and down to MacAkerns'. Brucie was sitting on the front steps, looking across the bay and humming to himself.

"Hi," he said when he saw me. "Nobody's here."

"You are."

"Nobody else."

"*I* am."

He blushed at being teased. "I *m-mean* Robbie and Wallace and M-M-Melissa and Aiden and Bailey. *They* aren't here."

"Where'd they go?"

"Wallace is out c-c-campaigning, Bailey and Aiden went to the library, and Robbie went to the beach with M-M-Melissa to see you."

"I must've missed them. What did they want me for?"

"Nothing."

I strummed a chord on my banjolele. "Wanna jam?"

"Yeah!"

He sang "Deep, Deep in my Heart" and I plucked along and harmonized on the chorus in simple four-four time. About halfway through I changed to a Caribbean rhythm, and after the song ended, we did it twice more, once in each style.

A ball of dust appeared at the far end of the road and the pickup truck came barrelling across the causeway and into the yard. Wallace sprang out, dressed in a shirt and tie which made him look like a particularly fashion-blind

Jehovah's Witness. He walked up to us just as Robbie and
Melissa appeared down the trail from the beach.

"The beach is beautiful" said Melissa. "You should check
out Christian's campground."

"Are you building something down on our beach, Whoever-The-Hell-You-Are?"

"Just fixing up the campground," I said. "I'm in love."

Everybody looked at me.

"With what?" said Wallace. "A warthog?"

"No." I looked back at him, offended. "She's the most
beautiful woman on the face of the earth."

"*OooooOOOOOoooooooo!*" said Melissa and Brucie
together.

"Who is she?" said Robbie.

"New girl at the office."

"What's she like?"

"Perfect," I said, stating a fact.

"Well, maybe you should aim a bit lower," said Wallace.
"I mean, your face being the way it is."

"Why? What's it like?"

But nobody wanted to be the first to say. They glanced at
each other and I put my fingers to my lip, felt the bump
there, and wondered again how bad it looked.

"Here," said Melissa, rummaging in her handbag.
She found a small
mirror and handed
it to me.

After the first day
it had not given me
any discomfort, so
I'd assumed that it
looked all right, but
this was the first

time I'd actually seen my face since my fall off the truck, and it was deeply shocking. One large black eye like a Dalmatian puppy was paired on the other side of my nose with a sad-sack purple line like a football player, and around this and over most of the rest of the face was an asymmetrical bruise of greenish-yellow. The bridge of my nose was raised in a lopsided lump, my lip was swollen slightly, and my jaw was scuffed. The new shape of my lip created an indentation in the corner of my mouth that caught and held a collection of small bubbles of spittle. The sunburn on my forehead had furred up with dead skin around the edges, and near the tip of my nose, in an independent attempt at ugliness unrelated to the abuse that the sunburn and ball-hitch had inflicted, a large pimple had started, a distraction which I now realized one eye was constantly being drawn to, making me vaguely cross-eyed. I adjusted my expression to the rakish face I had used when I had met Claire and what looked back at me was a zombie's idiot younger brother.

"Can't see why she wouldn't fall for you," said Wallace. "Unless she's blind. She isn't blind, is she?"

"No."

"Then you're fucked. Or, more to the point, *not* fucked."

"Wallace!" said Robbie

"Sorry," said Wallace. "I'm sure she's very important to you. And you never know, that look of yours worked for Quasimodo. Or not. I can't remember. Robbie? Did Quasimodo ever get laid?"

"No, Wallace. Quasimodo never got laid."

"Well then, Whoever-The-Hell-You-Are, you are shit out of luck."

"I have some makeup if you want," said Melissa.

"That's all right," I said. Though it wasn't. I was in shock.

"I'll give you some before you go," she said.

"Could I have some scotch?" I said.

"What did I tell you?" said Wallace. "A hound for the liquor. And as it so happens…" He walked back to the truck, dropped the tailgate, dragged out two crates stacked on top of each other and carried them back towards us, setting them down on the porch. He took a bottle out of the crate, unscrewed the cap, and handed it to me. "Remember now," he said. "No swilling."

"Where'd you get those?" said Robbie.

"Dunbar," said Wallace.

"I thought Dunbar hated your guts."

"Not really. Smooth Lennie screwed him over once, so he hated the whole family for a while just by association, but I made up to him and we're all the best of friends now."

"You and Dunbar?" said Robbie.

"Politics makes strange bedfellows."

"You *slept* with Dunbar?"

"A manner of speaking, Robbie."

I took a sip, then another. It didn't seem as bad as two nights ago. The trick was to administer it in small doses.

Bailey's van appeared in the distance, roared down the causeway and wobbled into the yard where it came to a halt and backfired. Bailey and Aiden got out and came toward us.

"How did da canvassing go, mon?" said Bailey.

"We are sipping the fruits of that adventure right now," said Wallace, toasting him as he approached.

"What's all this?"

"I got Dunbar's vote, and two cases of scotch as a campaign contribution."

"No shit?" said Bailey. He took the bottle from me and took a belt. "Just what the doctor called for." He handed the bottle back and took from my other hand the mirror, peered into it, then removed his tam and ran his hand over his skull, which was hanging with short dreadlocks in little knots like baby fingers. "Time to re-enter Babylon. My hair will be shorn like Samson, and then I will be weak enough for the fight. Ha!"

Aiden said, "That's brilliant, Bailey."

"Why don't you just marry him and get it over with?" said Melissa.

Bailey put down the mirror, took another belt of scotch, and clapped his hands once. "Campaign Mode!"

"Wait!" said Aiden, "I'll take some before-and-after shots," and started taking his camera out of its case.

"What's c-campaign mode?" said Brucie.

"It's where Bailey transforms himself from a clown into a horse's ass," said Melissa, and she rummaged in her handbag and took out a small set of folding scissors.

"Off they go, Melissa," said Bailey, pointing at his head and dropping his Caribbean accent. He sat down on the porch as Aiden snapped some photos. "And this will also mean there will be no more marijuana for the duration. For me, I mean. You can all do whatever *you* want, of course."

"Oh, I plan to," said Melissa, crosslegged behind him as she snipped, and with the first dropping dreadlock, Bailey's back stiffened and his eye cleared and steadied.

"From now until our victory, I will confine myself only to scotch. And a very fine scotch it is. Who's Dunbar again?"

"Our neighbour across the bay."

"Where'd he get it?"

"He makes it himself," said Wallace.

"They let you do that in Canada?"

"Not if you use a still, but he just ferments the barley mash, leaves it out in the cold to freeze the water in it, then pours off what doesn't freeze."

"And that's legal?"

"Well, it isn't *il*legal. Yet. But probably only because they haven't heard about the process."

"Hunh! Why'd he give it to you? "

"Dunbar's got a problem with drink, so he can't touch the stuff himself. He just likes trying to make a perfect batch."

"If he can't touch it, how can he tell if it's any good?"

"Sip and spit."

"I guess that means he can't be a real alcoholic."

"Worse. He's an artist."

"Well, it's certainly fine scotch."

I agreed. I was starting to feel the drink's particular charm, its warmth and the magical way it instilled a sense of possibility. Claire wouldn't mind my face. She would see through my outward appearance to my flaming spirit. Had I not just developed and gathered evidence toward a sanderling hypothesis that would, at the very least, be a valuable contribution to modern marine science? I sipped some more and listened to the conversation.

"So, Wallace," said Bailey. "How are we going to win this election?"

"Would you like to hear my strategy?"

"I would."

"OK. Do you know how much a Canadian MP gets paid?"

"Tell me."

"Twenty-four grand, and an additional ten grand expense account. And do you know the number of votes cast last election in Barrisway Riding?"

"No."

"Twelve thousand eight hundred and eighty seven. Which means you only need six thousand four hundred and forty four votes to win."

"Are you just making up all these numbers?" said Robbie.

"I swear I'm not. I phoned El'ner at the library and she looked them up for me."

"Continue," said Bailey. "You were saying you needed six thousand votes to win?"

"Right. Now, if you divide thirty-four thousand six hundred (my future MP's salary) by six thousand four hundred and forty-four (the number of voters we need to win) it comes to five dollars."

"Five dollars and thirty-six cents, actually," said Bailey.

"OK, smartass," said Wallace. "Five dollars and thirty-six cents, then. Around five dollars per vote, anyway."

"Fine."

"So. How's about this for a campaign slogan...?" said Wallace.

But Bailey anticipated him. "'Vote for me, get five bucks'?" he asked.

"You got it."

Melissa stopped snipping. Bailey looked right at Wallace, nodding slowly with respect. "I *like* it," he said. "It does mean, of course, that you will forfeit any salary if you do win."

"I'm not in it for the money. I'm in it for the power."

"That's what I like to hear," said Bailey. "I can work with

that." Melissa started snipping again.

"I go door to door and offer five bucks to anybody who will vote for me," said Wallace, "and, *voilà*, I'm in!"

"And, don't forget, that salary is per annum," said Bailey. "You can give them five dollars next year, too."

"Jesus! Fuck! That's right! And the next!..."

"And you can legitimately claim that by financing yourself in this way, you are more impervious to outside political influence."

"Right! I can't be corrupted. Unlike my respected opponent, the right honourable Shit-For-Brains-What's-His-Name?"

"Robert Logan Head," said Robbie. "And maybe you should learn his name if you're gonna be running against him."

"Minor detail," said Wallace.

"Well, here's another minor detail you may have overlooked," said Robbie. "Where are you gonna get the money for all this?"

"What money? That's the beauty part. I don't *need* anybody to bankroll me."

"Think it through, Wallace," said Robbie. "You go to your first constituent, and you say what?"

"I say vote for me."

"And he says 'Why?'"

"And I say, 'Because there's five bucks in it for you' and he says 'OK'..."

"And then?"

"And then I say, 'See you at the polling station!'"

"And he says, 'Where's my five bucks?'"

"And I say..." Wallace stopped. A difficulty loomed. "I say that... as soon as I'm in power I...One second, I got it! I give him a promissary note..."

"And he says, 'Yeah. Right! Like I'm gonna trust *you!*' And he slams the door in your face and sics the dogs on you."

"I could print up a sort of...coupon... 'Pay the bearer on demand...' only if I win of course, *you* know..." But you could see his excitement starting to trickle away. I think he'd had this mental image of going around to every door in his riding and delivering one crisp five dollar bill for the promise of the vote. "I could put a picture of my face on the coupon..."

"Jesus, now you *really* want to lose," said Robbie. "Forget it, Wallace. You're going to need some money up front."

The Old Problem. Silence fell around the table where seconds before there had been so much possibility. 'The rich they just get richer and the poor are left to rot, The bastards inherit everything and the meek inherit squat' went the lyrics of the song. The Barley Boys had hit the nail on the head.

"Oh well..." said Aiden.

I looked around at everybody. Bailey was the only one who seemed unaffected by the gloom.

"You can still do this," he said.

Everybody looked up at him.

"How?" said Wallace.

"I'll bankroll you," said Bailey.

"Really?" said Wallace, perking up.

"Absolutely."

"I don't know what to say..."

"Don't worry about it."

"Well...*Thank* you."

"You're most welcome," said Bailey, speaking now entirely in the accents of Old Money Boston.

Melissa snipped the last two dreadlocks off the back of his neck. "There. You'll want to shave the rest off with a razor."

"Yes," said Bailey, holding up the mirror. "That *is* better. My suit is in the van, isn't it?"

"I suppose so," said Melissa.

"Very well, then," said the new Bailey.

The girls prepared a meal and we ate. I drank two glasses of water with aspirin before I left and Melissa went upstairs and came down with a makeup kit, a small pouch crammed full, which she handed to me.

"Here," she said. "It'll cover the worst parts. Don't overdo it."

***

I awoke next morning three hours before I had to get to work, and at low tide made a note of the time. I lit a fire, boiled a potato for breakfast and thought that perhaps I should leave another note at the vegetable stand suggesting the occasional carrot or turnip as an addition to their stock. I picked and ate some raspberries but they were coming to the end of their season and I couldn't get as many as I wanted. I needn't worry, though: I came upon a Saskatoon berry bush and filled up on those.

One way or another, things worked out. There

was nothing to worry about. Claire would see past my bruises.

To help her do that, however, I went to the tent, opened the case Melissa had lent me and found face powder in a flat pearloid container shaped like a scallop shell, a tube of foundation cream, a stick of flesh-coloured lipstick and red blush. Everything was packaged and accessorized with brushes and applicators and, for the powder, a soft pad of the downiest feather. I laid everything out on a flat piece of driftwood, and went and wet my hair in salt water and combed it with my fingers into what I considered a romantic front curl with smoothed sides.

I didn't have a mirror, but the tin-foil I used for cooking had a somewhat reflective surface. When I flattened it out and looked into it, though, what looked back was a smear of colours like an impressionist painting by an artist with cataracts, so I just painted over my face wherever I could see any sign of bruising. By this time my hair had hardened into a matted felt helmet, which I considered lucky, as the bike ride to the park office wouldn't disturb it.

Finally, considering that my pyjama top wasn't stylish enough, I first removed the mangled collar and then put on my "Dad's shirt". On the way to the road, I picked and stuck into my top buttonhole a sprig of thyme.

When I parked my bike at the park office I could hear Fergie and Rattray talking while loading something around the back door. I started to join them but just before I came around the corner of the building I heard a sudden outburst from Rattray, and I stopped.

"Look," he was saying. "Everybody knows you're a friend of MacAkern's, but you're also an employee of the federal government, and that means there's a conflict of interest." It sounded rehearsed.

"So it's for my own good?" said Fergie.

"Yes."

"That sounds like a threat, Barry."

"Take it however you want."

"Very dramatic. And now you can go back to your uncle, who's obviously set you up to tell me all this, and tell *him* that if it's conflict of interest he's talking about, everybody knows he and his cronies have been buying up land around Barrisway, hoping to cash in when the park goes through."

"So what? That's just business."

"Yeah, but Barry, he's supposed to be a Member of Parliament, not a land speculator. And if he thinks he can...." Then Fergie suddenly sighed and stopped. "...Ah fuck it. Now. Let's get about *our* business, shall we?"

I can't imagine how they hadn't heard my feet on the gravel before, but now, around the corner out of their sight, I stood perfectly still. The longer I stayed there, the worse was my transgression, but they would definitely hear me if I tried to sneak away.

"I thought we were in this together," said Rattray.

"If we were in this together, would you be trying to get me fired?"

Rattray's voice dropped. "Who told you that?"

"You're not the only one with friends in high places, Barry."

"Well, I don't know what anybody told you, but I never..."

"Oh, spare me." And then Fergie walked away, around the other side of the building.

I thought Rattray might be coming my side, but then I heard him snort and follow.

I let out my breath and retraced my steps to the front of the building, then waited with my bike so if they saw me, I could pretend I had just arrived. I wondered how I had let myself become such a sneaky bastard. I peeked around the corner to see if they had come around the other side yet, but they didn't show up, so I left my bike and walked to the front door of the building.

I put my hand on the door handle but when I pushed it open and stepped inside, somebody behind the door gave out a yelp.

I knew that yelp. Claire was standing in the corner where the diorama was to be, holding one hand out to stop the door hitting her and turning to look at me. I felt an electric thrill and immediately forgot the guilt from having listened to something I was not supposed to. She saw my face and yelped again.

"Hey there," I said casually, just like a cool guy on TV.

She sighed angrily, frowned, then squinted and peered more closely. I basked in her attention and smiled goofily, ready to explain my makeup. But shaking her head and showing me the palm of her hand as if she didn't have time for any of this, she turned away and focused her attention back on her work.

I couldn't help but notice that she didn't seem as happy to see me as I was to see her. I had read somewhere that every love affair has one person who loves and one who allows themselves to be loved, and either way was fine by me. No point in her being downright miserable at my sight, though.

Perhaps her behaviour was evidence of a professional side which I hadn't seen before. She was certainly dressed more professionally today, in severe shoes and a woven skirt made of a tweed so thick it was almost burlap, with a jacket of the same material strapped across her like armour, and at her throat only the top button left undone. The key today, I thought, was to stress my professionalism.

"Oh! Claire. There's something in regards to my report I would like to talk over with you and get your opinion on."

"I have to do this," she said.

"Of course. At your leisure." I almost clicked my heels.

Her only response was that without looking away from her work, she reached up and fastened that last button at her throat.

I felt the hint of a distant tremor on the far side of the earth.

The best thing to do now was bustle through to the washroom, a busy man in a hurry to start his workday, but just as I turned away I heard sounds outside and Fergie and Rattray appeared on the other side of the glass door. Fergie's muffled voice was saying that he was going to town. Rattray, carrying a box, nodded. I turned to get to the bathroom before he came in, but Claire's hand shot out, grabbed my arm and stopped me. This was more like it.

"Tell me something," she whispered quickly.

"Anything," I whispered back.

She was looking away from me, through the glass door. "Who's that guy there?"

"Which guy?"

"The good-looking one."

"Fergie?" I looked

at her quizzically.

"No. The other one," she said, but there was no other guy around except Rattray, so she must have been mistaken, or hallucinating. Perhaps I should put my hand to her forehead to see if she was running a fever, and if so, administer mouth-to-mouth resuscitation.

Right then, Fergie headed towards his truck, leaving one person only to whom she could be referring. "Him," she pointed.

"You mean *Rat*tray?" I felt like spitting, to rid my mouth of the contamination of his name.

"Rattray?" she repeated, making even the ugliest two syllables in the universe seem almost musical. Then she turned to me eagerly. "What's his first name?"

"I don't know," I said, hoping to suggest that nobody knew his name, nobody cared enough to find out, and that it was rumoured he hadn't even been given one, his own parents never having felt he was worth it.

Apart from everything else that distressed me about this conversation, I *did* know that Rattray's first name was Barry, and it occurred to me this was my first real lie to her.

"I'll ask him," she said, seeming not only to be curious, but positively excited.

And on the far side of the earth, as though that tiny tremor had dislodged something, the tectonic plate slipped a min-iscule distance.

"Do you want something from him?" I said. "Because I could ask him, if you wanted."

"He's coming in," she said. "Introduce me," and with a quick motion she undid the top button of her shirt.

Appalled but obedient I waited till Rattray shouldered his way through the door, his eyes not yet accustomed to the lighting inside, and not particularly interested in seeing anybody anyway.

"Rattray? This is Claire," I said, trying not to make it sound like she was the most special thing in the world. I was no longer celebrating, but denigrating her, and dark and twisted feelings squirmed out of my soul where before had been only truth and purity.

"Oh yeah?" said Rattray barely looking up, and he turned away.

Rattray seemed not to see her beauty. Yes! Good man Rattray! And in a further twist of perversity, I found myself actually grateful to him. Everything was upside down.

But now his indifference seemed only to increase her curiosity. She took a quick step after him, following him to the counter. "Putting in boxes, eh?" she said.

"Yep."

"Need a hand?"

"No."

"I don't mind."

"There's only a few more," said Rattray, thumping the box on the counter and then crossing back towards the bathroom, still ignoring me.

"I guess those are the boxes of new stationary we were promised," I said to Claire. "High time, too. Those guys in Ottawa! I've been asking for them for a week now. Phoned in a requisition just yesterday. I needed some for that report I'm doing. Which is something I wanted to ask you about, like I was saying. I was wondering if you'd be up to

making some illustrations for it." I knew I was babbling, but I couldn't stop myself.

"What?"

"Illustrations, like the ones you made in *The Flora and Fauna of Barrisway Park*."

"I guess so," she said, but she wasn't thinking about what I was saying at all.

"There's no real rush, of course, but I liked your drawings so much that I thought, well, why not? I mean you're right here anyway, not that even if you *weren't* right here I wouldn't still try to get in touch with you, 'cause those drawings really *are* great, like I was telling you yesterday, remember?" The main thing was to keep her involved, or get her involved, or somehow have her still a part of my life.

"What? Oh, sure. See ya." And she went into her office and closed the door.

The way my strategy was supposed to unfold was, having built on, as I saw it, her initial attraction of yesterday, fueled as it was by my effusive praise of her drawings, she would continue a growing and deepening interest in me, then, during the course of the morning, or by lunch hour at the very latest, I would invite her to the beach. I could make the invitation sound like a semi-official walkabout, an introduction to the flora and fauna of the park which I had been instructed to take her on, a completely sanctioned and professional outing. Identifying and explaining to her what-ever it was that we came across would cause her first to be impressed, then awed by my incredible knowledge. I could suggest a swim, she would say she didn't have a bathing suit, and I would say completely naturally that I always swam in the nude as it promoted more vital skin tone. She would have to accept this, coming from who, by now, she would see was an authority figure in all the sciences, and she would strip.

But this wasn't happening at all. In fact, as painful as it was, I had to admit that the way she was behaving could be explained only by her finding Rattray attractive. Which was simply impossible. I could not see how somebody so outwardly stunning could possibly be so mistaken. She could have anybody. Well, not *anybody*. I wouldn't like that. To hell with everybody else. She could have *me*.

And then, from the farthest point on earth from where I stood, the antipode a thousand miles off the southwest coast of Australia, a faint tremor, the far echo of an impossibility, reached me and once more registered its huge but distant vibration.

My makeup had to be the problem. I must check.

I went straight to the washroom, just as Rattray was coming out, and he grabbed the inside handle at the same time as I grabbed the one on the outside. He pulled, I pulled back, he pulled again, I let go, he opened and stepped outside and we stood face to face. Although he hadn't looked at me before, preserving a contemptuous facade which ignored me completely, now he was forced to observe me directly.

He yelped. "What the..?" he said, forgetting completely to give me hell about Priority Entry and Exit Regulations as outlined in the recent policy decision of the Department of Door-handle Manipulation. Instead he just looked me in the eye. I expected anger, but he

seemed almost... *curious*, like he was seeing some new facet of me. It was uncomfortable. I pushed past him and he turned his head, still looking at me, as I entered the bathroom and the door behind me closed. I was alone. I looked at myself in the mirror.

I yelped. The zombie's idiot younger brother had apparently been trying to disguise himself as a transvestite by hiring the services of a spastic makeup artist. And it was not just my face that was an appalling assault on all that was good. My hair was like a primitive Frisbee constructed of straw, a nest built by one of the less-talented species of pack rat, a tangle of hemp and beach-wrack. Bits of sweet grass were stuck in it like an actress overdoing the part of mad Ophelia. My doctored shirt without the collar made me look like the minister's son in some Appalachian snake-wrestling cult.

I filled the sink with warm water and immersed my whole head in it, emerged and scrubbed my skull with my knuckles and wiped my face with paper towels. Then, I washed my face again. The swelling was going down somewhat on my bruises, but the colouring was still yellow and green. I was back to a somewhat less damaged Swamp Thing.

It must've been the makeup that was putting Claire off, or my bruised face beneath it. I walked out of the washroom, went to her office, knocked, heard "Come in!" and entered.

"Hi again," I said.

"Oh. Hi." She seemed disappointed that it was me, and looked back down at her work.

"My face isn't usually like this."

"Oh?" But she didn't even look.

"It was just that, you know that fight I was telling you about? Down at the wharf? Not that I *look* for a fight, but sometimes you gotta... It's just...I...My face isn't usually like this."

"That's good," she said, stood up, came around the desk and passed me on the way out.

Could she be avoiding me? I had to find out, so I followed her. She went through the door next to hers, into Rattray's office. He was at his desk, blank paper in a square stack exactly at the centre, sitting as straight as the pencil aligned beside it. He looked up with an expression like he didn't hold well to being interrupted, although he had obviously been doing nothing.

"So, if I can get the funding, what do you say?" I said, as if I was continuing a conversation from out in the lobby.

"What?" said Claire.

"For the illustrations in my report?"

"Ex*cuse* me..." said Rattray.

"One second," I said. "This is important."

Rattray straightened even further in his chair.

"OK," said Claire, turning to me finally. "I'll talk about it *later*, but right now I want to talk to Barry."

For the first time, Rattray looked directly at her, and saw, looking back at him, her adoring eyes. He was puzzled, glanced at me and saw me staring at her with my adoring but desperate eyes. He was even more puzzled. He looked at her again, then back at me. There was a long pause as something rear-ranged itself in his brain. The wheels started moving, whirred, clicked into gear, and then Rattray settled back into his chair. He had figured out

something, and what he had figured out could be worked to his advantage. Smug and superior, he *grinned*.

What was so funny? What did he have to act smug and superior about? He looked from me to Claire and back once more. The room was vibrating with so many waves of attraction and repulsion it felt like it might explode.

"I've gotta go," he said, still grinning, standing up and scooping the truck keys from his desk, the coolest man on earth. "Nobody's allowed in my room when I'm not here," he said. We followed him out of his office, which he locked. Then he crossed the lobby and walked outside, Claire following him and me following Claire, to the parking lot, where he stopped and pointed at me.

"You," he said, like he was whistling for a dog. And I went over to him, hating that I did. "You can bring in the rest of those boxes from around back, can't you?"

"I will," said Claire.

"No," I said. "I'll do it." I would show her that I was man enough to withstand even this humiliation.

"As long as it gets done," said Rattray and went across the parking lot toward the truck. It was the first time I'd seen him happy, the prick. So desperate for power, and now having it fall into his lap, there was actually a swagger in his walk.

"I'll come with you if you want," said Claire.

"Sure," said Rattray. Like one of the cool guys on TV.

I was close to despair. Knowing as I spoke that it was pointless, I blurted out anyway, "Claire?"

"I'm going with Barry now," she said.

"I was wondering if, later, you wanted to come see my tent."

"Your what?"

"I'm living in a tent on the beach. I was wondering if you

wanted to come see it."

"Sounds uncomfortable," she said, and went around the other side of the truck. Rattray looked directly at me and smirked.

"I thought we might go for a walk," I said to her, louder. "I could show you some of the flora and fauna..."

Rattray snorted, as if he was taking pity on me. She caught his eye. They seemed to agree on something. She looked at me from across the box of the pickup.

"Look" she said, taking a deep breath in preparation to making what she was about to say absolutely clear. "I want to go with *Barry*. I don't *want* to go to the beach with you. Now, don't you have any work to do?"

She got in and closed the door, and Rattray, still smirking, not about being with her, I thought, but with the idea that *I* was somehow now in his power too, got in the driver's seat, started the truck and spun out of the parking lot. The truck pulled onto the pavement and up the road where I had once bounced on my bike with my heart like a horned lark. They drove over the hill and out of sight and the dust from the wheels settled over the parking lot, and over me.

At the furthest point on earth from where I was standing, the continental plate lurched and the largest earthquake the world has ever known jolted the ocean floor. A tidal wave snapped out from its epicenter and swept over the planet, reached its widest circumference, then, rising in height as its aperture narrowed on this side of the

globe, it closed in and towered above me where I stood in the parking lot of the Barrisway Park office. A hundred miles above my head, filled with the jumble of world civilizations it had destroyed and picked up, the waters closed together like a drawstring on a purse, hesitated, then crashed down, driving me and my world inside out and leaving me standing alone in a landscape of mud and smashed things, waterlogged garbage, shit and dead bodies.

I walked inside, stiff and empty, went to my office and sat down behind my desk.

I stared at nothing for half an hour.

I picked up a piece of paper and started to write.

"The Survival of Life on Earth depends upon competition for a mate, and morality has nothing to do with it. Winning is everything, no matter how vicious the battle or how destructive the forces unleashed. Love is Pain.

These truisms are abundantly clear to anyone who has studied the fauna of Barrisway Park on Canada's East Coast. The sanderlings eat the small organisms that feed off the detritus left at high tide, but they give little thought to the havoc they wreak in that community when they do so. It's the immutable law of cruel Nature, red in tooth and claw. Victory goes not to the worthiest, but to the dirtiest fighter, and anybody who thinks differently will be chewed up and spat out, cast aside for a more worthless mate. Jungle Justice. It's a battlefield out there. Don't think it isn't. Life sucks.

Take, for example, the horned lark, which displays and nests in zone four of Barrisway Park. When he comes into sexual maturity, the male of the species first typically prepares not just one, but as many as six or more nesting areas for his prospective mate, which, if it so pleases her, she can choose from, while he, preening, singing and putting on aerial displays to make himself more desirable in her eyes, awaits her decision.

And if she deems none of these abodes suitable, then without giving it another thought, even in some cases without examining the work he has so painstakingly achieved, she will from pure whim pass him over and make the devastating choice of some other mate. She doesn't care. It's not her concern. He can be left a hollow shell, emotionally crushed, but what's that to her? And so the timeless breeding ritual continues. It starts with the attempt at attracting the mate, and ends with misery and waste.

Why it is that the female almost always makes the most unsuitable choice is a problem best left to philosophers or poets and not humble naturalists such as myself. It is not my place to suggest that there is perhaps something missing in the mental equipment of the female of the species, as though the double X chromosome lacks any normal human sympathy, allowing her to so cold-heartedly reject those who love them most, even though the flaws of the mate they have chosen will almost certainly show themselves as time passes and his worthlessness becomes more apparent. But by then it will be too late. He will have moved on, as the female, more and more trapped by her ever-advancing age and decreasing allure, becomes more pitiful. How will she feel then, eh? Oh, mark my words, she will rue the day that she so blithely rejected he who was to be her one true love.

And what's the unsuccessful suitor

*supposed to do? Confront his rival in a mano to mano duel
and pound his face into a bloody pulp? God knows he'd
like to. Oh yes, indeed. Give him half the chance and nothing
would feel better than delivering a few well-chosen and
painful blows to his face, or one clipped uppercut to the
jaw of his rival, sending him in a graceful arch backwards
through the air to land on his neck.*

*But we humans are civilized. We have laws, entitlements,
social consciences, Bills of Rights and Freedoms which
state, amongst other things that "...no law of Canada shall
be construed or applied so as to (b) impose or authorize
the imposition of cruel and unusual treatment or punishment;" Even though that document never states what
exactly constitutes "punishment"? Eh? Or "cruel"? for that
matter.*

*Thrown away? Cast aside? Would that be "unusual"?
(Oh no, all too usual by my findings!) But that is the Bill
of Rights of Canada, and the female horned lark has a
different law, doesn't she? The destruction of the very
spirit which makes life meaningful. And although it is not
the mandate of the humble naturalist to quote poetry, a
line from the anonymous folksong "Deep, Deep In My
Heart" sums it up best.*

*"For how to rise and forward go
My boat drifts from the shore
Now all my sails are slack and slow
and meaning means no more"
Which just about says it all, don't you think?*

I wrote it in one draft, the words roaring out of me like
from a flamethrower, and on re-reading I found it excellent.
I had said what I wanted to say, I had told the truth. I was
aware that it was not couched in the normal scientific language expected in a paper like this, but that simply meant

that they would now have to change the rules for what constituted normal scientific language. This was better.

I worked all the rest of the morning and the words kept pouring onto the paper. I heard trucks arrive and people go into their offices, and like the discordant drones whining behind everything in "Softening Shades," my thoughts kept telling me that Life Was Unfair.

Was it *me*? What did Rattray have that I didn't? A uniform? Where could I order one? How soon could it get here? Perhaps I could buy one in Barrisway.

I stayed in my office until quitting time and when I thought I heard that everyone was gone, I left the filled notebook on my desk and walked out of my office, wondering if I should wait till Fergie got back so that it wouldn't be left unattended. Then I thought the words "Fuck it" and felt the happy rebellious release of expressing myself naughtily. Fuck it fuck it fuck it I said, but feeling each time less of a thrill, that negative excitement which passes for joy amongst we the damned and loveless.

The door to Fergie's office was open. "Oh," he said as I passed. "You off?"

"Yes."

"I'll close her down, then. But first I think I'll have me some more vodka. I mean, I'll have *some* vodka. Wouldn't want anybody to think that I drink vodka during the day. Nossir. This job is far too riveting to make you want to go down that path, drinking at work. But now

that the workday is over I think I *will* have some. Would you like a shot?"

"No thanks. I gotta go to Barrisway."

"Of course you do. Shouldn't've offered it to you in the first place. OK then. See you tomorrow."

"Tomorrow's Saturday."

"So it is! No wonder I'm drinking, or, excuse me, *will be* drinking. Well, well...Don't worry about it. Don't worry about anything. Be joyful and live life easily, I say. See you Monday."

"OK."

I walked out and got on my bike and pedalled to Barrisway, purposefully and maturely all the way into town, obeying all the rules of the road stringently, tight-lipped and steady.

The man behind the counter at the hardware store seemed better disposed to me now that my spirit had been crushed. I was one of his brotherhood now. He had only been trying to warn me, I hadn't listened, and now I had seen for myself. He showed me to the back of the store where, no, they didn't have any uniforms, but perhaps these matching work greens with severe creases in them made from material as stiff as cardboard would do. Who cared? Mark it up as yet another of my failures. My brogues, unorthodox when worn with checked pants and pyjama tops, would now fit in with my new more conservative look.

I bought a tie and knotted it like a noose around my neck under the collar of my new shirt. I looked in the mirror, and with my lightening bruises and sad damaged pout, I now resembled a ward of the state, some work-farm inmate whom the guards had taken out back and unofficially convinced to give them no more trouble. But my hair was still definitely wrong. Since I had washed out the pack-rats' nest, it had resumed its usual goddamn fluffy curls, which jarred

with the rest of the Society's Victim look I was going for. I
had a small set of scissors in my Swiss Army knife, but
before I left the store I also bought a metal camping mirror
and a Hair Whiz ("As advertised on TV") with which they
claimed you could create "The Latest Teenage Razor Cuts."
I didn't want that, but the picture on the box of the sorry-
looking bastard they'd roped into modeling it reflected the
attitude I was going for exactly. I walked out of the store
wearing everything I had just bought and carrying my old
clothes in a bag.

I got on my absurd bicycle, which was now completely
unsuitable for the complicated brooding man I had become,
and which I would have to throw away or sell. Perhaps with
my first paycheck I could put a down-payment on a car,
something either stodgy and practical, or dark and menacing, anything but joyful or fun. I could work on the engine
in MacAkern's yard, drop the block and rework the spark-
plugs or manifold or whatever the hell you reworked on a
car. The point is, I'd renovate it myself. Or "repair" or
whatever it was called by people who did that sort of thing.
It occurred to me that I didn't know anything about cars:
another of my failures. Rattray probably regularly changed
entire engines, the prick. I might also have to take some
lessons in martial arts as it might come to combat between
me and him, and if
it did, I must re-
member that he
was bigger, so the
best strategy might
be to clip him from
behind when he
wasn't looking.
All's fair in love and

war, a phrase which wasn't actually in the Canadian Bill of Rights, but should be. Grim thoughts of violent revenge powered my pedals all the way back. At the vegetable stand I paid what I owed from before, so I wouldn't be beholden to anybody.

Back at the beach, the sea was grey and brooding, the sky threatening rain, and I didn't give a shit where the tide was. I set up my mirror on a piece of driftwood and I snipped at my hair randomly till I had reduced it to a manageable mass, but the scissors that came with the Swiss Army knife could remove only one small lock of hair at a time, and the result was uneven. I couldn't see the back of my head with only the one mirror, so I just took wild grabs at what felt like the longer locks back there until I nicked myself and stopped. I took the Hair Whiz out of the box and without reading the instructions, tried to even out what I had done so far, and the first swipe cut a bald spot on the side of my head which made me look like a brain-surgery patient prepped by drunken orderlies. Also, the Hair Whiz hurt like a bastard. Good. I deserved it.

Eventually I got the sides down, and the top more or less under control. There were patches of hair that sprang out like parts of a forest after a gale, but who cared? I went for a swim to wash the hair off my shoulders, taking no joy in the ocean. The Society For the Prevention of Fun had teamed up with the Ministry of Emptiness to form a task force whose mandate was Happiness Intervention. I stood on the beach and looked out to sea.

"AAAAAAAAAAAAAAAAAAAAAAAAAAAAAAAAAAAAAAAA *AAH!*" I said.

Back at my tent I kicked the pathway of shells, stirring them with my feet back into the sand until I was panting heavily, then I caught my breath, paused, and nearly burst into tears. I swore instead, and started to fantasize a scene where *I* was the one who had rejected *her*. "Sorry babe," I said out loud. "I'm a solo act. I'll always be a loner."

This was better. It wasn't my fault, it was the world that sucked. I flipped up my collar against the wind and felt a few drops of cold rain from way up as a keen wind blew from the northeast. Good again. I liked it that way. Cold and pain were the only things that made me feel alive. I spat and wished I'd been smoking a cigarette, not to impress what's-her-name, just another sour addiction, momentary compensation on my way to the grave.

I crossed the dune to the road, picked up a stick and lopped off the head of a wild carrot. Don't mess with me, I'm trouble. I hunched my shoulders and thrust my fists in my pockets.

But it was no good being a loner if there was nobody around to see it, so I slumped down towards MacAkerns', barely containing my sneer, peering through my wounded youth at the hypocrisy of the world. My world-weary eye would see through other peoples' shams. I would show up their phoniness with the real wounds of the martyrdom I bore in silence. My presence at any gathering would shame them all and I would grow old a tragic figure whom they would avoid like the Truth. Flipping up my collar against the wind, I turned my head and squinted over the chip on my shoulder.

I walked into the MacAkerns' yard with the high tide bucking up and down on the bay, waiting for a channel to flow out. When I climbed the

stairs onto their porch I could hear arguing in the kitchen and I stopped just outside the door. It was like when I had overheard Rattray and Fergie, but this time I didn't feel badly about it. So what if I really was a sneaky bastard?

"Best book I ever read," Wallace was saying.

"The only book you ever read," said Robbie.

"Take it for what it's worth," said Bailey. "I just picked it up at the library for some background about your political system. Most of the actual ideas in it are cribbed from Machiavelli."

"Who?" said Wallace.

"Renaissance philosopher from Italy."

"Don't tell Robbie that," said Wallace. "She'll probably drag out some book to say he's from Scotland."

There was a pause in the conversation and I heard a chair squeak.

"Is somebody there?" said Bailey. And I came right in and nodded hello as though I had just arrived. I think Bailey was about to ask me what I'd been doing standing outside, but Wallace spoke first.

"Oh my fuck. What did you do to your hair?"

"I cut it."

"It looks like shit."

"Good," I said.

"I *liked* your hair," said Melissa.

"Me too," said Robbie.

I didn't answer.

"Well," said Wallace, in consolation. "Nobody's gonna be looking at your *face* now, anyway."

I didn't care. I leant against the wall inside the door and put one foot behind me on the wainscoting in a pose I'd seen on the cover of *The Mighty Spear of Jah* tape.

They resumed their discussion. I stayed silent, but leant

forward and picked up the book from the table and looked at it with disdain.

It was entitled *So You Want To Be An MP?* the front cover showing a cartoon character slinking away from the House of Parliament with a suitcase crammed to overflowing with dollar bills, while in the distance a Mountie was impotently shaking his fist to make him to stop. On the back the publisher wrote that "Ward Morris", the author, was "*a pseudonym for a high-powered Ottawa insider who spills his guts on how to succeed in the bare-knuckle world of Federal politics.*" Below was a blurb from somebody I'd never heard of: "*This is the real scoop on attaining and maintaining power in Canada*".

I flipped it open. "*...when they find out you've lied, lie some more. When the lies start to backfire, blame anybody in your way. Don't give me any of that goody two-shoes Pollyanna crap. There are no saints. They're just better liars than the rest of us. Learn how they do it and use it against them. Wipe that saintly smile off their faces. Everybody does it. Don't be a sap.*"

I could see his point. This burden of always trying to do the right thing, where'd it get you? Alone, that's where.

Brucie came in to the kitchen. "Did you hear?" he said. "Somebody stole some food from B-B-Blake's last night!"

"*What?*" said Wallace.

"B-Blake's vegetable stand. Stuff was stolen."

"Jesus! Some people!" Robbie shook her head in disbelief.

"The nerve! Probably somebody from Charlottetown."

"Or a Mainlander. No offense, Christian."

I still didn't say anything.

"He even l-l-left an IOU!"

"Cocky prick!"

"All high and m-m-mighty. Sarcastic-like."

"I...um..." I said.

"What is it, Christian? You know anything about this?"

"Yeah, well. It may be nothing..."

"Go on."

The tide-bouncing water found a channel, the weight of it poured through the sand wall and flowed. "It's just that I saw Rattray around there last night," I said. Immediately I wanted to take it back, but Robbie, Wallace and Brucie instantly weighed in.

"Of course!"

"Rattray!"

"Who else?"

"T-Typical!"

"But I didn't see him actually *steal* anything," I said.

"Oh it was R-Rattray all right..."

"Exactly the sort of thing he *would* do."

"When I catch him I'm gonna kick his teeth in," said Wallace.

"Yeah. One by one," said Robbie.

"S-Slowly."

"Stopping only to enjoy his cries of pain mingled with his pleas for mercy."

"And when he's lying there weeping and moaning, I can act like I'm taking pity on him, all 'oh I'm so sorry, have a nice glass of water,' and when he drinks it he finds out it's *battery acid*."

"Then I could come back and start kicking his teeth out

some more."

"Yeah, it probably *was* Rattray," I said.

***

A warm sickly breeze was blowing from the south and it was almost dark when I got back to the beach and saw him. He couldn't have known what I'd been up to, so it must have been for some other reason that he was standing outside my tent.

"Hi Rattray. What's up?"

The reason I could be so casual was that, having made up that story about him, I felt in control. I'd been having twinges of conscience about that, but now, seeing him here in the flesh, I didn't feel badly at all, in fact I was almost thrilled at the power I was wielding.

"I hear you've got a new friend," he said.

"I've got lots of new friends," I said, but, close to him now, my cockiness was holding only by a thread. He looked a bit scary, to tell the truth, and although I did feel a bit afraid, I still hated him like poison and saw no reason why I should give him the pleasure of seeing me that way.

"Like Monroe, for instance?" he said.

"I guess so. Why?"

"He's getting you to deliver mail for him, I see."

"What are you talking about, Rattray?"

"The letter. To MacAkerns'. I know about it."

153

Why shouldn't he know about it? And who cared whether he knew about it or not? "And so..?" I said.

"And so I was wondering why he gave it to *you*."

Seeking me out like this long after work for something which was clearly so insignificant only confirmed that he was an idiot. "I have no idea what you're talking about," I said, and moved to go past him and into the tent.

But he blocked my way and faced me directly. I smelled liquor on his breath. "What are you?" he said between clenched teeth. "Gay?" It seemed to hiss out of him like steam off acid. "Is that what you are? A kissy little gay boy queer? You're a pansy, and Monroe's your faggy friend?"

I supposed it was because he had seen me in makeup and riding a girl's bike, and it explained that look in his eyes when we faced each other at the washroom door. But he was mistaken, and this made me feel on top again. "*Rat*tray..." I started.

"...I know Monroe's a drunk. But is he a faggot too? Eh? Does he like to kiss boys?" And he stepped even closer.

What was wrong with him, anyway? He didn't make any sense. Why, for instance, was he *not* attracted to the most lovely woman in the world? And since I *was* so plainly attracted to her, how could he think I was not straight? And what was that look in his eyes now, and this ignorant rant..?

And then the obvious answer occurred to me.

Rattray himself was gay, and furthermore, unable to admit it, maybe even to himself, he took the pain of it out on the world around him.

It all seemed very clear, and also meant that Claire would not therefore consummate with him, which was excellent news. Unless Rattray was bisexual, goddamn it, which was just the nasty two-faced sneaky bastard thing he *would* be...

I looked at him again and what I saw drove this out of my

mind. He was looking back at me unblinking with his eyebrows scowling down and the whites of his eyes showing under his pupils.

I was the object of his desire.

I wondered if I could stoop down quickly enough to pick up a rock for a weapon. Instead, I took a deep breath, and because legal babble had worked before, I tried it again, not from memory this time, but completely improvised.

"Rattray," I said, "although this is not my personal property, I do have permission from the owners to be here, which you don't. And since that tent is my lawful domicile, under the Canadian Bill of Rights section four (c) I am entitled to not be interfered with or prevented from entering or leaving said domicile, or having its contents, my possessions, disrupted or removed. So I am hereby formally putting you on notice to vacate the premises, or I will be forced to inform the authorities."

"Who's gonna make me?"

"The uttering of a threat is an illegal act as well."

"Who's gonna know?" By which I guess he meant to say that if he killed me and hid the body, nobody would be the wiser.

"Wallace MacAkern. Robbie MacAkern. Bailey Hendershott..." I started to count off..."Aiden, Melissa, Brucie..."

He blinked.

"I only came back here to pick up some food," I continued. "I'm supposed to be back there in a few minutes and if I'm not, they'll come

looking. I already told them that I saw your footprints on the beach here last night, and Fergie knows what you think of me, so you'd be the first suspect." I think I preserved a placid face, but I could feel my heart thumping. "You're right about one thing though," I added, "I do have a lot of friends."

"You little prick..." he said, but he took a step back and looked around shiftily. I watched as he backed away, then walked away down the beach, turning to look back over his shoulder at intervals, the whole way to the point of land to the east, which he disappeared behind, following the path he had made the night before. When he was out of sight and I was sure he really had gone, I crawled into the tent and lay down. But I couldn't get to sleep for a long time.

6

The next day I woke up thinking that since I was being threatened, I should at least be armed, so I went to the field of driftwood for some sort of club to have by my side if he came back. I found a nicely-weighted five-foot pole, thinking that by standing away and using it to lay into him with wide swings, I could keep him at arm's length. And in case he broke through, I found a handy little piece like a shillelagh for close-up work. For good measure, I also picked up a hatchet-shaped tickler like an Iroquois war-club with which I could soften up his skull in a clinch or throw at him to bring him down from a distance. By

God he would rue the day he'd messed with me, The Bruised Avenger.

I practiced with all three weapons, swinging them around and bashing at the air, imagining him falling under my carefully placed blows. Then I propped up on its end a log, and attacked it, administering a flurry of stabs, swings and one-two combinations. I was particularly effective with the long club, which I wielded like Little John's long-staff, using both ends in a rat-a-tat attack, then taking three steps back, running forward and pole vaulting into the target with both feet, knocking it over. I tried the move again, but this time I hit myself on my nose with the other end of the staff, right on a bruise. I swore loudly and took out the rest of my anger on the log in an unprecedented hail of destruction. When it was lying wounded and unconscious, I finished it off with a deadly thrust to the solar plexus and then walked away down the beach, the movie camera in my imagination tracking me, cold-hearted but finally avenged, as credits rolled.

I took the back way to the MacAkerns', which was friendly territory, so I placed my weapons behind the dune to retrieve on the way back. I walked into their yard to find the place hopping with energy: Campaign Mode.

A television van was parked down by the shore, a camera set up on a tripod in front of two chairs, and a cameraman was strapping a battery belt around his waist. Bailey, in his three-piece campaign suit, was talking to the interviewer, Wallace was sitting in one of the chairs, and Melissa and Robbie were standing with Brucie out of the camera's line of sight.

"What's going on?" I said.

"They've come to interview Wallace," said Robbie. "They were down at the Barrisway wharf for that big tuna that was supposed to be coming in this morning, but apparently that was all bullshit, so anyhow, Bailey was there and he saw them and convinced them to hop over here. Turns out Bailey's a pretty good campaign organizer."

"He is," said Melissa. "And he needed this."

"It's nice you're looking out for him," said Robbie.

"What else can I do? He's my brother."

"I know the feeling."

The interviewer was picking over himself now, grooming like a nervous monkey, then I heard him starting in on a vocal exercise, practicing his professional accent. I wondered whether all the people in the news media adopt this voice because there is one person, their hero, whom they all imitate, or if perhaps that by agreeing on an accent which was not found anywhere in the world except in the news media, they reduced the risk of slanting their viewpoint and damaging their journalistic objectivity. I stepped back and tried the accent a few times myself, saying, "The Jah voice come, the mighty run, like salmon always upstream, but down they go, one to and fro and shine the light eternal." I found that by stressing some arbitrary syllable it imposed the illusion of meaning on anything I said and whatever I uttered would come out sounding considered, evenly-weighed and truthful. It was an interesting sensation, as if I had cut off the wiring between my brain and my tongue.

I went over to Brucie. "Can you do his accent?"

Brucie considered, then took a breath. "Well, let's see. Why yes, I find that I can, in fact," he said, without

stammering.

"Cool."

"Are you suggesting that if I wish to speak without a stammer, Christian, I simply have to talk like this?" He cocked his eyebrow down at the end of the sentence, just like a newscaster.

"Seems to work."

"Why yes, it does. The only problem, though, is that it *would* mean I would have to go through life sounding like a complete horse's ass."

"True."

"I'd rather s-s-stammer," said Brucie in his own voice. He was a talented little guy.

The interviewer took a seat beside Wallace, who coughed once into his hand and looked into the camera. The cameraman said, "in five...four..." then counted down the rest with his fingers in silence while the reporter looked into the lens of a box full of wires and transistors as though he was addressing a real human being.

"Thank you, Keith," he said. "It's a beautiful North Shore day up here in Barrisway riding where there has been an interesting development on the electoral front. With the entire country plunged into an election, the choice seems to be narrowing down to between the two leading parties..." He paused. "...Or *is* it? Wallace MacAkern, well-known to Island residents for his steadfast refusal to move from his home in response to a government expropriation order, has thrown his hat into the ring as the independent candidate for Barrisway riding, and we're here to ask him about his controversial platform, 'Vote for me. Get five bucks.'" He turned to Wallace. "What do you say to people who may claim that you are corrupting the practice of democracy, Wallace?"

"I'm sure some would say that," said Wallace, "and some others would say that it is the other candidates, whose names I will not even mention, who are doing the corrupting, and that whoever gets in, it'll be the same old horse... crap, excuse my French, and that my campaign is providing a much needed service to the democratic process as laid down by the founding fathers."

"That's the United States which has founding fathers."

"I am speaking about the Fathers of *Confederation*," said Wallace without dropping a beat, " who *founded* Canada. I'm not an idiot, Ben," he added, looking at him steadily.

"Of course not," said Ben. "I didn't mean to suggest you were."

"Well watch it, then," said Wallace. If I hadn't known he wouldn't hurt a flea, I would've been alarmed.

"Sorry."

Wallace resumed, all forgiven, "No, Ben, in terms of the democratic process, the only difference between me and the other candidates is that on the morning after the election, the people who vote for me will be five dollars richer." He lifted the five dollar bill he was holding and snapped it in front of the camera.

"But, Wallace, because it's a private ballot, what is preventing the voter from only *saying* that he or she has voted for you, and then just taking your five dollars?"

"The natural honour of Islanders," said Wallace, shocked that it was even being called into question.

Steely accusation crept into his gaze. "And if you are im-pugning Islanders by suggesting that we have no honour, then you'll have to fight me first." His steady gaze was now an open challenge.

"I'm not," said Ben. "I'm saying that some people might say that."

"Yeah? Well, give me their names, and I'll fight them too."

"OK then. But, look...."

Wallace dropped the accusatory tone again. "Ben, it's like those serve-yourself potato stands you see around the Island. There is absolutely nothing to stop people from just *taking* the produce, but *do* they? No. There has never been one reported case of theft...until just this week where this honour system has been breached for the first time in our history, by an employee of the proposed park no less, someone already sucking on the government teat, excuse my French again, and who must have performed this heinous deed just for the fun of it, as he clearly has enough money, being a salaried employee as he is, paid by the government in power, that is, by us, the taxpayer."

"I see..."

"His name is Barry Rattray, and he works at the Park Station..."

Oh Jesus, I thought.

"...He's a longtime Conservative supporter, and a nephew of, well, I won't even mention his name, the Conservative Candidate, which probably explains how he got the park job in the first place, an obvious patronage appointment where he pulls down a tidy little salary for doing precious little, and whose behaviour in this case is sadly typical of the arrogance of office, and is yet another reason why you should vote for me and receive your five dollars."

"I have ten seconds to wrap up."

"More than enough time to say that this brings us to the real problem with big projects like the park. They are simply using *your* money to hire more people to keep *them* in power, and whoever doesn't believe that is probably on their payroll too. Who are you voting for, Ben?"

"I...haven't made up my mind yet."

"Well, vote for me, then. Remember, there's five bucks in it for you." He snapped the five dollar bill in front of the camera again and looked directly into the lens for his final statement. "At least you'll be getting *something* back."

"Ben Malone, CBC News, Barrisway, Prince Edward Island. Back to you Keith."

"And...we're...*out*," said the cameraman.

Wallace invited the cameraman and Ben Malone for a cup of tea but they said they had to go and cover a housefire in Georgetown. Wallace said, "But it's Saturday," and the cameraman said with a glint in his eye that that meant time-and-a-half, and started packing up.

"Good job, everybody," said Bailey. "And Ben, I'm impressed! You really know how to ask the tough questions."

"Just doing my job," said Ben Malone, but you could see he was pleased at the compliment.

"Sure you don't want the five bucks?" said Wallace. "All you got to do is vote for me."

"Better not."

"Well, take these anyway." And Wallace handed them each a bottle of scotch. They departed amid more thanks, and everybody moved up

onto the porch and into the kitchen.

"Nice work, Wallace," said Bailey. "I liked your jab at that Rattray guy. It shows you've got the killer instinct."

"I only said I saw him lurking around the stand is all," I said.

"Oh, it was Rattray all right who stole the potatoes," said Wallace. "Who else?"

"No question," said Robbie.

So I told myself that I had made my protest and was therefore absolved from blame. I didn't feel good about what I had done, but I did feel empowered. Real things actually happen, for real reasons, and if you look at them honestly you can sometimes find real answers, but I found it liberating, this idea that you can change the way reality is perceived and actually win, not just observe and record. Mere truth seemed like an impediment on the way to affecting the world. Part of me suspected that I was taking a step down a dangerous path, but even that danger made me feel more alive and alert.

And anyhow, Rattray may not have deserved this precise injustice, but he certainly deserved *something*. It was *his* fault if he behaved in a manner which caused people to spread false rumours about him.

"When did they say it'd be broadcast?" said Melissa.

"Tonight at six o'clock," said Bailey. "Now, pep talk, everybody. Gather around." We did. "I think we can say that the campaign is now officially under way, and a most auspicious beginning it has been indeed." His shaved head oddly complimented his perfectly-pressed suit. "Our job now is to continue to get the news out. And *how* are we to get the news out, team?"

"By any means available," said Melissa as if she was being examined for a test.

"Including?"

"Letters to the editor, press releases to the media. Television, radio, print."

"Don't forget personal encounters. Wallace? You up for it?"

"Where do I start?"

Bailey unfolded a roadmap onto the kitchen table. "This map shows Barrisway riding, which I've squared off in a grid. I want you to go door-to-door and complete one square every day. Strictly one-on-one. I'm going to save your public speechifying for the debate."

"What debate?"

"The all-candidates debate at the Barrisway Legion, two weeks from now, to be broadcast live on the radio. The main thing is to concentrate on talking to everybody you run into until then, so when you do go onstage, they'll be on your side. Let people know you."

"But, what do I say?" said Wallace.

"No hard-sell. Just invite them to our big picnic."

"What big picnic?"

"The one we're planning."

"Where?"

"Here."

"When?"

"Next Saturday. Now, Wallace, how does this riding break down?"

"What do you mean?"

"How are people divided?"

"Same as the rest

of PEI," said Wallace. "There's a line between the Irish, the Scottish and the French, and also between Catholic and Protestant, though that's less of a problem now. Indians and White, too, I suppose, though the Indians don't seem to vote a lot."

"Can't imagine why not, having benefited so much from European democracy... Anyhow, what are you?"

"Scottish Catholic."

"So, everything else being equal, can you count on the Scottish Catholic constituency?"

"Och aye," said Wallace.

"Great, but can you *count* on them."

"What? To vote for me?"

"Not even that yet. Just to hear you out."

"That depends on what family."

"So the real divisions are along family lines."

"I see. Yes, I suppose."

"Kind of like New Hampshire, then. Melissa, get the PEI phone book from Robbie, then both of you list the twenty most numerous family names. All right. Who was the next you mentioned? French? How many in our riding?"

"Not many who actually speak it, but quite a few families claim a connection. Arsenaults, Gallants, Chiassons. Anybody with a name like that."

"What about the married-intos?"

"The who?"

"If a French woman married, say, an Irishman, she'd take *his* name."

"Oh. Like my grandmother. She was a Taillefer."

"Really? Well, you can use that."

"How?"

"Stress it when you're in a situation where there are any French. Come on, Wallace, catch up."

"Sorry. I never really thought about it."

"Well, think about it now."

"OK then."

"Who's next? Irish?"

"No Irish in me that I know of."

"So how do we make a connection?"

"Give them free booze?"

"Which is exactly the type of thing you should refrain from saying in this campaign."

"You mean, 'just the type of low ethnic slur we've come to expect from my opponent, and the kind of thing that our Irish brothers and sisters, fellow Celts, have had to endure after having contributed so much to Island culture...'"

"Exactly."

"...Like drinking," he added.

"*Wall*ace..."

"Don't worry. I'm not stupid."

"Since when?" said Robbie.

"People! Focus!" said Bailey. "So the question is, how do we include the Irish?"

"How about getting The Barley Boys to perform at the picnic?"

"Who?"

"Irish band. Big around here."

"Do you know them?"

"Not really..."

"OK. I'll look into it. Make a note, Melissa. And can we get a liquor license for the scotch?"

"Don't need a license if you just give it away, do you?"

"Could always use more funds though. Robbie, can you check on that?"

"Yep."

"Right. So. Picnic. Debate, and door-to-door. Ready?"

"I guess so," said Wallace.

"Don't worry about it," said Bailey. "Just act natural."

But Wallace looked a little more weighted down now, feeling the new burden of his responsibilities, and the speed with which things were happening. "How do you *do* that?" I heard him say under his breath. "You either *are* natural, or you're *acting*."

***

"Six o'clock," said Melissa. We gathered around the TV and Robbie frittered with the tin-foil on the coat hanger that acted as an antenna. "Here we are!"

And we all watched. At the end of the item everybody applauded and Wallace bowed politely. He looked good on TV, substantial.

"Nice the way your underwear was crawling up outside your pants," said Robbie.

"What can I say?" said Wallace. "I have the common touch."

"And maybe you shouldn't pick your nose on air."

"I was *scratching* my nose."

"Looked like you were p-p-picking it."

"I'll pick *your* nose," said Wallace, throwing an arm around Brucie's neck and getting him into a headlock.

I had been preserving the hope that they might have edited out the Rattray comment, but no chance. In fact, it turned out to be the most effective moment in the interview, Wallace looking directly into the camera with an accusatory glare like a contestant in the World Wide Wrestling Federation issuing a challenge to his sworn enemy. He clearly enunciated Rattray's name too, unmistakably. The only thing he'd left out was his address and telephone number.

So it shouldn't have been much of a surprise when later, just as I was leaving for the night, Brucie hung up the phone in the other room, re-entered the kitchen and took centre floor.

"Rattray's been b-beaten up!"

"Who by?"

"Toe and G-Gump, I heard."

"Bad?"

"He's in the hospital, b-b-but nothing permanent."

"Well, you can't say he didn't deserve it," said Wallace. "Stealing from their stand!"

"He k-k-keeps saying he didn't d-do anything."

"Weasel."

"Should beat him up again for refusing to admit it."

"Serve him right."

"The prick."

It would have been better if he had actually stolen the potatoes, because now that he had been punished for it unjustly, the moral high ground was shifting disturbingly to his side. Uncontrolled forces were being unleashed, and for the first time in my life I felt the insecurity of power. You lash out with one end of the long-staff and the other end hits you in the nose.

I started back to my camp, picking up my weapons on the other side of the dune. The moonlight was bright enough to allow me to see if Rattray was lurking somewhere in the woods, but of course he was in the hospital tonight. Good, I thought, he deserved it, then I tried again to unravel exactly

how. It went back to when I first saw him, when I suggested he was a pervert, although I *hadn't* really...No, before
that. When he was mocking Brucie's stammer, no, even
before that, when he told me to get off the dunes... Oh, who
cared? Rattray had, after all, threatened me, sort of, on the
beach, with what might have been attempted rape.

And it made me feel better that I had potentially found
something that put him in the wrong. As long as that was
the case I didn't have to think about the confusing grey area
of the "theft" and the beating I had initiated. It also crossed
my mind that I shouldn't feel good that he was in the wrong
because surely something bad should not make me feel
good...

Everything was mixed up. For instance, Robbie and Melissa
were gay, but they were nice, while Rattray was gay, but a
horse's ass. Did this mean that all gay men were horse's
asses and gay women nice? It couldn't be that simple, but
if people didn't fall into recognizable categories it was going
to make life a lot more difficult. It should be like *The Field
Guide To The Birds*. If the tail of the swallow is forked, then
it is a barn swallow. If it is boxy and square, then it is the
cliff swallow. You knew where you stood. With the Things
of Man, though, it seemed that good and bad, right and
wrong were not as easy to separate.

And then an even more confusing possibility occurred to
me, that everybody had both good and bad in them, and in
varying amounts. But that would mean that Rattray was
not all bad, which, oddly, I found even more disturbing.
Also, the fact that I did find it disturbing made *me* bad (or
partly bad) and how was I to know whether my bad out-
weighed my good...

I quickly grew tired of all this moral hair-splitting, and
as if I was turning a channel to a crappy show on television,

I turned my mind to the movie I was constructing in my imagination where I stood over Rattray's prone and wounded body and in an unemotional tough-guy voice recited to him the Canadian Bill of Rights. "No person shall detain...." and the camera tracked back and faded out.

7

The weather the next morning was like the weather on Jupiter. I lay inside the crazily flapping tent, watching from underneath shadows of raindrops blowing upwards across the stretched vinyl of the roof, like isopods under the microscope.

The mad weather had gotten into my dreams, only parts of which I could recall fleetingly, flashes of dread where I was looking at the beach from the ocean, unable to stop drifting away from the shore.

Something else was bothering me too, and this was at least more identifiable. When I thought of that encounter with Rattray on the beach, it occurred to me that I had never knowingly been the object of desire, and it gave me a sudden sharp insight into what it must be like to be an attractive woman. I had an acute and embarrassing memory-glimpse of what my behaviour towards Claire must have been like from her point of view and I whimpered out loud, then chewed the corner of my knapsack until I stopped thinking about it.

I stuck my head outside my tent. Contrary winds shook the spruce trees and waves slapped the shore as if they were angry at it. Two crows were blown across a blustery grey sky, feathers ruffled backwards. I rose and ate one raw potato for breakfast and washed it down with water. It occurred to me that if I could describe the contradictions I was feeling, I could stand outside them and see them for what they were, but the rational methods of science no longer seemed able to do the job. The most meaningful line in my beach report yesterday was when I quoted "Deep, Deep in My Heart," so I should write something like that, and to hell with science. Clearly the pain and confusion that I was feeling had given me a unique insight into the Fall of Man, Innocence and Experience, and Man's Inhumanity to Man, all of which I would delineate once and for all in a great work of literature, a huge and heavy novel perhaps which any number of publishers would sob with regret for having rejected when it was finally released to unparalleled acclaim.

But that implied the possibility of future success, so perhaps a long epic poem would be better, arcane and grandiose, comprehensible only to teams of scholars who would dedicate their lives to its study. The mysterious woman in these verses, part Dark Lady of the Sonnets and part Dante's Beatrice, would never be named, and entire university departments would be set up to crack the almost impenetrable code of my language and discover her identity. By virtue of being read only by the worthy few, this poem would slowly become an undisputed classic, but only long after I was dead. Then she'd be sorry.

Under a turbulent sky, I walked up the road and into the front yard of the MacAkerns', mounted the porch and scowled into the kitchen.

A cheap Korean television was set up on the counter with the volume down, and two radios were tuned low to different stations. The phone from the parlour had been dragged through and placed on a milk stool by the wall and five different newspapers lay strewn across the tabletop, all three Island publications as well as *The Chronicle Herald* and *The Globe and Mail*. Next to them Robbie sat drawing on the stencils for a mimeograph machine and beside her, Melissa was sitting straight-backed and typing furiously, all ten fingers attacking the keys like sanderlings at the surf. A sheet of white plywood had been set up in the far corner and Bailey was writing on it with a lump of laundry blueing "Speaking Points". The room was bounding with activity like the choppy waves at the mouth of the harbour. In direct contrast to my solitary poetic aloofness, here everybody was engaged with each other.

"Make a note, Aiden," Bailey was saying. "Buy real chalk. Also, a longer cord for the telephone. And typewriter ribbon. Then we should hide the van and rent a car. Wallace, you keep driving your pick-up truck. It makes you look like a Man of the People... "

"How the hell do you tie one of these things?" said Wallace, turning around from the mirror. The knot on his tie was a double granny, pulled tight enough that the sides of his neck bulged over it. He saw me in the doorway. "Whoever-The-Hell-You-Are!" he greeted me.

"Quarter in the swear jar," said Robbie.

"It's his name!" said Wallace.

"No it's not," said Robbie. "Twenty-five cents." She was efficient and formidable.

Wallace took out a quarter from his pocket and put it in the jar. "Well it's what I *call* him," he protested.

"You're lousy with names," said Robbie.

"What's wrong with 'Hey, You'?"

"Yeah. That's much more personal."

"Well, I don't know. How do those greeter and backslapper types do it, anyway?"

"They take the time to be actually interested in the other person."

"That's out of the question then," said Wallace, then turned to look around the room. "Is somebody gonna help me with this, or what?"

I was getting sucked into the energy of the room like flotsam into a rip-tide, but I walked over reluctantly, hoping my brooding poetic mood would at least be noticed, even as I felt it slip away. Wallace was clutching the miserable knot like a victim of a lynching. "Shit," he said.

"Quarter in the swear jar," said Bailey.

"Not again. Fuck!"

"Fifty cents," said Melissa.

"Do we *have* to have a swearing jar?" he pleaded.

"It works," said Bailey. "Now. Fifty cents."

"I'm broke."

"Write an IOU then," said Bailey. "Go through the motions. And don't think we won't collect. I don't want your potty mouth giving some old lady in Barrisway a heart attack."

Wallace turned to me. "Can you help?" he said. I took the tie off him and tied a neat Windsor knot around my own neck, slipped it off and handed it back.

"Good man, Christian," said Bailey. "Now, sit down here and take a dictation."

I thought I owed it to the rapidly fading memory of the persona I had fashioned for myself that morning to state my own intentions for coming here.

"I want to know how to write a poem," I said.

"You've come to the right person," said Bailey.

"Who? You?" said Melissa, still typing. "You can't write poetry worth sh…" then she caught herself and stopped typing. Everybody looked at her. "…sh… *Sh*eilah Cudmore, NDP Candidate for Barrisway riding."

"Good one," said Robbie. They high-fived and bent back to work.

"Don't listen to her," said Bailey. "I can tell you how to write poetry in one simple lesson. Here's a pen. Sit down."

Surprised at the speed things were happening I said, "OK."

"To the Editor of *The Guardian*," said Bailey.

"What?"

"Write, '*To the Editor of The Guardian. Dear Sir.*' You getting this?"

"Yes, but…"

"Write, 'Let me add my voice to the growing number of people who seem to be responding positively to Wallace MacAkern's straightforward plan to give money back to the taxpayers. Not only is it an eminently workable scheme and an effective protest of a failed system, it also shows great courage and fortitude on the part of Mr. MacAkern. Prince Edward Island needs more like him.

Yours Truly: A Citizen for Wallace MacAkern.'"

I did as he said, but when I finished I protested, "I wanted to know how to write a *poem*."

"Just warming up. Now, Melissa? That letter is for Monday's *Guardian*. For Tuesday, Christian, you can type this one up on the other typewriter."

"Why?"

"To make it seem like somebody else is writing."

"But this isn't poetry…"

"Poetic fiction...of a sort...Well, OK, pure lies. But before you start writing poetry you should always prime the pump with a bit of prose. Now, 'Dear etc etc... Date it tomorrow. Melissa, you can fill that in after Christian's finished?"

"Got it."

"Good girl. Now, take this down, Christian. 'Who's Wallace MacAkern think? He should be shot. Say the word and I'll shoot him, that's for sure and no questions asked. They shoulda done it with Hitler and they shoulda do it with him.'"

"Hey!" said Wallace.

"Don't worry. Just setting up a lunatic tone to destroy its credibility. 'If anybody falls for this they're idiots. What are Islanders anyway? Brain-dead?' Sign that 'Anonymous' and be sure to spell it wrong. And Melissa, I want that out for Tuesday. Now, take one more dictation, Christian."

I was starting to get interested.

"'It has come to my attention that the last letter in the growing Wallace MacAkern story is a set-up. If you check the stationary, you will see that it was sent from Robert Logan Head's campaign office, a typical low trick from the Right Horrible MP and Conservative candidate, and is a good example of why we need more citizens to act with the courage of Mr. MacAkern and declare themselves as less corruptible Independent candidates.'"

I finished typing. "What's this got to do with poetry?" I said.

"Nothing.

"But you said..."

"I know what I said."

"You lied."

"No I didn't."

"You *led* me to be*lieve*..."

"Welcome to politics," said Bailey, and everybody else in the room nodded and snorted. It was like a slap in the face, but, at the same time, it felt bracing.

"I'm starting to see how Smooth Lennie did it," said Wallace.

"Don't fool yourself," said Bailey. "It's how they *all* do it. How does Ward Morris put it? 'Lie, deny, and never say die.'"

"I'll say this," said Wallace. "That book may be shameless, but it does make you understand that type of character,"

"What type of character?"

"The politician."

"Like you, Wallace, you mean?"

"I have the perfect answer to that accusation," said Wallace.

"What?"

"I'm *different..*"

"That is a circumlocutious tautology."

"And this is my middle finger."

Brucie came into the kitchen. "Rattray's out of the hospital," he said.

"Oh yeah?"

"It was nothing. Didn't have to g-go anyway, the wimp. And he was brought there by a g-girl!"

"Who?" I said.

"That g-g-girl, what's her name?"

"Claire" I said. It physically hurt to say it. She didn't offer to bring *me* to the hospital when she saw *me* all bruised and battered. What was I? Nothing? Oh God. I *am* nothing...

"Focus, people!" said Bailey. "Now, sign that lunatic moron letter. Who? Anybody? Who's the most hated prick..."

"Twenty-five cents!" said Wallace.

"You didn't let me finish...The most hated, prick-*ly*, irritable, and detested person on the Island?"

"Rattray," I said. Everybody looked at me. I forgot completely about poetry.

"Perfect!" said Bailey. "Now go ahead and sign it."

"Barry Rattray," I said as I typed. "Assistant Chief Warden, Parks Canada. I can get a park envelope to put it in, if you want."

"Better not. They might be able to trace it back to you."

I saw the way it was done. Harness your anger. Work with a vengeance, literally. Come out on top by whatever means, justified or not. Just like Ward Morris said. I had a brief memory-flash of my dream of the night before. Somebody, a man or a woman, I couldn't tell who, was looking at me from the shore, but I shoved the thought away. It was not even a thought: a memory of a dream. This was the real world and it's a battlefield. I felt angry and pure, waiting for a chance to strike out.

"You're going to need a sparring partner to practice for the debate," said Bailey to Wallace.

"I'll do it," said Melissa.

"Somebody not stoned all the time, who is less likely to giggle."

"How about Whoever-The-Whatever-I'm-Supposed-To-Call-Him-Now?" said Wallace, cocking a thumb at me.

"My name is *Christian*."

"See? Perfect," said Wallace.

But I was sick of his fooling. "Fuck off."

Everybody stopped. Wallace kept looking at me, but not offended, guessing, perhaps, what was wrong.

"What's up?" said Robbie. Nobody mentioned the swearing jar.

"Nothing," I said, and by that I meant Everything, but nothing they could do anything about. Somehow I had cornered myself, and all there was to do now was fight.

"Come on," said Wallace. "What's wrong with me running for office?"

"Go on Christian," said Robbie. "*We* give him shit all the time."

So I said, "OK, then. First of all, the only reason you're getting into politics is to stop the park."

"Yeah? So?"

"Well, what's wrong with the park? You got something against letting other people enjoy this place? You're just as bad as them. You just want what you've got and you're manipulating the whole goddamn system to have it your way. I mean, Christ, you've got rusting hulks of cars in your yard, the dune is moving into the back of your house, Robbie is sleeping under a leak, and Brucie is running wild. You can't even take care of your own household, for God sakes, let alone a constituency. You're like everybody else, just some loser trying to spread it around."

"Is that all?" said Wallace.

"No," Robbie chipped in. "You're also ugly."

Melissa giggled.

But Bailey ignored the awkwardness of the moment. "Well done, Christian, although you didn't observe the no swearing rule. The opponent has three minutes to respond."

"Well," said Wallace. "First of all, I would like to thank my honourable opponent for his frank assessment, as he sees it, of my unsuitability as a candidate for office, and I agree with him that sadly we all in life do have private failures, some, as he points out, in the maintenance of a household, and for which I must take full responsibility, even though his critique is rather condescending to Robbie and Brucie, implying as it does that they are somehow underprivileged. But my point is that yes, we all, in one way or another, have failed. Some with money, some with family.

Some with women." He looked at me and I felt a shaft of loathing enter my heart. He wouldn't dare. "However, I must protest as to the nature of his attack. It would be unworthy of me if I were to launch a scathing personal accusation of his failure with What's-Her-Name at the park office, Daphne..."

"You... *prick!*"

"The incumbent will refrain from comment. And twenty-five cents in the jar, Christian," said Bailey.

"But..."

"No more freebies. You will have a chance to defend yourself with your first rebuttal."

Wallace was smiling with annoying feigned innocence. "What is so galling in my honourable opponent's remarks," he said, "is his anti-democratic slant. Even if it were true that I am, as he claims, some sort of incompetent hick, we cannot degenerate into mere name-calling. Otherwise I would be justified in calling him, for example, a drunken little face-bashed rich boy. Or refer to his would-be girlfriend, what's-her-name, Cecilia?"

"Claire...Don't you bring her into this!"

"Whoa!" said Bailey. "Stop both of you right there. Now, back in your corners. You are going to have to learn to deflect criticism, no matter how close it is to you. If you try to think of it as just a game it might give you some emotional distance."

Wallace regarded me with an unbearably smug look on his face. I wanted to smash it...

But it's best not to describe that whole debate, which was after all only a rehearsal for the main event. Enough to say that I needed it. White hot at first, like a son blaming a father for bringing him into the world and accusing him for everything wrong in it, I attacked Wallace with all the force of somebody railing against the global tragedy his life had become. Wallace easily countered with needling and mockery, and Bailey calmly and persistently reined me in, redirecting me away from what was driving my anger, and steering me back to the points I was trying to make, the arguments themselves, and not just my coded personal torment. Anger lost ground but reason regained it. And gradually by focussing my thoughts on these more exterior challenges, I found that, temporarily at least, I could distance myself from my own deeper pain and sidestep my humiliation and confusion. When I thought about what had happened it still made me wince, but at least I could now think of other things. After the tsunami which had engulfed me, the re-formed earth was starting to harden into something I could walk steadily on.

Afterwards on the porch I felt cleansed and happy. The sun was down and I could hear the tide lapping on the shore. Everything was blue and dark and beautiful. I could see why Wallace didn't want to leave here.

"No hard feelings?" he said.

"No hard feelings," I said.

"Really?"

"Yes."

He looked into the darkness. "Girls!" he said. "They'll drive you nuts." Then he added, "I was married once."

"Oh?"

"Yep. And I loved her."

"What happened?"

"She didn't love me. Broke my heart."

And that's the last I ever heard about it.

Bailey came out of the kitchen. "Sorry, Christian," he said. "We gotta get through this election first, then we'll do that poetry thing, I promise."

"Politics is more fun," I said. More engaging, I should have said. More obsessive.

"Watch it," said Bailey. "You gotta be able to switch it off." He exhaled mightily. "Now, where's that scotch?" He reached for the bottle and said with a sigh to nobody in particular, "It's never the booze or the pot or the swearing that's dangerous. It's the power."

8

During the next week, time seemed to speed up. I went to work and hid out in my office avoiding Claire, not that she noticed. Only part of me wanted her not to notice, but the other part, because I knew she was not noticing, galled me.

She was indifferent. I tried to fool myself that since being indifferent to her was what she seemed to have found attractive in Rattray, I was on the right track, and I even practiced in my mind my lack of emotion towards her, imagining the scene where she came into my office to see me. "Could you check these reports, Christian?" she might ask, and I would look up from my work, accommodating and efficient but mildly bored. "Sure," I'd say. And that was only one of the hundreds of romantic dialogues I had devised to woo her back with my lack of caring.

It was hopeless. I walked past her open door with my best purposeful stride, as though focussing on the task I was pretending to have to do, hoping to make an impression with how unimpressed I was with her, but she didn't even look up. I hung a sign on my door which said, "Do Not

Disturb." She didn't.

So, I tried to lose myself in my work. I closed my door and sat behind my desk from nine to five reading reference volumes and working up my notes. Then, from five-thirty to eight, I went back to sit on the beach with my binoculars, ferociously identifying birds. "Come *on*," I admonished all of nature. "Is that the best you can do? A Black-Backed Gull? That's three this *week* for God's sakes. Oh, what? A *Gannet*. Could you make it any easier?...You *gotta* do better than *that*..."

The morning of the third day I wrote up an argument on a sheet of paper and went into Fergie's office to gave it to him.

"What's this?"

"A new schedule I've worked out."

"Oh yeah? Why?"

"For after work. I've been doing a bird count and making some tidal readings."

"And you're doing this on your own time?"

"Yes."

"We got ourselves a keener," said Fergie to whomever he imagined he was talking to. Then to me he said, "No need to go overboard, though. Why don't you just do the field-work during office hours?"

"I thought I had to hang around here."

"I don't see why." It was the best news I'd had for a while. "Look, Christian, I don't know what you're supposed to be doing here...Frankly, I don't know what *I'm* supposed to be doing here, if it comes to that..." He drifted off for a while as his lips kept moving. "...Well, they also serve who only stand and wait," he said out loud, "Boy, you can tell it was a bureaucrat who wrote that one, that's for sure..." Then he seemed to recognize me again and snapped back.

"Like I was saying...What was I saying?"

"That I didn't have to hang around here."

"Right! Better in fact that you don't. It'll keep you out of Barry's way."

And because I should probably let somebody know, I said, "He came down to my tent the other night." At least there'd be a suspect if my body was found.

"Who did?"

"Rattray."

"Really? Why?"

"I don't know."

"Did he..? There weren't any... problems were there?"

"Not really. It was just weird."

Fergie put his head between his hands. "Oh Rattray, Rattray, Rattray. I don't know what his problem is? Well, actually I do. He's jealous...."

"Of what?"

"Sorry? Was that out loud?"

"Yes."

"Oh. Well... He's jealous of...almost everything, actually. Me. My job. Your job. Anybody else who has a job anywhere..."

"Why?"

"Who knows? He's Rattray. When you first showed up he'd already asked me whether *he* should take that letter to the MacAkerns and I said no, see, because he would have made a big confrontation about it. But when you said that you were a friend of theirs, I figured I'd give it to you to deliver."

"So?"

"So, being Barry Rattray, he makes a big deal about me allocating tasks to junior adjutants who are only sectioned to, and not employees of, the federal park system, and who do not have priority and seniority, et cetera et cetera... and now because of that, and some other stuff, I guess, I'm an enemy too, apparently, as well as you..."

I was jealous of Rattray, he was jealous of me. I wanted the girl who wanted him, but whom he didn't want. All personal feelings aside, it was easy to see that it would be better for everybody if Claire simply started loving me. Then everybody would be happy, except Claire of course, but somebody had to make a sacrifice for the good of the community.

But that, as I knew with a pang, wasn't going to be. Why was I torturing myself?

"Enough to drive a man to drink," said Fergie, then seemed to hear what he was saying, caught himself, looked at his desk drawer, and said, "Fuck it. It's coffee break. Want one?"

"No thanks."

"Of course not. Proper thing. I shouldn't even have asked you. Take a small one myself, though. Be sure not to tell anybody, will you?"

"Don't worry," I said, and as I left he was already opening the drawer.

***

Now I spent my days on the beach, where I observed the wildlife and wrote up my observations. I also made notes on the tide, the delay in its descent caused by the expulsion of water from Barrisway Bay, which, meeting the clockwise coastal current around Prince Edward Island, pulled to the east. I modeled the shore and ocean floor in a sand sculpture from Barrisway and MacAkerns' Point to the park's eastern boundary using the depth measurements of a navigation chart from the office, which I amended. I put pieces of wood into the water and watched through my binoculars where they floated, then drew where the currents brought them. I finished my first notebook and filled up two more.

I would wake up angry and sit on the beach, making my observations and occasionally yelling at the ocean. Underneath the objective style of my notes, my mind crawled around looking for things to be angry about.

And in the evenings, I went to MacAkern's to debate with Wallace, which cleansed and left me empty. Then I could go back to my camp and, calm now, look over my notes on birds and tides. These things were comprehensible.

The Things of Man, though, at the office and with the election, had too many waves intersecting from too many sides. There was no pattern, and if one could be identified, then someone could use that knowledge to bend the advantage toward them.

***

We were at the MacAkerns' when Bailey entered the kitchen with a copy of *The Guardian*.

"We have a problem," he said. "The Conservatives are claiming that according to the elections act, paying for votes is illegal."

"How's it any different than promising jobs?" said Wallace.

"Hey, *I* agree," said Bailey. "But don't worry. It was to be expected."

"But..."

"Don't get hung up on it, Wallace. It's a good thing."

"That was the main plank in our platform..."

"It did its job. It got us some attention. Also, frankly, I don't think we could have sustained it financially."

"I thought you said we had enough in the war chest?"

"I lied. Now, we need some other enticements."

"How about a forward thinking platform of meaningful policy?"

"Yeah, right," Bailey snorted. So did Melissa, Robbie, Aiden and Brucie. I thought I might as well snort too.

"OK. Now. Press release. Can you do the typing, Melissa?"

"Go ahead."

"'Ottawa Makes It Illegal To Get Your Money Back.' New paragraph. 'While admitting that he will submit to the decision of Elections Canada to close down his innovative salary give-back scheme, Independent Candidate MacAkern says, "Vote for me and I'll get those laws changed." He also said that while on the subject of campaign regulations, how about the fact that Robert Logan Head has been hiring paid government workers to help out in his campaign?"

"I said that?"

"Yes."

"What did I mean?"

"Rattray's working for them."

"Really?"

"Yeah. Seems they read the letter we published using his name and they contacted him. So that kinda backfired."

"Well, that's gonna backfire on them too, cause everybody thinks Rattray's a tool."

"Good. Now. Next order of business. Somebody tell me what is the meaning of this?" He laid the "People" section of *The Guardian* open in front of Wallace.

"Shit," said Wallace.

"Twenty-five cents," said Bailey. "And who's Eleanor Beardsley?"

"Widow of the late Elmer Blake," said Robbie. "El'ner and Elmer."

"Toe and Gump's Mom," said Wallace.

"Does she have ties to the Conservative Party?"

"Not that I know of."

"She must've been played, then."

"Why?" said Robbie, leaning in.

"She's written a story about Smooth Lennie."

Robbie looked at Wallace. Wallace looked at Robbie.

"'Prince Edward Island has long been a breeding ground for colourful Maritime characters,'" Bailey read, 'but Leonard "Smooth Lennie" MacKay, the Island's own Sam Slick, would have to top the list of the best known of them' ...And yes. Here it is, in the sidebar: '...Uncle of Wallace MacAkern who is running as Independent Candidate in Barrisway this summer...'"

"Oh Christ," said Wallace, taking the paper and scanning it. "She lists the scams...Fixing the Gold Cup and Saucer Race...The crab license kickback...The Irish moss subsidy... It's all here...The Georgetown arson trial, the tide-wall... Oh Jesus, she's written up the tide-wall!...The Island whiskey project..."

"Who's feeding her this stuff?" said Bailey.

"Could be a coincidence."

"Don't believe it. They must've had this in the works since they heard you'd thrown your hat into the ring. And there's going to be a daily selection from her upcoming book, *Island Characters* for three weeks. Until election day, which is rather convenient." Bailey sat down heavily. "Is this going to be a problem, you being related to him? I heard that Head is starting to refer to you as 'Smooth Wally.'"

"Clever."

"Yes. But you're gonna need a better comeback than that."

"How about 'I loved my uncle, but I hated his politics'?"

"Not bad."

"May I remind you that he was also a Conservative?" said Robbie.

"That's better. People! From now on it's never 'Smooth Lennie MacKay,' it's '*Conservative MP* Smooth Lennie Mackay'. And let's get some dirt on Robert Logan Head's relatives."

"Why'd this have to happen now?" said Wallace.

"Because it was orchestrated to do exactly that. Now it's time we started to get some information on them."

"Like what?"

"Like how are they getting information on us. We need an insider."

Wallace cheered up. "Right! An insider. Of course! Ward Morris recommends that. Chapter Four, 'Getting the Skinny.'"

Bailey thought a bit, sucking his lip. "Melissa, we need somebody to go work for them."

"A spy?"

"Exactly."

"Do I get to wear a message ring?" She had rolled and lit a joint, and was sharing it with Aiden and Robbie.

"Does she get to write notes with invisible ink?" said Robbie.

"No. I just want you to volunteer at their riding office."

"Maybe I could use a false name?"

"Whatever..."

"Who'll I say I am? Natasha Sloventsky?"

"Ivana Katerina, Woman of Mystery," giggled Robbie. I had never heard her giggle before.

"I want you to volunteer for Head's campaign, and once you're there, keep an ear open for any news."

"Do I get a spy car?" said Melissa. "Dress in a long mink coat?"

"With nothing on underneath! Oh! Yes! *Dahlink!*"

"I'll photograph you!" said Aiden. And he picked up his camera and started to click at her, while Melissa pouted and posed. "Work with me! Baby! Beautiful!... Gorgeous!"

Robbie pranced around like a photographer's assistant, moved in to puff Melissa's hair, "Oh! Yes! Perfect!" she said, then pecked her on the cheek. "Fabulous!"

They all collapsed into their seats laughing.

"Well, nothing wrong with having a bit of fun with it, I suppose," said Bailey. "So this means, I take it, that you're OK with the idea?"

"Not really," said Melissa. "Why me?"

"Robbie is Wallace's sister and if she shows up there, they'd obviously suspect something."

"Wait! Robbie can't come with me?"

"No."

"Well, I definitely don't want to do it, then."

"Aren't you sweet," said Robbie, and they kissed.

"Do I have to hose you two down?"

"Sounds like fun."

"Look," said Bailey. "If we're going to *win* this campaign, we're going to have to make some personal sacrifices...."

"Bailey..?" interrupted Aiden.

"Yes?"

"I can do it?"

Bailey turned. "Aiden! Of course. Thanks. And maybe that would be better."

"I gotta go into town? To get some pictures developed? I'll volunteer at their office on the way back? I'd better not live here, though? Somebody might follow me home and find out?"

"Good point."

"I can find some place? And stay there? But how do I

contact you." That last question, of course, he said like a statement.

"Let me think…"

"When I get anything, I could sneak away and phone you?"

"Sure. Simple. That'll work."

"I could run m-m-messages to your place," said Brucie.

"Thanks. Yes. That might be helpful," said Bailey. "You could be our secret messenger."

"All r-r-right!"

"But don't tell anybody anything about what we're doing."

"Don't worry. I won't b-b-blab."

It was agreed that Melissa and Robbie would drive Aiden down to rent a car and leave him there to find his way back to Conservative headquarters. Everybody said goodbye and good luck and Aiden departed like a hero, which in retrospect, turned out to be quite ironic.

9

The next day I snuck into the park office to pick up some more paper, looking first to see that Claire wasn't around, and crossed the lobby towards my office. As I passed, Rattray's open door a voice inside said, "Hey. I want you."

I looked in and saw Rattray. He didn't look up, just sat there pretending to be casual, and made a gesture for me to approach, still without looking. He was clean-shaven and newly pressed and had undoubtedly just calibrated his epaulets with a micrometer. But I was pleased to see there was still a little bruise on the side of his nose. I wondered if I should ask him if he would like to borrow my makeup, but instead I said, "What do you want?"

"Come here," he said.

I came in, letting it be known by my demeanour that I wasn't obliged to just because he had told me to. "What?"

"I found your notebook." He looked up to see my reaction. He must have been rehearsing all morning.

I paused. "Give it here."

"Not so fast. I was reading it."

"That's my business."

"Not entirely. There's something in it that concerns me".

"It's private," I said.

But he was in charge now. "There's some notes about birds and shit. And a whole lot of other crap, and then, what? A poem? Jesus!"

"Give it."

"...But right in the middle there's something really interesting. It's the first draft of a letter..."

I didn't say anything, though of course I knew what he was getting at. "It's all about how you really like the idea of that vegetable stand and how you're going to leave some money for them."

"So?"

"So I'm thinking it's an awful lot like that other letter."

"What other letter?"

"The one they accused me of writing."

I looked at him for a while. "So, they're punching and kicking you and you're saying 'oh please don't hit me! I didn't do anything?' Is that what it was like?"

"There were *two* of them..." he said, and stopped.

I didn't say anything, just stood there with one hip cocked, looking back at him. Might as well go down fighting. "Did it hurt?"

"Go fuck yourself," was his witty retort. He looked at me some more and then got back to the point. "I'm keeping the notebook, and if you give me any more shit, or refuse to do anything I tell you to, I will make it public. Got it?" My eyes must've flicked around the desk, because he said, "No, I don't have it here. I've hidden it. I'm the new recruitment officer for the Conservative Party," he said, and he pointed his finger at me and sighted down it like a pistol. "And I'm recruiting *you*."

"Did they give you a shiny badge to wear?"

His face fell. "You do what I say. And you can start by telling me about the MacAkerns."

"What about the MacAkerns?"

"Noticed any, oh I don't know.... illegal activity there?"

What I needed was a bone to toss him to give me time to retaliate, and which wouldn't mean prison for my friends. Marijuana could mean just that, but from everything I'd heard about the whisky that Dunbar had given Wallace, it seemed to inhabit a legal grey area. I didn't know whether freezing was in fact a legal form of distillation, but it sounded like it hadn't as yet been legislated against, so that came to the same thing, didn't it? Or did it? Surely they couldn't lock somebody up for leaving something out in the winter in Canada. Not yet, anyway.

And right then I had a brief and awful vision of what could drive legislation if you let it: the will to control. The free use of The Things of God (in this case cold weather) being reined under legal control by the Things of Man.

I also saw the resistance which must be set against that to achieve, if not victory, at least balance. And in that moment I became a rebel, a real one, not just pretend. I saw the future as it would be if the Rattrays of the world were in charge, cruel because they were afraid, needing to get something on the world because the world had something on them, having to control so they wouldn't be controlled.

I started to say something, then caught myself. He had to think that he had forced it out of me.

"What?" he said.

"Nothing. It's nothing. No..."

"I have your notebook," he threatened.

I turned as though I was hating myself for what I was doing. "Fergie asked me to see if he could buy a case of bootleg whiskey from them."

"Monroe did?"

"Yes."

"From MacAkern?"

"Yes."

"Perfect! That's exactly what I mean! We can set him up! We can catch him red-handed."

"We're not the police, Rattray."

"We can tell the police how to catch him red-handed. Just as good."

"Why?"

"High time I was in charge of things around here. Fergie's a drunk. He's been screwing up since forever."

"You were drinking the other night."

"What other night?"

"On the beach."

"I don't know what you're talking about," he said, and really looked like he didn't know. Maybe he didn't. The possibility remained that he was simply insane. He continued, "Now. You're going to phone the MacAkerns."

"What? Now?"

"Phone them."

So I dialed the MacAkerns' number and Melissa picked up.

"Campaign Headquarters for The Wallace MacAkern Campaign. Vote Wallace!" Her joyful energy even came down the telephone wire, the direct opposite to here where everything was seething, locked down and destructive.

"Hi, Melissa, it's Christian. Is Wallace there?"

"Sure, Christian."

I waited until he took the receiver. "Hello?"

"Hi Wallace. Listen, Monroe says he wants a case of scotch."

"Fergie? OK. Sure. Why not?"

"He says he'll pay for it with a contribution to your campaign."

"Great!"

"But he wants it delivered."

"Why doesn't he just come and pick it up?"

"I don't know. He's weird."

"That's a fact. When's he want it?"

I covered the mouthpiece and turned to Rattray. "When should I say he should make the drop?"

"Tomorrow night. No! The day after. I have to set up some stuff first. Tell them the day after tomorrow."

"Why would Fergie wait that long?"

"Tell them he's paranoid."

"Where should we do it?"

"I don't know. Make up something."

"Two nights from now," I said to Wallace. "On the beach below the park office. He wants you to bring it in by boat." I looked at Rattray. He nodded OK. "That's what he says," I said to Wallace. "It has to be by boat. There's been a lot of surveillance around and he doesn't want to risk it by road." I looked at Rattray, who nodded back, "Good."

"Is there somebody else there with you?" said Wallace over the phone.

"Monroe," I said.

"Put him on."

"No," I said. "He doesn't want to talk to you directly."

"Weird. But OK. So..." said Wallace.

"Tell you what, Wallace," I said. "I'll find out the rest of the details and tell you tonight."

"OK. See ya."

I hung up and Rattray actually smiled.

***

I'm not too proud of this next part, so I'll get through it fast.

I went over that night to MacAkerns' and said, "I got a way to mess with their campaign."

"Do tell," said Bailey.

I left out the part about how Rattray was threatening me with the notebook, and when I was finished, Wallace said to Robbie, "It's not supposed to rain for another four days."

"So?"

"We're gonna need that tarpaulin off the roof."

***

The next day I went to Rattray's Office.

"It's all set up for tomorrow night," I told him, and left him to think. With Rattray, that might take some time. And sure enough, later that day he told me to meet him tomorrow evening, an hour before the drop was to take place, by the phone booth near the park office.

After work I went directly to MacAkerns'. Bailey and Wallace had dragged the skiff out of the mud where it had sat half-sunk at the water's edge. They had taken the tarp off the roof and opened it out on the lawn, then laid the boat onto the center and wrapped the skiff with it, tucking the edges of the tarp up around and into the boat, nailing it all around on the inner gunwale and bending the nails over so that the tarpaulin wouldn't pull off. They assured me that it should be perfectly all right, and sure enough, when they put it in the water it worked. It was ugly as hell but it floated like a cork. They placed a case of scotch in the centre behind the thwart. Robbie and Melissa found some oars in the barn.

"You take it around and do your thing," said Bailey to me. "Tomorrow night I'll row it from your campsite."

"You know how to row?" said Wallace.

"I was on the sculling team of the Charles River Boat Club for two years."

"Good, 'cause I'm useless at rowing."

"I suspected as much."

"Oh yeah? Why?"

"You lack the lithe grace and aristocratic manner of the born oarsman."

"Fuck off."

"*Voilà, la preuve.*"

"Jesus, where'd you find him?" Wallace asked Melissa.

"Ask him what he *did* on the rowing team."

"Well?" said Wallace

"I was the crew manager."

"So you don't know how to row, either."

"Strictly speaking, no, but I have a good grounding in the theory. Fifty cents in the swear jar, incidentally."

I had to poke holes through the tarp at the oarlocks for the oars, but they'd work fine. I wouldn't use them much to get around the point anyhow, just keep them handy if I hung up on the shore. I wanted to see how the tide took me. We waited for just when it was beginning to ebb, at 7:43 p.m., and I rowed out and waited off the dock until the water began pulling me away. It started so subtly that I didn't realize I was moving until I looked ashore and saw that the MacAkerns' house was wheeling out of sight behind the dune that curved around the side of their property. I was being towed by the moon, up there in broad daylight, almost full. I started to move faster, but because I was on the body that was moving, I still didn't feel it, but when I looked up again, I was around the big dune, and I could see the point, and the highest dunes behind, and, across the inlet in the other direction, the harbour of Barrisway. Down by the end of the point terns were twinkling above the water, rising in excited flocks and suddenly dropping. How they saw what they were diving for was anybody's guess.

Where the bay flowed into the channel the rip grabbed and pulled that idiotic blue-wrapped boat and shot it through the narrows. The tide running out hit the waves coming in at the mouth, all jumping and joyful. Perhaps in this stirring-up was what the terns were feeding off. I spun out onto the ocean, then was swept around the point in an eddy which would have then pulled me back towards the inlet, but here I took the oars up and rowed parallel to the shore towards my campsite. I didn't notice any east-moving current, as was marked on the navigational charts, but perhaps that was a general observation and not specific to today, which was good to know. I saw my tent ahead and approached and beached the skiff, nudged the boat into the shore and waited, looking at my watch and making notes. I had to wait only a few minutes before the tide left the boat solidly aground where it would be until the next high tide. I would still have two more chances to make the necessary observations before the rendezvous with Rattray.

***

The next night I biked to the park office, mostly by starlight. The moon was behind a large bank of clouds moving north-east towards Newfoundland, but the rest of the sky was clear. I even saw a shooting star, but it was too quick for me to make a wish.

Rattray was under the street light that illuminated the phone booth, more excited than I'd ever seen him. He was holding a piece of paper, looking at his watch, dancing his weight from one foot to the other like he was nearly peeing his pants.

"I *own* you," he said, taking his dialogue directly out of the crappy films he undoubtebly watched. *Jungle Justice*, starring Barry Rattray as The Horse's Ass. I got off my bike and came toward him.

"Time to arrest your friend," he said. "Phone the police and tell them there's a bootleg deal going down at zone two of the park."

"Why don't *you* just phone them?"

"Because, I'm Conservative recruitment officer for Barrisway Electoral District, and an arrest of the Opposition candidate cannot be seen to be politically motivated. Though it is," said Rattray. He barked a short ugly laugh, overjoyed at his cleverness.

"For fuck's sakes, Rattray. Just give me back my notebook."

"You phone first."

"How do I know you're not lying?"

"You have no choice."

"I could just tell everybody everything."

"And have your friends know you betrayed them?"

"I haven't betrayed them."

"You are about to."

"Not if you don't give me back my notebook."

"The old Mexican standoff," said Rattray. Oh yes, there was no doubt about the cool-eyed competence of Barry Rattray. How could a tight negotiation fail with someone who clearly had seen so many shit movies as him?

"Well, fuck this," I said, and started to walk away.

I've learned since then that it always comes down to some moment, in fact, the moment of truth. And when it does, both sides are always damaged, so it's pointless, but apparently the only way that things move on to something else. Then, though, was my first time. And I didn't care. My strength was in my indifference. So what if everybody knew everything? So what if they didn't like me. Anything was better than this pointless power deadlock. And Rattray saw that I was serious.

"Wait, wait, wait, wait, wait," he said in a weary sing-song, as if he was dealing with somebody who was obviously unable to take a joke. "Here's your notebook." He held it out.

I took my time coming back, letting him know by my manner that I was willing to turn and leave any time. If he snatched the book back at the last moment, I would leave for good, and he seemed to know that I would. I watched him in the eyes the whole time. I took the book.

"Now make the phone call," he said, hiding his sudden vulnerability from me. It occurred to me that I could leave right then and there, just run away into the dark and hide, but that would make an already complicated situation even more so. See this through at least, I thought, the better to start again from something more solid.

I opened the phone-booth door. Rattray told me the number to dial. I talked to the person who answered.

"I want to report a crime that is being committed. On the beach below Barrisway National Park office, there's a bootleg alcohol deal taking place. Now...Yes...As soon as possible. No. I don't want to leave my name." The girl on the other end asked for details.

I hung up.

"I told you to tell them your name," said Rattray.

"I didn't want to."

"Well, don't worry. Everybody will know who squealed. I'll make sure of that."

"Go fuck yourself, Rattray."

"No. *You* go fuck yourself." We were now equally witty.

I deserved the total lack of joy I was feeling, considering that I was betraying something I never thought I would. But then Rattray absolved me even of that. "And just so you know," he said. "That notebook? I photocopied it."

Perversely, this new information made me feel better. Now *he* deserved it. I walked over to my bike, got on, and pedaled out of his sight.

Away from the light, you could see the stars again in half the sky. Down the causeway ahead of me I saw a dark shape parked beside the road. I stopped before I reached it and laid my bike on the ground beside the pavement.

I waited. The moon came out from behind that bank of clouds and everything was bathed in a silver wash. I started to walk towards the shore between the clumps of wind-stunted spruce. The sand on the path beneath my feet was silent. When I got to the low cliff edge where my hiding place was, I could see the ocean, as calm as oil, rising from low tide. I scanned to the east and it was bright enough now to see Rattray fifty yards down the shore, crouched behind a spruce. The moon was full and luminous, so bright now that you couldn't see the stars nearby. It was positioned exactly where predicted, riding its elliptic, a sure constant that real plans could be built on. When it had moved across the sky a little more in this direction, its increasing influence would drag one part of the film of water which was all the oceans of the world, releasing another part from its gravitational pull, and the tide on this shore would rise higher. It would be at its greatest height, according to the tide chart, at eleven-fourteen in Barrisway, but by my calculations, corrected for our position further along the coast, closer to eleven twenty. The boat would take about three minutes to float if Bailey and Wallace dragged it up just so. But I shouldn't worry. The moon would do its job all right, and the weather couldn't have been better. Human error was the only possible weak point.

I waited some more. Over the horizon towards the Magdalen Islands was a huge thunderhead.

I saw Bailey row around the point from the west, his oar-locks squeaking. As he approached I could hear Wallace, the big oaf, in the stern singing quietly, "I am a bold deceiver, murrah ringum madurrum madah..." Bailey's theoretical-only knowledge of rowing, and the inefficiency of the boat itself, made for a clumsy crawl up the coast, but perhaps the current that was missing yesterday was helping him tonight because he was steadily advancing.

I saw a dim flash of sheet lightning on the horizon which, in the same instant, illuminated the underside of that thunderhead. Bailey, pulling an oar, skipped the blade out of the water, lurched back, then resumed rowing again. The rumble from the thunder reached me faintly.

I saw Rattray crouch lower in his hiding place as Bailey and Wallace passed in front of both of us, then ran the boat ashore and pulled the prow up from the water's edge exactly two lengths of Wallace's feet, as we had calculated. I saw them leave the boat and fast-walk up around the headland to the east.

I waited.

The tide rose slightly and bumped the boat.

I saw Rattray half-stand in the moonlight, crouch again, then stand fully upright like a gopher, look up and down the shore, then at the boat, gently rocked now by the small waves. I was close enough to the road to hear Bailey and Wallace panting back to the van, which was the dark shape I had seen further down the causeway. I heard the van start up and drive toward the park office, but only because I was listening for it. From where Rattray was hiding it would be inaudible.

I saw the rising tide float the stern, as it swung around bobbing.

I saw Rattray creep out on the beach, then stop, indecisive. He was in a tizzy as to whether the tide was going to float the boat and take away the crate of bootleg liquor, his lovely evidence. Where was Fergie? he must have been thinking. All his plans hung on Fergie showing up.

I saw the bow of the boat bob loose and the boat begin to drift off the shore.

I saw Rattray run down to the water, in up to his knees to retrieve it and pull it onto the beach lest it be lost and Fergie not be caught red-handed. And just as he grabbed it I saw the strong light of a high beam flashlight, and heard a voice through a megaphone.

"Stop! Police!" Just like on TV.

Rattray stopped. "Oh, good..." I heard him say.

A big beefy policeman and a younger policewoman walked toward Rattray. "Hands up, sir. Hands up!" she said.

"I was waiting for you..." said Rattray.

"We are arresting you for the charge of trafficking in illegal alcohol, or possession for the purpose of trafficking," said the policewoman, who then took off her cap, and shining the flashlight in it, started to read from a paper she had taped inside. "'It is my duty to inform you that you have the right to retain and instruct counsel without delay.' Are you listening?"

"Officer," Rattray explained. "I was waiting for you. I was

the one who called. Then it looked like the boat was floating away so I came down to stop it."

There was more jiggling with the flashlight as she continued to read him his rights. " 'You may call any lawyer you want. There is a 24-hour telephone service available which provides a legal aid duty lawyer who can give you legal advice in private...'"

"I wanted to make sure the evidence didn't disappear."

"Quiet please, sir," said the policewoman. "'This advice is given without charge and the lawyer can explain the legal aid plan to you. If you wish to contact a legal aid duty lawyer, I can provide you with a telephone number. Do you understand? Do you want to call a lawyer? You are not obliged to say anything, but anything you do say may be given in evidence.'" She put her hat on again and took the handcuffs off her belt.

Bailey and Wallace approached from the direction of the park office, from where they had directed the cops.

"You got him, I see," said Bailey.

"Oh my God!" said Wallace, grossly overacting. "It's Barry Rattray!"

"Do you know him?" said the cop.

"He's working with the Conservative Party, isn't he?" said Bailey.

"I phoned *you*..." said Rattray to the cop.

"Didn't sound like you, sir," said the policewoman.

"Well. No. Not me personally. I got somebody else to do it."

"Why would you do that?"

"Because...I wanted..."

She waited, but Barry didn't want to say what he wanted. It occurred to him for the first time that this could be serious.

"Better take up on that free call to the lawyer," she said.

"It was that little asshole, Christian. I got *him* to phone you."

"Do you know anything about this?" the cop asked Wallace.

"Christian?" said Wallace. "I don't know anybody by that name."

"Anyhow," said the policewoman. "It was a woman's voice."

In the phone booth, while Rattray was giving me the number of the police station, I had been dialing the Mac-Akerns'. Robbie, who'd been waiting for the call as planned, had answered, and then made an anonymous phone-call to the police and told them that she knew where the drop was going to take place. After Bailey and Wallace left the boat and whisky, they met the police by the park office and directed them to Rattray. Fergie was home asleep and didn't know anything about any of it.

"I'm not guilty..."

"That remains to be seen. Now, come along." And they walked him to their car.

You can't control the Things of God, but sometimes, if you observe them honestly, some of them are predictable. Things couldn't have gone better, but pedalling home to my tent across the causeway, I didn't feel proud of myself. I had never thought of myself as the sort of person who did the sort of things I was now doing, and it felt like I had betrayed something. That night, I had that same dream with that same sense of loss, and I thought I knew who it was on the beach I was drifting away from. He looked like me.

10

All next morning I still felt uneasy about what I'd done, but it couldn't have been the memory of the look in Rattray's eye that bothered me, I couldn't even see his face as he was led away. So, it must've been what I imagined that look to be. For someone who was nervous even with legal language, who had probably always felt guilty, it must've been a nightmare for him. It had been only three years since homosexuality could get you up to fourteen years in prison.

I was helping the MacAkerns set up for their picnic. We'd opened the house and swung wide the front door, an ornate double-winged monstrosity with a great rusted brass twist-bell and beveled glass, one pane which had broken and which had been replaced with a stained slab of chip-board. Windows painted closed with coat after coat of thick paint had been jimmied and propped up, and the musty smell of moldering parlour wafted out across the lawn where it was baked away by the sun.

Where the front porch wrapped around the western corner of the house we had created a stage. The corner of the porch was cut off at a forty-five degree angle with two pillars twelve

209

feet apart, and the banister between them was obligingly half-falling down and easily removed, making for an open proscenium, which would work quite well if you avoided the great ugly rusted spikes sticking out from one side. Wallace had asked Brucie to hammer them out but had got him to stop when the pounding had threatened to bring down one of the pillars. Loudspeakers had been taken out of Bailey's van along with his amplifier and mixer and set on the porch floor on either side. There were two microphones on stands in the centre.

The table was set over by where we had moved the tractor on the first day I had come to their house. It was as though Wallace had somehow divined even then what would need to be done, but there was probably nothing magical about it. The way he worked was with a vague plan as to the direction he wanted to go, and then he'd arrange things in a way which might at the time seem pointless, but which insured that he was never out of opportunities. It meant that his life was full of uncompleted projects, but with always enough other options to follow.

He was standing with Brucie on the front steps and he gave me a handbill announcing the time and date of the event: "MacAkern Potluck Picnic (and Antique Auto Show) with The Barely Boys!"

"That's 'Barley Boys,'" I said. "You spelled it wrong."

"No I never. People will naturally *think* it's the Barley Boys, but we may not be able to get them, and if we can't, our ass is covered."

"So who are the *Barely* Boys then?"

"You and Brucie," said Wallace. "Robbie tells me you sound pretty good."

I turned to Brucie. "What songs do you know?"

"'D-d-deep In My Heart.'"

"What else?"

"Th-th-at's it."

"We have kind of a limited repertoire," I said to Wallace.

"Don't worry," said Wallace. "You'll come up with something."

Bailey came out of the house and approached.

"Maybe you could sing 'Speed Bonny Boat,'" I suggested to Wallace.

"I suppose I could…" he said. "You know the chords?"

"I can learn them."

"And you and Brucie could come in with the harmony," said Wallace, and his eyes started dancing with the thought.

"No you don't," said Bailey. "You're not getting up on stage at all."

"Why not? I could also do 'My Love Has To The Lowlands Gone.'"

Bailey put one hand on his shoulder. "Wallace."

"Yes?"

"You can't sing worth shit."

"Ah, come on…"

"You know that bagpipe thing you got on tape?"

"'As Softening Shades Of Evening Fall'? What about it?"

"You're worse."

"Really?" said Wallace, dismayed.

"Don't worry. We want you doing what you do best. One-on-one. 'How you doing?' 'Lovely day today.' And only talk politics if they bring up the subject. This whole shindig can't look in any way self-interested. If they think you got them here just to get their votes, it will harm your reputation for generosity."

"I didn't know I had one."

"Well you do. 'He's generous,' they say. 'I'll give him that. If he's got something, he'll share it.' I don't understand it

211

myself. I mean, when was the last time you actually *bought* a meal for somebody else."

"This party will make up for that."

"It's a potluck. They're bringing their own food."

"Which I will generously share with everybody."

"Nice."

"What about the scotch? Who's bringing the scotch?"

"Dunbar's bringing the scotch."

"But I've arranged that he should."

"You are a river for your people," said Bailey.

"Are the Barley Boys actually g-g-gonna show up?" said Brucie.

"I don't know," said Bailey. "I went down to see them and asked, 'How'd you like to do a benefit concert?' 'We'd love to!' said the leader, what's-his-name, Niall. 'But it'll cost you a thousand bucks.' 'How's that a benefit?' I ask, and Niall says, 'It would benefit *us*.' So, it looks like we put you two guys on stage and claim it's some sort of community service. Go for the pity vote."

"H-hey!"

"Ever worked on a stage before, Brucie?"

"N-n-no."

"Christian?"

"No."

"Well, it's tougher than it looks. The very thought of being in front of the public can rip your soul out and hang its tattered remnants in the wind. Don't worry about it, though, you'll be fine. As long as you don't get stage fright."

***

The first guest to arrive was Fergie. He came down the causeway in the park truck and Wallace poured him a scotch and talked to him about what had happened to Rattray, making it sound as if he was only piecing it together himself from what he'd heard, rather than mentioning his part in it. Soon after that, Toe and Gump showed up with a lady who turned out to be El'ner, their mother.

"I want to pick your brains about your uncle," she said to Wallace.

"Well, we're trying to soft-pedal that, what with the election and everything."

"Oh pooh!" she said. "Nobody gives a hoot about who you're related to."

"Maybe not," said Wallace, accommodating and genial. "And you know, he wasn't that bad anyway..." And he told her a long and completely improvised story which stressed Smooth Lennie's good points, chief among which being his total and utter loyalty to the Conservative party. She even took notes, so that looked like it was working out.

Others started arriving until there were a good thirty people, then fifty, and growing. Some brought food, which was laid out on a table and picked at. Wallace served the scotch. Dunbar, a man with eyebrows like wooly caterpillars and the largest Adam's apple I'd ever seen, followed around nervously and asked people their opinion on its taste, without drinking any himself.

"Not too smokey?"

"Not at all."

"How about the peatiness?"

"Not too peaty, I think."

The fall of Rattray was discussed extensively. Apparently, somebody had filled El'ner in with what everybody else knew because I overheard a conversation between her and her sons.

"But, he's queer," said Toe.

"Well, that's no reason to beat him up!" she said, tapping with suppressed anger a rolled newspaper against her forearm. "Now, I want to know. Is that the reason you attacked him?"

I could see Toe watching her warily, hearing the accusatory tone which implied that if that had been the reason, it would be a bad thing.

"No," he said.

Gump, catching on, supported his brother by shaking his head vigorously.

"Why, then?" said El'ner.

"Why then what?" Toe stalled.

"Why did you beat him up?

"Because....when we told him he was, he said he wasn't," said Gump.

"Well, if he'd admitted it, you'd have beaten him up for that!" said El'ner.

But by now Toe had assembled his argument. "No! I said we *didn't* beat him up 'cause he was gay."

"So why did you, then?"

"Why did we what?"

"Why Did You Beat Him Up?"

"Because he's gay?" said Gump, who'd lost track.

"No, we didn't. Shut up, Gump," said Toe. "We beat him up because... I know! Because he stole stuff from our vegetable stand."

"And that's all?"

"Yeah."

She smacked Gump on the head with the rolled up paper, and then again to punctuate every word. "Don't...Beat... People...*Up!*"

"Come on, Mom! Stop! He's a horse's ass!"

El'ner stopped hitting him. "Well, that's true," she said.

"He deserved it."

"Yeah, Mom. I don't give a shit if he's gay or not," said Gump

"You wouldn't," said Toe.

"What's that supposed to mean?"

"You're gay."

"You calling me gay?"

"Yeah."

Toe punched Gump on the shoulder. "You're the gay one."

Gump punched back, harder, and they left, punching and accusing each other of homosexuality.

El'ner sighed deeply. "Its not the sexuality. It's pretending to yourself that you're something you're not. Life's not complicated enough without that?" she said it to nobody in particular.

Fergie was standing to one side. "One lie breeds another," he said to his invisible friend.

I didn't have to be there at all. In fact, it was time that I should go tune up my banjolele.

But right then, a large town-car rolled into the parking area and three familiar-looking men dressed in expensive clothing of the bell-bottoms and leather jacket variety stepped out: The Barley Boys.

"Gentlemen, Gentlemen, Gentlemen!" greeted Wallace, moving toward them with his hand out in welcome. "So nice to see you! Caught your show at the Mall, when was it? Two weeks ago, and it was great! But here now, in the flesh! Live! In person! Well, I never. We're your biggest fans. Come in! Don't be shy! There's food and scotch. Help yourselves."

All this was met by The Barley Boys with silence and a sullen scanning of the grounds, not even acknowledging Wallace, a buzzing noise in their ear. They stood like a pride of lions still too lazy from last night's meal to move in quite yet for the kill. After a long pause the largest, most heavily-bearded head swiveled around. Niall didn't even look at Wallace's outstretched hand. "You're Wallace MacAkern."

"I am! The very same! Independent Candidate for Barrisway riding in the upcoming election. Hope you vote for me!"

"Your man came to see me." A thick Belfast statement.

"My man?"

"Your man, what was his name? B- something."

"Bailey?"

"Aye, that was it." Though he seemed to get no joy from solving that puzzle. "He asked if we wanted to perform a benefit concert."

"Yes. He was telling me..."

"And we said no."

"Yes."

"In no uncertain terms."

"I understand."

"There was no ambiguity in our refusal whatsoever that I remember, was there boys?

"There was not," said another Barley Boy.

"None," said the third.

"So what I am saying is that by 'No,' if you catch my drift, we didn't mean 'Yes, we'd love to.'"

" I see of course..." Wallace started but was cut off.

"...So you can imagine my surprise this morning when, upon opening *The Guardian*, I see an advert in the entertainment section that said we *would* be playing here this afternoon."

"Well," said Wallace, as though it would be a bit of an imposition, but one he could perhaps work around, "I suppose...I mean...we have a band already, but, well, I don't

see why we couldn't make room in the program for such a
fine... Sure! Why not? The more the merrier!"

"You misunderstand me, Mr. MacAkern."

"Oh?"

"Yes. We didn't come here to ask to play at your 'picnic.'"
He managed to make both syllables of the word sound
independently distasteful and collectively foul.

"Then...why?"

"We came here to see who has been using our name to
draw a crowd without our consent."

Wallace played it for innocence. "I don't follow..."

Niall snapped the wad of newspaper he was carrying under
Wallace's nose. "Read," he commanded.

"'This afternoon,'" read Wallace, "at MacAkerns' farm in
Barrisway off Route 3. The first annual MacAkern Family
Picnic. Come one, come all. Free food and refreshments.'
Yes, but I don't see..."

"Read!"

"'Entertainment provided by the B....'" Wallace stopped,
shocked. "But this is terrible!" he said, all concern for having
become somehow involved, no matter how remotely, in any
annoyance of people he so clearly admired. He looked at
the advertisement again, confirmed that his eyes were not
playing tricks on him and took charge and demanded,
"Who's the copy writer?" He looked around as though before
another minute passed one of his staff would get to the
bottom of this. In the full force of this performance, Niall's
lidded eyes looked deeper into Wallace's, his lips turned
from sneer to question.

"*Barely* Boys," said Wallace. "*Barely*. I won't say that we
didn't have you in mind when we named them, but I had
no idea..." He leant in and explained how this awful mistake
must have happened. "Brucie and his friend here had a few

songs they wanted to do, and a couple of us were sitting around trying to think of what we'd call them, and they were boasting about some great feat they had performed that day, like you would, you know, at their age, and somebody said, 'Yes, there's no doubt about it. You're both Real Men' and Robbie (was it?) said 'Barely that!' and Melissa said, 'Mere boys is all.' Then I said, "Barely Boys! There's your name!' So we went with that. I won't say we weren't *thinking* about you, I mean with the greatest respect of course, as a tribute really...but...Oh! My God! Trust *The Guardian* to get it wrong! Well, that's the last time I leave it up to them to edit the final copy. Melissa! I want the money back for that advertisement. We could probably sue them for damages as well." He turned back to Niall. "I'm so sorry. What can we do to make it up to you?" Robbie handed Wallace the handbill. "There!" said Wallace looking at it. "See, The *Barely* Boys."

"Where's the scotch?" said the Terrorist Gnome.

"Scotch!" said Wallace. "The Barley Boys want scotch! Here, take a few bottles. There. Perfect. Try some of El'ner's lasagna, too. Relax. Enjoy yourselves. Could I perhaps get you a 'Vote MacAkern' sign for your lawn?"

"No."

"Of course not. Still. Enjoy yourselves. And my deepest most heartfelt apologies." And Wallace walked away, shaking his head in sorrow at the number of details that can go awry in this world.

It was time for me to get ready to go on stage. I don't know quite how I felt about that, because I had been furiously avoiding thinking about it since I had first agreed to it, but it was taking a lot of nervous energy not to think about, and it was soon time to actually do it. You couldn't die from stage fright, but what about this mounting anxious stressful heart-pounding extreme discomfort? I looked around at the crowd of people in the sun, talking and drinking and eating. What right had I to demand their attention? Though maybe they would pay as little notice to me as to the tape of fiddle music now playing over the speakers. That would be a blessing. We could just get up and do the one song we knew, and then slip back into lovely anonymity.

"Are you r-ready?" said Brucie, quite at ease with it all.

"I have to get my banjolele." I walked up onto the porch and around behind the house.

Under the roof of the porch and in the shade of the dune creeping close on this side, it was cool, dark, and quiet. Melissa was there with Robbie, smoking a joint.

"Want some?" said Melissa.

"It doesn't work with me."

"Then you might as well," she said, although I didn't quite follow the logic. But I was about to go on stage, and the photo on the front of The Mighty Voice of Jah tape showed three very relaxed people getting ready to do just that while smoking up, and right now I could do with some of their apparent self-possession. So, if only to get into character, as it were, I took the joint and inhaled, held it in my mouth to cool it as I'd been taught, and sucked the smoke into my lungs without coughing. It was so successfully executed that I took another, held my breath like a pearl diver, then exhaled. Just taking charge of my breath like that calmed me somewhat. I tuned up the banjolele for a minute or two, until it sounded quite perfect.

"What are you going to play?" asked Robbie.

"'Deep, Deep in my Heart,'" I said. "It's the only song we know. We haven't rehearsed, really. It probably won't be very good. I hope Brucie doesn't freeze up."

"Naw," said Robbie. "He's a natural."

I paused for quite a long time. "Yeah," I said, gradually more amazed that I hadn't seen the connection before. "A *natural*, that's it...

"You're stoned," said Melissa.

I looked at her. No, not stoned. It's just that I'd figured out Life. The key was that you had to be *natural*...

If necessary, by artificial means. "Give me another toke," I said, and she did. "But how do you do that, just be natural? I mean, it's easy to say, but there's gonna be people out there looking at me..."

"Shit, *they* don't care," said Robbie.

I considered this. "Oh no!" I said. "That's worse."

"Show time," said Robbie.

Show time! Now? No! It couldn't be! Too soon! I wasn't ready! Why me? "I don't think I can go on," I said.

"Everything's going to be fine," said Melissa. "It's important to just keep cool when you're stoned."

"I'm not stoned. I don't *get* stoned."

"OK then. You're not stoned," said Melissa. "But everything is going to be fine. Say it."

"Say what?"

"Say 'Everything is going to be fine.'"

"'Everything is going to be fine.'"

"Just keep repeating it."

So, Everything Is Going To Be Fine, I told myself as I walked toward the front of the house. Everything Is Going To Be Fine. Everything is going. To be fine. Fine, then, that everything is going to be. Going Fine is to be Everything? Then, my best so far: To be is everything. Going, fine.

It almost overwhelmed me with its profundity. From its Shakespearean opening to the calm acceptance of a final parting, it seemed to sum up all of Life. It was brilliant. I would have to find some way to work it into my beach report.

Then I remembered that I was no longer repeating what I was supposed to. Wouldn't it be awful if I had forgotten what Melissa had told me I must recite?... And then I realized that I *had* forgotten it.

Terror gripped me. I had forgotten that everything was going to be fine! Everything *wasn't* going to be Fine. Fine was exactly what everything was *not* going to be! I was stoned! On pot. Which is illegal! ...I'll be thrown into jail! With Rattray! As my cellmate!...

But wait...Everything is going to be fine. That was it. A close call! Everything is going to be fine. Every sing is going two bovine. A Very Thinnest Go In To Beef Vine. Avery thinks he's going, Tubby Fein...

"Ready?" said Melissa.

"No."

"Let's go, then."

She and Robbie led me around the corner of the building into the sunlight. I concentrated on the details around me to stop myself from thinking about what was ahead.

The crawling tides moved the eel-grass on the shore. Leaves trembled like coins in a breeze through the Balm of Gilead...a lovely tree with a lovely name. Is there no Balm in Gilead? Why yes there is. This lovely moment. Now this one...and now...Oh, here's another. They just keep coming... until...until...

I blinked my eyes and some quick figure flicked across my imagination. Better keep my eyes open, I thought. I hadn't liked that. Make a mental note: Never blink again. This was better. Every song was going to be. Fine!

And while we're on the subject, I thought for no reason at all, this thing about me not crying at Dad's funeral? Maybe crying at funerals was just one of those things which you were *told* you should do, was in fact *un*natural, and as such would not, in its falseness, truly honour my father. So that was all right. "Everything was going. Too benign," I muttered, and I giggled at my own wit.

"What?" said Robbie.

"Nothing."

"You OK?"

"No." I giggled again.

There were maybe thirty people in front of the stage. Strangers and friends: Toe and Gump, El'ner and Dunbar, Fergie and Wallace. The three Barley Boys stood with their arms across their chests, holding their scotch in their fists, ready to let Wallace off with this one, maybe, if we were as harmless as we seemed and not the agents of some conspiracy to steal their name.

Melissa turned off the fiddle music and went to the microphone. "Hi everybody! And welcome to the first annual MacAkern Family Picnic! Great to see you all here, and could you please welcome, for your listening pleasure...The Barely Boys!"

There was some mild applause.

Far too soon I found myself onstage, standing beside Brucie, looking out at the audience, with the bright dune behind them seeming to pulse toward me. I gave my banjolele a strum. More people turned toward us. Brucie struck a mock operatic pose and sang the note "mi mi mi" into the microphone. His voice rang out like a bell across the lawn.

I strummed another chord and another, and laid down a rhythm. Natural. Brucie started singing, coming in perfectly on the beat, his voice beautiful.

He sang the first verse, and the significance of the lyrics almost overwhelmed me. I felt like when I had first set eyes on Claire. And when I joined in on the chorus, supplying the easy harmony, I wasn't nervous at all. The utter simplicity of things dazzled me. You could do anything on a day like this and it would work out. It was even okay when Brucie stumbled on the words and sang "La la la," and I started talking, like the kind of filler I had heard on the Mighty Spear of Jah tape. In "Jeremiah," they had sung, 'Is there no balm in Gilead? No physician there? Why then is there no healing for our wounds?' So I said that, but instead I said, '*Feeling* for our wounds,' getting it wrong, but it still worked, so I added, 'Healing for our feeling,' And the full import of this suddenly hit me. "Here we are on a summer's day," I continued,

"At MacAkerns' picnic,
With the tide going out,
And the sun going down,
Not yet, but soon, or soon enough..." I strummed the rest of the line without saying anything. I didn't know what to say next.

"Lalala la la la la," sang Brucie.

Then I heard myself talking again. "On this evening, in this beautiful home. And I want this family to do whatever they want....but I'm being paid by people who want to kick them off... so it's all very confusing..."

Then I stopped talking and just strummed and listened to Brucie. I had heard what I said as I was saying it, amplified and apart from myself, my own voice not from my mouth but from a different source in front of and to either side of me. It was the first time I had ever said anything over a microphone.

It also sounded, strangely, like my father's voice, and that reminded me that I should ask him about those Balm of Gilead trees when I next saw him, and then I realized, with a shock, that that was impossible now, and that I would never see him again, and my whole body filled with that realization and made me sadder than I'd ever been before. I stopped strumming.

Never again.

I was up to my neck in the world and he wasn't around to guide me through it. I was lost, as I had lost Claire, and plunged into a pointless war with Rattray...And right then I suddenly knew who was on the beach in my dream as I was drifting away from the shore: not me, but my father, and I remembered that look in his eyes, not conquered by the world, but aware of its enormity. And there for the first time in my young life I felt the pangs of painful wisdom.

I had never wept for him. That was the sad thing. And it was too late now, and this made me sad too. I had to blink my eyes a few times, as if I had opened them while swimming under salt water. I understood his demons; they were the same as mine. I saw what had saddened him, and they were the same things that saddened me. He'd had a father too, who'd had a father too, and all you could do in this world was weep.

So, I wept.

I wept for the dunes, for time, for life, I even wept for Rattray because we were all the same, after all, but mostly I wept for my father. Some dam I didn't even know I had built cracked and released with a sigh, and I was standing in front of the microphone, my shoulders shaking and my chest heaving, sobbing in public.

"I never wept for him," I said. " My father...when he died... at his funeral...afterward..."

Robbie had come up to my side and had an arm around my shoulder. "Well, you're weeping for him now," she said to me. How did she understand so much?

People looked on, concerned. I saw all the completely unearned care that had been given me, and I wept for my ingratitude. Then I saw how I would have to join this circle of responsibility, and I wept for that. Robbie started to draw me away, but I turned back to the microphone.

"I took the potatoes," I said. "It was me. I said it was Rattray, but it was me... *I* left that note. I didn't mean it to sound sarcastic.. I couldn't change any of my money when I went to Barrisway....Really..."

"That's all right, Christian..." said Robbie.

I was just eighteen years old, but sometimes I felt eighty and other times I felt eight. Melissa came over to my other side, put her arm around my shoulder, and even though I was shaking with sobs, I felt her un-brassiered breast against my side and it made me feel better and whole. Then sadder. I continued sobbing as they led me off stage. Toe and Gump were there, looking embarrassed.

"I'm sorry Toe," I said. "I'm sorry Gump."

"Don't you worry," said Gump. "You're from Montreal. Home of the Habs."

"That prick had it coming to him anyway," said Toe.

"And you knew Rocket Richard."

"I only met him once..."

"Still. Put it here." He held out his hand.

"We'll go beat that fucker up again anytime. Just say the word."

"No really. Don't..."

"What's this?" said El'ner, moving in.

"Nothing, Mom."

"Did I hear you were going to beat up somebody again?"

"No."

"I'm fairly sure that that is what I heard."

"We didn't mean it."

I heard behind me the scrape of a microphone stand, amplified. I looked up and saw that the Barley Boys had mounted the stage.

"All right," said Niall. "I gotta say that when we came here today we thought we were being ripped off…Our name, you know…But then, well, seeing those two, the little one with that voice of his, *beautiful*, and the taller one with the beat-up face…weeping like that for his da…I mean, publicly humiliating himself…groveling…sniveling…pathetic…My God… I think…Ah Jesus fuck…I mean, you can't…" He was close to tears himself, then he snapped out of it. "We're all here to teach the pricks who are doing this to our friends a lesson they won't forget." He jabbed his finger with his whole arm behind it at the house. "I suggest, right now, we take a can of gasoline and burn this fucking place to the ground!"

People in the crowd looked at each other. Bailey took two steps, tugged on Niall's sleeve and Niall leant away from the microphone. They conferred. You could see Niall off-mic talking with annoyance at being interrupted, then with an oh-I-didn't-know-that look on his face as he was re-briefed. He leant back to the mic. "Everything I've said before?" he said. "Well, what I meant to say of course was…that's just the sort of prickish thing *they* would be saying. What *we're* here for is to defend the right of our friends to stay here, and any prick who wants to come in and take away their home for the sake of some friggin' park is gonna have to come through us first!"

The crowd whistled and applauded, even Fergie.

"Boys," said Niall, "let's give 'em 'My Love Has To The Lowlands Gone.'"

It was an unaccompanied sea-shanty in three-part harmony, and a beautiful tale. Love was the cause of grief, but was worth it. I almost wept again.

11

"The great thing about being from some shithole back-water in the sticks," said Wallace, "is that the competition is so lame."

"If I were you I wouldn't bring that up in your opening remarks," said Bailey.

"Don't worry. I'm gonna give 'em my stirring message to the grassroots."

"A clarion of hope for these troubled times?"

"A grand oration to make the welkin ring."

We were in the truck on the way to the All Parties Debate at the Barrisway Legion. Robbie and Brucie were riding in the back with Melissa, I was in the front with Wallace and Bailey. Three days had passed since the picnic and things were getting interesting on the electoral front. Bailey kept saying that there seemed to be a growing groundswell of support out there, but when anybody asked for specifics, he'd just say "Never mind. We'll see." Robbie and Brucie would mention that somebody or other had asked them about Wallace, and since the picnic, while working door-to-door, Wallace had been met with courtesy and curiosity.

I think I may have been partly responsible for all this. A story had spread about how at the picnic a mentally deranged and battered orphan boy (who out of the kindness of his heart Wallace had taken into his home and cared for) had burst into tears in public at the thought of being dispossessed by those heartless bastards in government.

As we approached the Legion, we saw a sea of cars and pick-up trucks parked side to side and nose to nose. And still there was a line-up both sides of the road coming in.

"It seems that you're a draw, Wallace," said Bailey.

We all looked wide-eyed at the crowd, but when I glanced at Wallace I saw his eyes staring with something I'd never seen before.

"What's wrong?" said Bailey.

"What...do I *do*?" Wallace said. "All these people..."

"This part's easy. It's just a meet and greet. The petting zoo. I'll go park, you go mingle. Chat 'em up. Shake hands, kiss babies. Make your presence felt."

"But..."

"You'll get the hang of it," said Bailey. "Brucie, you go with him. You too, Christian. And remember to look pathetic. It seems to work for you. Ah!" he added, as if he'd been missing this. "The killing floor!"

Wallace took one step out of the truck, wobbling.

"Hey, Wallace!" said somebody in the crowd. Strangers looked around.

"Wallace! How you doing?" said somebody else.

"There he is!" said another.

"How's it going, Wallace? Ready for the big debate?" Smiling, greeting people were all over the place. He smiled back and nodded but it was as if he didn't recognize anybody.

A groundswell indeed had been building out there. Something Wallace had said or done, or more likely a combination of a lot of little things, had created a buzz. He had clicked. But from his point of view, it was a nightmare, or some neurological condition like The Old Hag where he was locked inside his consciousness, regarded but unable to regard. As I looked at his face, I thought: This is what fame is. This is what the media does to you. Our politicians and the people we go to for our public information, under their assured and acquired style, this is the terror in their lives.

"MacAkern!" yelled a no-nonsense stranger in a straw fedora and suspenders, striding toward him. "If you get in, I want you to see about my driveway. There's a huge pothole right where it joins the main road, so it's government jurisdiction, I've checked, and I've written four letters for Chrissakes, but nobody cares. Now, I don't plan to vote for you. Christ, I got screwed over by your uncle so bad once it's unlikely I'd ever vote for anybody in your family, that's for sure. And it's not likely that anything you could do or say could convince me otherwise, but still, just in case you do win, I'd like your promise that you'll do something about that goddamn pothole. Would ya? Would ya give me your word on that, here in front of all these people?"

Wallace smiled back. "How ya doing?" he squeaked.

"Fine. Now, will ya do that for me?"

"Hi," said Wallace and held out his hand again.

The man looked at him more closely. "What the hell's wrong with you?"

"It's his voice," I said. "He's got a touch of laryngitis, and he wants to save it for the debate. But I know that he will address your problem personally as soon as he is in the position to do so. Vote Wallace MacAkern."

"All right then," said the man and he moved away.

"G-g-good one, Christian."

A mother with three daughters in tow came up.

"Give 'em hell, Wallace. I saw you on the tube, and it's high time somebody shook these bastards up."

"Hi," croaked Wallace.

"Sorry," I said. "With all the speaking engagements and public demands on his time, Mr. MacAkern has developed a mild case of laryngitis, so he has to save his voice for the debate. It should be a good one, don't you think?"

"We're hoping," said the lady. "And lemonade and honey's best for the throat. We'll leave you, then. Be sure to crucify them for me, though, will you, Wallace?"

I took Wallace by the arm and we stepped around back of a van and away from the crowd.

Bailey rejoined us with Robbie and Melissa.

"Give me a cigarette," said Wallace.

"You don't smoke."

"I'm gonna start."

"What's wrong?"

"Full house."

"That's a good thing, Wallace."

"Jesus."

"*I* see." said Bailey. "So, it's stage fright..."

"It's not stage fright," said Wallace, peeved in a way I'd never seen him. "Why do you say it's stage fright? It's just... I've got this sudden deep terror in the pit of my stomach that I'm heading for a pointless and crushing public humiliation."

"In that case, I'm sorry. It's *not* stage fright then. Look, Wallace, what you're feeling is perfectly natural..."

"Natural? *Natural*? This is anything but...My God. I can't breathe."

"Of course you can breathe," said Bailey. "Inhale. Exhale. Sssssssss.....Again...Good...Now. Better?"

"No."

"It will have to do. A lot of people have gone to the trouble to come here tonight..."

"Yeah...to *laugh* at me."

"No. To hear you debate."

"Why? What have *I* ever done? I'm a loser. I've always been a loser. I'm a useless mound of crap. Everything I do is a failure. I got nothing to say to anybody. I just want to crawl away somewhere and die. They can have our house and land, I don't care. Oh Christ. I'm gonna join a monastery, though they probably wouldn't let me in. I'm a liar and I don't go to church..."

"You went to church last week."

"Yeah. To get *votes*. Christ, This is awful. What they're saying about me and Smooth Lennie is true. We're the same. Why the fuck did I ever get involved in this. Why? *Why?*"

"You can't back out now."

"I can so. That's what I do. Back out of things."

"Come on, Wallace," said Robbie. She took him by the hand and pulled him out from behind the van. "It's like Robert the Bruce and the spider. You gotta reach deep down within yourself and come out laying about with your claymore at the English bastards to win the battle for Scotland."

"*Fuck* Scotland!" said Wallace, probably more loudly than he intended. From around him heads turned, and three men in kilts who were coming toward him stopped and, offended, turned on their heels and strode off.

"Wallace," Bailey grabbed him by the shoulders and pushed back under cover. "Best not to say anything now."

"I told everybody he had laryngitis," I said.

"Good. Stay with that story. Melissa, Robbie, go get some

scotch. Come on, Wallace. We're going up to the hall."

Robbie and Melissa went back to the truck. We walked alongside the parking lot where there was nobody and around the side of the Barrisway Legion, past a CBC truck where large pythons of electric cables coiled out and ran in the side door of the building, which we entered.

The doors and windows were all wide open, but it was still hot inside the Legion hall. There were maybe thirty people standing around in the room, which was set up with auditorium chairs under fluorescent light, and was constructed with a stage set into the far end with a door to go behind on either side. It was the kind of room that any amount of festive decoration would only make sadder, but there was no decoration tonight, only campaign posters of the candidates and on one wall a large photograph of Robert Logan Head, smiling paternally. Apparently, the Conservatives had some pull with the poster-hanging committee. The remaining walls of the Legion were hung with framed photographs, mostly black and white pictures of soldiers, but also a few more florid colour snaps of older drunken ex-army types holding trophies and laughing. Queen Elizabeth was prominently displayed in a colourized portrait which probably came from one of the British holdings in the South Pacific, as Her Highness had been rendered with a distinct Polynesian cast to her facial features and colouring.

Robbie and Melissa came in with the bottle of scotch, excited. "You'll never guess what we heard!" said Robbie.

"What?"

"Robert Logan Head has hired a new political advisor."

"Ha! See, Wallace?" said Bailey. "That means we got 'em on the run."

"And guess who he got," said Robbie.

"Who?"

"Leo Murdoch."

"Who?"

"Perhaps it might ring a bell if you knew what pen name he sometimes goes by: Ward Morris?"

Wallace looked up and found his voice. "Ward Morris? The guy who wrote...Just a second. You're saying that Robert Logan Head has hired Ward Morris as his campaign manager?"

"Yes. But..." Robbie looked worried that she might have said the wrong thing.

Wallace sat down in an empty chair and stared at a point in the floor, then put his hands to his head. "*Fuck!*" he howled.

"Come along, Sonny," said a mother who had approached with her six-year-old, turning on her heel and clicking away.

"I thought you'd *like* the idea..." said Robbie.

"I'm sure Robbie's mistaken," said Bailey. "And even if what she says is true, all that means is, well, it means we know how he thinks, anyhow. And how would the electorate like to know that Robert Logan Head has hired someone like Ward Morris? Eh?"

"They wouldn't know who he was."

"Then it's up to you to educate them ," said Bailey. "No, the more I think about it, the more I believe this is perfect. All those quotes you've memorized? I want you to have 'em handy, to show the voters what we're dealing with here. But I want you to save it for the time it will do the most damage, Wallace...Wallace, are you listening?"

"They're going to slaughter us," said Wallace.

"Pull yourself together!"

"We've lost! Jesus, Jesus *Jesus*..."

"Snap out of it, Wallace."

"I can't."

"Wallace! Look at me. Now! You are going to...Look at me!...You are going to meet the opposition, shake hands like a gentleman, retire to your corner and when the bell rings, you are going to come out and kick the living shit out of him. Got it?"

"I..."

There was movement by the front door. At the opposite end of the hall from where we were, the growing crowd parting and reforming after him like the waters of the Red Sea, Robert Logan Head entered. With his two aides behind him, a younger man like a secret service agent and, shadowing his left shoulder like his familiar, an immaculately dressed wraith of advanced age, he began glad-handing his way around the room, clearly enjoying himself. He worked the crowd like a master, spoke a few words to a grandmother, moved to a family of five, while everyone else in the room arrayed themselves into a reception line like iron filings along his magnetic field. Taking all this as his due, Head moved from group to group, saying something personal to each without breaking rhythm or causing offense. Then he moved on, a busy man working for your good, leaving you feeling lucky to have had the few words he could spare out of his busy schedule of helping you, the voter. His face was immaculately shaved, his hair groomed and sculpted. He was bathed, scented and probably massaged. He was looking both sharp and relaxed.

Wallace on the other hand was a quivering wreck, sweating buckets and breathing hard, face red and hands shaking. Wearing his father's church jacket, too tight around the shoulders, and a pair of check pants, too short by an inch, which he had convinced himself might look casual and down-to-earth, but now only seemed laughable. His stage-fright was crippling in itself, but with the actual sight of his opponent, I saw his core confidence start to crumble.

"Follow me," said Bailey. "Melissa, Robbie, Brucie, save us seats up front." He led Wallace to the door beside the stage and we stepped in and up a small set of stairs to the backstage area.

"Give me some marijuana," said Wallace.

"No fucking way," said Bailey. "That stuff will rot your brain. Have some scotch." He unscrewed the cap of the bottle and Wallace grabbed it and gulped.

"Whoa! Enough!" said Bailey as he wrestled it back away from him. "Now, listen to me, Wallace. Are you listening? That bastard is out there right now, smiling and shaking hands and being friendly and amusing, but make no mistake, what he is doing is *castrating* you. Slowly. With a rusty knife. Carefully sawing off your testicles. And when he has done that, he will cast them under his heels and flamenco-dance them into a fine puree to spoon-feed them to you, in public, as the rest of the world looks on laughing. Got it?"

"I know…"

"Unless you screw him to the wall first."

"It's over."

"It's *not* over. Are you listening?" Bailey hauled back and slapped Wallace hard on the face.

"I deserved that," said Wallace.

"You didn't deserve that. Jesus! You should have kicked the shit out of me for that!" Bailey, for the first time, looked worried.

Then the door opened behind us and "Hello!" said the cheery voice of Robert Logan Head. He stepped in and up, accompanied, still behind his shoulder, by Leo Murdoch.

This leather-faced *éminence grise*, eyes masked behind dark glasses, looked, up close, as old as Methelusah, although every cosmetic aid, including undoubtedly long and expensive bouts of plastic surgery, had been employed to carve years off his body and face, or at least make him look human. It hadn't worked. His hair was dyed a coppery colour which doesn't exist in nature, and the top of his head had been replanted with hair-plugs like marram grass on a dune. A partial comb-over from just north-east of his right ear flipped and plastered over the remaining bald spot, completing his Tribute to Bad Hair, and his teeth were false and fitted oversized to force his lips into something away from the habitual sneer you could tell was his default expression. Under good lighting and with the right makeup, seen through gauze from a distance, all this might shave a week off his apparent age, but as it was, here and now, it only served to highlight his desperate seniority. He looked like Faust after the Devil had come to collect, as if any vital energy he possessed was created by some massive spiritual meltdown which had been happening since birth and sustained by God-knows what? Alcohol? Drugs? New transfusions administered in his subterranean vault below the Parliament buildings where ritual sacrifice of innocents were performed to feed him their sustaining lifeblood? Anything was possible with that face.

He whispered into the ear of Robert Logan Head, who acknowledged with a nod, and looked at Wallace, who was sitting, staring down and away, too afraid to look.

"I hope I'm not interrupting anything," said Head. "I saw you duck in here and thought I'd come and introduce myself. I mean, obviously we find ourselves on the opposite sides of this election, as well as many other individual issues, but we are after all living in a civilized democracy and I see no reason why we shouldn't behave to each other as respected colleagues rather than opponents."

"Go fuck yourself you slimy bastard you," said Bailey. "We

will personally eat you up raw and vomit you back into the sewer that spawned you."

Robert Logan Head didn't bat an eye. "What I mean to say," he continued, "is that apart from the political differences which beset us, and are bound to beset any two opposing forces in a healthy democracy, I still harbour a great respect for both what you stand for and the manner in which you have run your excellent campaign so far."

"You prick-faced dick-wad. We'll crush your eyeballs and feed them to the jackals. We will rip out your intestines, and strangle you with them, then bash in your brains with your own severed arm," said Bailey.

"Ah. Well. At least I tried the civilized approach."

"We will step on your nuts and eat your organs raw."

"Yes, yes. I catch the drift," said Robert Logan Head, with the first trace of mild annoyance, "but I think you might find it somewhat difficult to do any of those things you so glibly threaten, Mr. Bailey James Hendershott, from prison." He looked into Bailey's eyes, and now his voice had the edge of a low menacing hiss.

"How do you...my name?" stuttered Bailey.

"We have friends. On both sides of the border. And your cohort Aiden has been most forthcoming with photographs of you flagrantly flaunting the laws of our land. Or am I mistaken? Please feel free to correct me if I am wrong."

"Oh *fuck*," whimpered Bailey. He looked at Robert Logan Head in fear and awe and backed two steps into the shadows, wilting.

"And so, if you don't mind, let me at least *introduce* myself to Wallace MacAkern. I am Robert Logan Head. And this is my campaign manager, Leo Murdoch."

Making a humiliating, subservient effort, Wallace, who had been looking pathetically at the ground the whole time, raised his head, while he held out his limp paw, a wan smile on his face that as much as said, "Please don't hurt me." You could almost see him tug his forelock as his head swung up and he stole a humble glance at Leo Murdoch.

There was a rattling sound behind me and I looked to see Bailey, still backing away, knock over some brooms in the corner.

And when I looked back at Wallace, something was different. He seemed to have stiffened from the inside, straightened up to his full height and was now clasping firmly the hand of Robert Logan Head. I had missed something.

"Hello," said Wallace with strange new confidence. I guessed that, with his friend under threat, he must have somehow rallied and found strength.

"I'm sorry," said Robert Logan Head. "Have you two met?" And he indicated Leo Murdoch.

"I feel like I have," said Wallace, as though to an equal. "I *loved* your book! You're Ward Morris, aren't you? That's your pseudonym?"

Leo Murdoch was about to say something else, but Robert Logan Head put his hand up to field the question. "Why, yes he is, and you are, of course, referring to that parody of the Ottawa political process which he wrote a few years ago? That humourous satire on what *not* to do. That fictional account?"

"Precisely," said Wallace.

"Can you believe that some people not only took that book seriously but actually tried to use it to defame the campaign of one of the candidates he was advising last year? Do you remember that little scandal? No? Well, why should you? A small glitch in an unimportant by-election, quickly squelched by threats of a lawsuit and in fact showing them up as a group of backwoods low-rent hicks with about as many qualifications for leadership as so many swamp leeches. Awful isn't it, this game we're in? Well, best not to take it personally." He sighed at the imperfection of the world.

"I can see you're learning his lessons well," said Wallace. "That's pure Ward Morris right there. Deflection. How to return a threat. Chapter 6. Classic! But you misunderstand me if you think I plan to use that book as some sort of weapon in this debate." He turned to Leo. "I have far too much respect for you as a writer and artist to stoop to such tactics, Mr. Ward Morris... Or Mr. Leo Murdoch. Which do you prefer?

"Leo is fine," said himself, hoarse-voiced.

"Very well," said Wallace. "Leo. I'll make a mental note of that. I'm awful with names! Leo is the name you are going by. Got it. And thank you, Leo. I'm your biggest fan."

"You're welcome."

"Although, I may be lying," said Wallace. "Which is what you do after all advise in that book of yours."

"That satire, yes," said Robert Logan Head.

"Yes indeed."

Everybody paused. "Well, that's done," said Head, a little put-out by not fully understanding what had just gone on. "It's best if there are no hard feelings, don't you think?"

"Indubitably," said Wallace. "Let the best man win." He sounded sincere, looking deeply into Robert Logan Head's eyes and taking his hand in both of his. Then Head and Leo backed away, smiling and nodding, watching Wallace the whole time until they had left through the door they had entered and which now closed after them.

"Those pricks..." said Bailey.

"Don't worry," said Wallace, still smiling.

"What do you mean, 'don't worry'? I'm looking at extradition and ten to fifteen in Norfolk. I can't do this anymore, Wallace, I gotta pull out..."

I heard him start to slip back into a frightened version of his Caribbean accent. His spine had become cartilage, his voice a whine.

"Of course you won't pull out."

"I got to".

"Don't worry," said Wallace.

A bell rang outside, and, having found strength from somewhere, Wallace said, "That's us," and walked back down the steps and out the door into the large crowd who had gathered by now in the hall.

I don't know where it had gone, but the stage-fright had disappeared completely, replaced by a calm acceptance and joy of battle, like Arjuna in his chariot, filling him like wind in a sail.

"What's happening, Wallace..?" I asked, but I was interrupted.

"Feeling better now?" said the loud man in the straw fedora from before. "Because if you are, I want to tell you again, I'm *not* going to vote for you, like I said, and I want to be clear about that right up front, but if you do get in, I want you to look into that pothole for me."

"Let me get this right. You're *not* going to vote for me?"

"No."

"Then fuck off," said Wallace, still smiling, and he turned and left, leaving the loud man speechless.

I followed Wallace around the room as he shook hands and said hello to as many as he could. He did the complete circuit, waving and smiling at anyone out of reach. When he got to the front of the stage, he climbed the steps at a run, and I sat down in a seat that Brucie had been saving on the far side of Robbie and Melissa. On stage the moderator, who turned out to be Ben Malone, was speaking to Wallace and Robert Logan Head. Although not audible over the babble of the crowd to anyone else in the room, the microphones on the podiums picked up just enough for me to hear what was being said, through the loudspeaker I found myself sitting beside.

"The other candidates haven't showed up yet, which is goddamned unprofessional, if you ask me," said Ben Malone. "But we're going out live on the radio two minutes from now and can't have any dead air, so we're going to start with just you two. When I call your name, just take a bow. We'll take it from there." He looked at his watch and moved to the front of the stage and the babble and hum died down.

"Good evening ladies and gentlemen and welcome to the All-Candidates Debate for Barrisway riding. It seems that Liberal candidate Dwayne Evans and NDP candidate Shiela Cudmore haven't showed up, and we have somebody out trying to contact them now as we speak. Nevertheless, we can start the debate with Mr. Head and Mr. MacAkern. There will be an opening speech from each of the candidates lasting five minutes, and then a face-to-face, and for want of a better word, a free-for-all." The audience chuckled. "Both candidates will then take questions from the floor. Mr. MacAkern, as challenger to the incumbent, will go first. Any questions?"

Wallace spoke up. "I would just like to take the opportunity to send out a big hello to the Arsenaults over there in the back, a family who came over with my grandmother Monique Taillefer on the same boat from France. Claude, Gerry and Bridget! How are the kids?"

At the back of the hall the Arsenaults looked up and flushed under the attention, unaware till now of this connection with Wallace, which was understandable considering that it was entirely fabricated for the occasion.

"Very good, Mr. MacAkern," said Ben Malone. "And now, if you would be so kind as to come to the podium, I will tell you when to start your opening remarks."

Robert Logan Head, seated with a clipboard on his knee, drew out from his inside pocket reading glasses and put them on his nose, then extracted an expensive looking pen, removed the cap and looked up, ready to take notes. Wallace stood up and walked empty-handed to the podium.

"First, then, we will hear from independent candidate Wallace MacAkern." There was applause, then quiet. "I'm starting your three minutes...now."

"What you're all here for," said Wallace, "is the *debate*." He looked around for agreement and seemed to receive it. "And I have far too much respect for your time to waste it with the usual political platitudes. (I'll let my honourable opponent supply those.) So what do you say we let him drone on for a bit, then we'll get to the good stuff?" And he turned, walked back and sat down.

Ben Malone got to his feet. "All right, then...And...my, that was fast, Mr. MacAkern. Mr. Head, are you ready?"

Robert Logan Head had been taken off-guard. He fumbled with his papers and the reading glasses around his neck.

"Need some help?" said Wallace.

"No, no," said Head. He got to his feet, dropped a paper, picked it up, walked to the podium, coughed and took a drink of water. Ben Malone introduced him and he received applause.

"As any Islander will tell you," he started, "Islanders have a long history of helping fellow Islanders. It's the Island way. And on the Island, as all Islanders know, any fellow Islander, be they from the west of the Island or the centre of the Island or here on the dear eastern part of the Island, well, if Islanders know anything, they know that the Island is above all our home. On the last Island Day, do you know where I was?"

"The mainland?" said Wallace loudly. There was laughter.

Ben Malone made to intervene but Robert Logan Head answered back, "No, Mr. MacAkern. I was on the Island."

"Which one? Bermuda?" said Wallace, which struck home neatly. Two winters before, when PEI was snowbound after a massive storm, Robert Logan Head had sent a television message to his constituents saying that he wished he was back on PEI at this time to help out. The message was sent from an oak-lined room which was strongly implied to have been in Ottawa, but as it turned out the segment had been videotaped in the Governor's mansion in Bermuda, where Head was vacationing. When this was revealed there were strong anti-Head mutterings on the Island, and the name "Bermuda Bob" had started to gain currency.

"No interruptions, Mr. MacAkern," said Ben Malone.

"Sorry, Ben," said Wallace. "This is my first debate."

I looked at the crowd. Everybody in the room was smiling. And I understood something about Wallace then, the source of his political capital: people liked him.

"The candidate will refrain from further commenting."

"Absolutely," said Wallace. Which he absolutely refrained from doing, although as soon as Head started to speak again, Wallace's body language yelled volumes. Within thirty seconds of Robert Logan Head's starting in again on his speech, Wallace had adopted a look of accepting patience, which gradually turned to an expression that said that with all the good-will in the world, he found it impossible to pay attention to such non-stop thudding boredom and frankly unbelievable nonsense. He looked at his watch, held it to his ear to see if it was possible that it was still running. He shook it, tapped it, then assumed that it was doing its job and forgot about it, folding his arms and adopting a mildly contemptuous air. After a few heavy sighs, Wallace then slumped in his chair, crossed his legs, re-crossed them, adjusted his position a few more times, then opened his jaw and moved it around like a boa constrictor swallowing a sheep, in a yawn that threatened to suck out all the oxygen in the room. Finished, he settled back, folded his arms again, leant his chin against his chest, and started blinking rapidly as though only a monumental effort of the will was keeping him awake. Then he seemed to succumb to the inevitable, and you could see him lose the battle with himself, close his eyes for several moments, snap them open, try to pull himself together, find it impossible, and then close his eyes finally as though for good. There were stirrings in the audience as they wondered whether they should wake him up, but just as attention was shifting back away from this beautifully executed sideshow toward Robert Logan Head, a snore like ripping canvas shook the hall, and seemed to wake Wallace himself. Audience, Ben Malone and Head all turned to look at him. "Sorry," said Wallace. "Continue."

"No, that's all I have to say," said Robert Logan Head, his big tag line at the end of his speech ruined.

Wallace got to his feet and approached the podium. He looked at the audience. He looked at Robert Logan Head. "Fascinating speech," he said, and the audience tittered.

"Now," said Ben Malone. "If Mr. Head would approach the other podium we can move to the one-on-one portion of the debate starting with a question from Mr. Head."

"I would like to ask Mr. MacAkern why he is even running, since anybody that votes for him will be simply throwing away their vote."

"That," said Wallace, "is a circumlocutious tautology."

"It is not a...*what*?"

"In essence, all you are saying is that nobody will vote for me because nobody will vote for me. And it makes the *a priori* assumption that you will get more votes than me."

"We will."

"How do you know?"

"Historically, an independent has never won in Barrisway riding."

"Well, if that's the case, why have an election at all? I mean why not just say that since the Liberals have 'historically' won here, we should just give it to them? Are you saying that anybody who votes for the Conservatives are 'throwing away their vote'?"

"Certainly not. I'm saying..."

"Because if so, it sounds as though you have quite a bit of contempt for democracy."

"Nonsense. But Mr. MacAkern, if you are so innocent of the electoral process..."

"Innocent is exactly what I am," said Wallace. "And you, sir, are guilty of it."

I'm not sure what that meant, exactly, but it seemed to complete the exchange, and both Head and Wallace backed off from their initial parry and thrust. Ben Malone said, "Mr. MacAkern has the floor."

"I hardly know where to start," said Wallace. "But first of all, in the interest of hospitality, maybe we should say that Barrisway riding is truly honoured tonight with the presence of the Conservative campaign manager, Mr. Leo Murdoch, who amongst other things has carved out a successful career as best-selling author Ward Morris. I think it would be very welcoming if everybody were to give him a hand."

Leo Murdoch had been sitting in the shadows off to our side with his hand to his chin. He acknowledged the applause, but didn't rise, just lifted his hand as though he was too shy to do anything else, and then kept his hand up to his lower face.

"Maybe he could say a few words about how he wrote that truly fine book *So You Want To Be An MP?*"

Head broke in. "This is hardly the place to discuss what is after all a work of pure satirical fiction."

"Suit yourself. I just thought we should mention it."

"Well, if you are going to bring up our staff, I should bring up yours," said Head. "Bailey Hendershott, for instance."

"Absolutely! Bailey. Take a bow." Wallace looked out. Bailey behaved in almost exactly the same way as Murdoch.

"Particularly in light of certain rumours and allegations about him which are circulating."

"Of course those rumours are circulating. You started them!"

"Now, Mr. MacAkern, that's hardly a fair accusation."

"Neither is yours, unless you abandon the presumption of innocence. And anyway," said Wallace. "I wasn't attacking what's-his-name...Leo Murdoch, Ward Morris (I'm sorry, I'm bad with names)... As far as I know, there's nothing to attack. But since you seem intent on slagging our staff, maybe I should return the compliment by mentioning, oh I don't know, say, Barry Rattray..."

"We responded to that situation immediately and we can in no ways be held responsible for it. So let's move on."

"Suits me," said Wallace, "Although that's a bit rough on Barry isn't it? I mean where's your sense of loyalty?"

"In keeping with our tough-on-crime policy, we in the Conservative Party have no tolerance for, or loyalty to, anyone who would break the law."

"Supposing he wasn't guilty."

"I have personally reviewed the dossier and after a thorough examination of the facts I am satisfied that justice has been administered."

"Not thoroughly enough apparently. I heard that when the evidence was finally examined, it turned out the bottles were filled with nothing but brown pond water."

You could see that this new information came as a surprise to Robert Logan Head. He stopped, looked offstage at Leo Murdoch, who looked back with nothing. "Well...I'd have to look at the dossier to see about that..." said Head.

"I thought you already 'thoroughly examined' that dossier."

"As I say, we'll have to look into the matter."

"So there we have it," said Wallace. "A perfect example of where being tough on crime gets you. A loyal employee, working in your own office, for godsakes, finds himself up on charges of buying bootleg liquor, and was immediately and falsely accused by you..."

"It was the police who..."

"...I am saying that he was falsely accused to the extent of you firing him from your organization. Where he had blamelessly volunteered out of his own free will! I mean to say, if that's what you do to your own people who are dedicating their time to try to help you, well, God help the rest of us with your tough-on-crime policy."

"Excuse me, Mr. MacAkern, but aren't you doing the same thing?"

"Same thing as what?"

"Aren't you now making unfounded accusations about us?"

"So you admit that it was an unfounded accusation?"

"What was?"

"Your insinuations about my good friend and campaign

manager Bailey Hendershott.

Head took a deep breath and backed off. "Insinuations?" he said. "I was merely trying to make the point that....Look. Forget the rumours..."

"Yes. Let's."

"...And move on to some more important topic."

"Like what?"

"Like jobs, the number one priority of our Government, whose very campaign slogan is 'Jobs, jobs, jobs.'"

"And if you create two more you'll have filled your mandate?"

This got a laugh from everybody except Robert Logan Head.

"Very humourous, Mr. MacAkern, but I imagine you wouldn't find it so funny if you were one of the unemployed."

"I *am* one of the unemployed," said Wallace.

"Yeah, well, if you...were..." You could see him trying to bluster his way out of the hole he had dug, and he went on the attack. "If you're too lazy to try to get work..." and then realized what he was saying. Too late. He looked at Leo Murdoch, who looked back, absolutely still.

"Oh? 'Lazy' is it?" said Wallace. "So that's the reason the unemployment figures are so high? We're too 'lazy'. It's *our* fault that the jobs aren't here? Take note, my friends," he addressed the audience. "They promise the jobs, they get jobs themselves by claiming that there will be jobs, but when the jobs aren't there, it's *we* who are too 'lazy' to find them. We just aren't looking hard enough. Apparently what we should be doing is hopping into our cars (which we all own thanks to the huge pay-cheques we've all been receiving), then taking the ferry across to the mainland to New Brunswick where jobs grow on trees, oh, no, that's not true. I remember now. Moncton riding, thanks to the Conservative candidate there, has a job market which is about the same as ours, and so I guess we'll have to continue down the highway to Fredericton, where, oops! Same thing, sorry. It seems we're going to have to keep moving up the Saint John Valley until Edmundston and then Riviere-du-Loup where the numbers *are,* in fact, slightly higher, but then *they* elected an independent candidate, Manny Poirier, if I'm not mistaken. No, Mr. Head. I was up at six this morning preparing for this debate (although I was not paid to do so, as you were), because thanks to eight years of Conservative and Liberal misrule, it is, in this way only, that I at least have a twenty-five percent chance of getting a job, which is better than what your mismanagement of the Island economy has delivered to the 'dear eastern side of the Island.'" There was some applause but Wallace did not act in any way triumphant. "Thank you," he said to the audience, and then as though with great grace, he added, "But I don't want to demonize my respected colleague, the Right Honourable Richard Logan Head..."

"Robert," corrected Head. It wasn't much, a minor slip, but you could see Head wondering if he could use it as part of a handhold to start climbing back.

Wallace didn't seem to register. "I reiterate, I have nothing personally against Richard Logan Head..."

"That's *Robert,*" said Head, his eyes brightening a little. Wallace, as he had just admitted, had always had a problem with names, but it was beginning to get embarrassing as he ploughed on unlistening.

"It's the policies that Richard is espousing that are so damaging to the already fragile Island economy."

"Robert," corrected Head again with a well-played concern that perhaps we were dealing with some sort of serious mental defective. The audience glanced at each other too.

"But as to the point you're trying to make, I, of course, disagree."

"As is your right, under that most sacred of documents, the Canadian Bill of Rights, which is after all the basis of our society, along with civil discourse, without which the tenor of politics is lowered, the quality of debate is debased, language is corrupted, and wit becomes non-existent." As his words took on a life of their own, Wallace straightened up, seemingly unaware of the subtle shift in power away from him. "When I am elected Member of Parliament for Barrisway riding, let me pledge here, that if I can do one service to my constituency and to the Canadian people it will be to bring back to Parliament the grand old days when people followed what was happening in their country partly, of course, because it affected their lives, but also because it was where the most *sense* was on display. Wouldn't that be a good thing, Richard?" said Wallace. "I hope I can call you Richard?.."

"Robert..."

"...There's no reason why we should be enemies, is there? I may despise what you stand for while still considering you, as a human being, a friend and colleague. And so I extend my hand and let me say, please, call me Wallace. Or why not let's be even more familiar? Call me Wally..." and he held out his hand... "And please allow me to call you my good friend, Richard..."

"Excuse me..." Robert Logan Head started, smiling openly now in anticipation of the blow he was about to deliver, but Wallace marched on, cutting him off.

"...No," he corrected himself, "that's still not familiar enough. Let me here, for the sake of the good-will upon which our society rests, publicly shake your hand and call you my good friend...Dick Head."

You could have heard a pin drop. Nobody breathed. The only faint sound was through the walls of the Legion and the intervening space beside the building where, from the not-quite-soundproof-enough Mobile Media Truck, there erupted muffled joyful yelps of disbelief at what they had just heard.

On stage, Wallace stood innocently with his hand out, and The Right Honourable Robert Logan Head, with a sallow smile on his face, wondering what had just happened to him, extended his hand tentatively and took Wallace's in a weak clasp. Wallace played it beautifully, with a bland waiting smile of innocence, absolutely sure that he was doing the gentlemanly thing.

"That's Robert," Head corrected.

"Sorry?" Wallace asked politely.

"My name is Robert."

"What did I call you?" Wallace was all contrition, lest he have committed some unpardonable *faux pas*.

"You called me 'Dick.'"

"Excuse me?"

"'Dick!' You called me 'Dick Head.'"

"Dick Head?" repeated Wallace

"Yes! Now, let's..."

"I don't think so. Did I?" he looked out at the audience who were nodding and smiling, understanding exactly what he was doing.

"Yes. Dick Head! You called me that."

Wallace looked convincingly befuddled. "Robert it is then." And in a stage whisper that everybody could hear, he muttered to nobody in particular. "A bit sensitive, isn't he?"

It was very infantile, and extremely effective.

A fissure appeared in Robert Logan Head's smooth façade, and I glimpsed a scorpion in his eyes as he withdrew the next knife from his sheath.

"Your uncle, correct me if I'm wrong, is Lennie MacAckern?"

At the mention of the name the mood of the room shifted suddenly and a low seething mutter emitted from the audience. Wallace didn't even seem to hear it.

"Smooth Lennie?" he said. "That old bastard (excuse my French). Everybody still wonders what happened to him. He still owes money to more than one person around here, myself included."

"But let me get this right. He is your uncle?"

"Sure. Or was. Like I say. Nobody knows what happened to him. You wouldn't happen to have heard, would you?"

"Of course not."

"I ask because some said he went to Bermuda. I thought you might have met him there."

"And others said he went to Monte Carlo. Or Tangiers, Bangkok, or Las Vegas..."

"There's a worse rumour than that," said Wallace.

"Really?"

"Yes. I heard he went to Ottawa."

Which not only got a laugh, but some applause. Wallace was back on top.

"But let me make my point..." said Head.

"Go right ahead."

"Well, he *is* your uncle..."

"You heard me."

"Well..?" Head left the question hang until Wallace seemed to grasp what he was asking.

"Oh. I see what you're driving at. That because I am related to him he somehow transmitted to me his...what? Aberrant political behaviour gene?"

"You said it, not me."

"Well, I don't want to be guilty of misrepresenting your position."

"Fine then. For the sake of argument, let's consider that possibility."

"Fine then, for the sake of argument, we should also consider the possibility that if behaviour of any kind is an inherited trait, then I would have to also allow that I was genetically instilled with the let's call it "behavioural DNA" of the courageous Wilf MacAkern (there's a picture of him over there on the wall), killed at Mons, July 15th 1916 with the Abegweit Light Infantry. Or Luke Taillefer, over there on the wall, sniper, DSO.... Should I go on?"

"I don't think it's necessary to..."

"Well, I'd like to, if you don't mind, since you brought it up, you understand..."

"That's all right...." said Head.

"Audience?" asked Wallace.

"I want to hear," said someone in the front.

"You go ahead, Wallace," said El'ner Beardsley, offended that Head was trying to rob her of some important information that Wallace might have. And it seemed to be an opinion supported throughout the crowd by widespread grunts of agreement and affirmative nodding of heads. So Wallace launched into an expanded version of one of the points we had argued thoroughly in our practice debates.

"Because," continued Wallace, "the pernicious suggestion that genes determine character would mean that you would be somehow tainted with your own father's blood, Lionel Head (a much closer relative than Smooth Lennie was ever to me I might add), who was trumped out of the New Brunswick Legislature in 1956 for what was it? Suspicious activity surrounding a certain Saint John wharf scandal if I'm not mistaken? Or was it the Richibucto lobster license scandal or the crab fisheries scandal (one of those scandals, they're almost too many to list with Lionel). Or The Shediac Bridge kickbacks or the Miramachi Salmon Lodge weekend giveways? But I would certainly never claim that that was the case, (not that those scandals didn't take place. Oh no! There was hell to pay). What I mean to say is that I would never claim that the deep personal connection to your own father has any genetic influence on your behaviour at all (although being raised in a household where that was the culture is another question). No. I believe that our fate dear Brutus is not in our genes but in ourselves, to coin a phrase. And if you believe that genes do determine ethical behaviour, then it seems you are in agreement with Herr Adolph Hitler, who my other much closer relative Eugene MacAkern died fighting against during the Battle of Falaise in 1942. If you'd like to confirm, check that plaque out on the wall there, right next to the Queen."

He waited for Head's response.

Head coughed once. "Precisely my sentiments on the question of inherited traits..." said Head, beating a hasty and ugly retreat. "And...I...my father...well...our family never...It doesn't matter...though I, for one, think our armed forces are doing a *great* job...don't you, audience..?" This appeal didn't raise a single clap of the hands. The audience waited.

Leo Murdoch looked concerned. You couldn't see his eyes, but he was as motionless as that rabbit I had seen in the dunes that day, just before I'd met Rattray.

"No," continued Wallace. "We choose our own fate as we choose who we associate with and the people we work with. Assuming we have a job (which is unlikely ever to be the case if you get re-elected). You didn't choose your father, "Tricky" Lionel Head (to recall only the most polite of his nick-names), and I didn't choose Smooth Lennie (who was after all my mother's sister's husband, and no blood relative anyway).

"Well, of course I agree..."

Then Wallace pulled the pin on his grenade. "You did, though," he said.

"What...do you mean?" said Head.

"Your campaign manager. You chose him to work for you."

"Yes, but...who? Leo Murdoch?"

"Yes. Leo Murdoch. Also known as Ward Morris."

"Yes. But if you're saying that comic satire of his in any way is..."

"I'm not saying anything about that book at all."

"Well then?"

"What I'm saying is that Leo Murdoch AKA Ward Morris..." Wallace paused.

"Yes?"

"Also goes (does he not?) by the name of... Smooth Lennie MacAkern."

The name dropped into the room like a bomb. Everybody looked over with intensely focused interest at the man who claimed to be called Leo Murdoch. His eyebrows above his dark glasses rose and a blush of fear flushed through his phoney tan. He rose part way from his seat.

"How's it going, Uncle Lennie?" said Wallace. "What you been up to?"

Then all hell broke loose. A chair squealed. Somebody shrieked.

"He owes me money," yelled Dunbar, standing up in the back and pointing. In an amazed pause like the eye of a hurricane passing over, where everything goes silent before hitting with just as much force from the opposite direction, Smooth Lennie stood up and quickly walked out the side door of the building.

The crowd rose, looked around and started to swarm out the front, and we dodged out the side door and up toward the parking lot. By the time we got there a reporter from the CBC truck was following Smooth Lennie just as he was stepping into the limo, urgently telling the driver, "Get out of here! Get *out* of here *now*..." The door closed and the motor started up as the crowd reached the car and as it spun out of the driveway someone pounded on the trunk with his fist. The car rolled onto the pavement and everybody stood around watching it disappear down the coast road.

When it was out of sight, everybody looked at each other, then turned toward the front door of the Legion where Robert Logan Head was emerging, talking rapidly and making placating movements with his hands. We all moved back toward him. Ben Malone moved up close from behind with his microphone, like a crucifix to a vampire.

"...Assuming he is, we don't know for sure. Look. I'm just as much in the dark here as you," I heard as the crowd settled down and listened.

"I'm not in the dark," said Wallace who had joined the crowd. "And I'm here to tell you, that's Lennie all right. He hid his eyes under those glasses, but I caught a glimpse of them backstage and I'd know them anywhere. Everything else...well, he's changed all that, hasn't he?"

"Let us not prejudge the situation until more information comes our way," said Head.

"If he wasn't Lennie, then why'd he leave so fast?"

"All I can say is that we'll get to the bottom of it as soon as possible, and you can't be absolutely sure that he was who you claim."

"Well, as you were so eager to point out," said Wallace, "he was my uncle."

"Yeah, that's him all right," said Dunbar.

"One of my aides has ordered a cab," explained Head to the crowd, "and as soon as it comes, the first place I will go is the riding office where I will immediately put a call through to the Conservative Party headquarters in Ottawa..."

"Think they'll want to talk to you now?" said somebody in the crowd, raising widespread rueful laughter.

"...and get to the bottom of this, rest assured. And if this bizarre story turns out to be true, somebody's head will roll."

"Yeah! Yours!" said the heckler.

"Hope it ain't somebody innocent like what's-his-name."

"Rattray," supplied someone else.

I saw Head lean over to his other aide and hiss under his breath something that could have been, "Where's that fucking cab?"

And, as though he had summoned it, the cab arrived, although it turned out to be hardly the rescue vehicle that Head had hoped for. It roared into the driveway as Head stepped down the stairs of the Legion, the crowd parting and letting him move toward it, and as it came to a skidding halt, immediately both back doors opened and a man and a woman, who I recognized from their campaign posters as being the other two candidates, got out. They strode directly to Ben Malone, who, seeing the look of anger on their faces, revolved away from Head and held the microphone to them.

"First of all, I would like to extend my deepest heartfelt apologies to the people of Barrisway riding, who I see have turned up in such numbers for this debate," said the woman. "Let me explain that I was looking forward to this gathering with great anticipation and that it was certainly our intention to be here, mine anyway, I'll let Dwayne speak for himself. But when both me and he left our offices, both in different parts of the riding, in something which cannot reasonably be considered a coincidence, we found that our tires had been punctured."

There was a melodramatic "Ooo!" from the crowd and some voice said, "Smooth Lennie rides again."

"Oh yeah," said another. "That's our Lennie, all right..."

12

As the evening sky darkened into night and the long day of the northern summer came to an end, the buzz and babble in the parking lot moved back first to the Legion hall, and then, when that closed up, the crowd finally dispersed and we went back to MacAkerns'. Before I left the Legion I checked the pictures on the wall, and for the life of me I couldn't find Wallace's Uncle Eugene, or Wilf MacAkern. But it didn't matter. Wallace had the momentum. Word was spreading and, against all odds, it was looking like he might actually win, or at least beat Robert Logan Head.

"Well done," said Bailey.

"Got lucky, is all," said Wallace.

"Or unlucky."

"What do you mean?"

"The fun part's over."

"That *was* fun, wasn't it?"

"Yeah. Now, work."

"How?"

"Win the election."

"Then what?"

"Assume power."

Wallace cocked his head to one side. "Yeah, but *then* what?" he said. Suddenly it all seemed real and possible.

"Then you serve your constituents."

"How?"

"By working with the opposition."

"But...and then what?"

"Christ, I don't know. Up the ladder. Into the system."

Wallace considered. "It seems the obvious choice."

"That it does. But don't be fooled. It comes with a price."

"I suppose so. What, exactly?"

"Exactly? I dunno. But don't kid yourself that you'll be *in* power. Nobody ever is. You're going to be in a *balance* of power. Constantly trying to outwit and set up your opponent, constantly being outwitted and set up by him, in a world where you're forced to befriend people who stabbed you in the back yesterday, and who are trying to stop from being stabbed by threatening to be the stabber and not the stabbee. Until you're double-crossing the person nearest to you."

"Aiden."

"Can't blame him really. They had something on him."

"What?"

"Same thing they had on me. Pot. I think that's why it's illegal. To give the people who make the laws something on people they want power over."

"That's ugly."

"That's power."

"Hmm."

"I always thought there was something suspicious about him," said Melissa. "Sucking up to you like he did."

"Forgive and forget," said Bailey. "And anyhow, how's what he did any different than what we've been doing? They found his weak point, and exploited it to find my weak point. Luckily Wallace found theirs and exploited that. Politics. And does it really help anything?"

"Keeps things moving."

"Yeah. Revolution. Good name for it. Around and around... Anyhow, Wallace, what's it gonna be? Cut your losses or move to the next level?"

Wallace didn't say anything, but next day, he went and visited Robert Logan Head.

***

Wallace is the hero of this story not because he slew the mighty dragon. I am of the belief now that the mighty dragon is never slain, not completely. Wallace is a hero because, lest he become the dragon itself, he used the high point he was then occupying to help the people around him. When he guessed at the things that could be given to him, when he felt the temptation of an audience who liked him, he saw at the end of those tunnels something worthless, another trap. So he traded off on what he had.

Discussions were held behind closed doors. Political aides were flown in from Ottawa, an angry group of people, publicly smiling and privately swearing, held together, it seemed to me, by the mutual fear that if they were to expose anyone in their immediate circle, secrets that were held on them would be exposed. And for all their bluster, they were helpless, having lived in that world too long to escape, locked in the same death-grip that Rattray and I had almost assumed, and would have assumed permanently if I hadn't publicly confessed.

Some new deal was worked out between Wallace and Head. First of all, Head agreed to sign an affidavit wherein it was stated that he knew but had not informed the police about Bailey's marijuana use. This ensured that if Head were ever to exploit this information again, Bailey could thereby incriminate his accuser, and so a measure of protection was afforded to Bailey, and a balance of power was achieved.

Also, when all Wallace's other "rejectables and deal-breakers" were eliminated, it was agreed that he and his family could stay on in the MacAkern home and Wallace would be hired by the park as a historical interpreter. The house would be repaired and the front parlour turned into an interpretation centre, which pleased Robbie no end, and meant she'd get her roof fixed. They could live in their house until the death of the last of them, whether it was Wallace, Robbie, or Brucie. They would each in turn receive a salary from Parks Canada as "Interpretive Officers," though nowhere near the hundred thousand a year which had been one of Wallace's original demands. If all this could be put into place before the election, Wallace would drop out of the race.

A phone call to the Minister of the Environment fast-tracked the agreement, buttons were pushed, strings were pulled, and it was done. But, as it turned out, all the wheeling and dealing was a waste of time for the Conservatives. The Liberals won the riding.

It was not long after that I saw Wallace's first historical presentation. It was questionable in its historical accuracy, but full of drama and action. His Taillefer family saga, easily as lively as his epic "Exile from Castle MacAkern," was lifted in large part from Dumas, but he also fabricated a royal connection, the Sieur de Montlouis Taillefer, who saved the Queen but was exiled as a threat to the power of Cardinal

Richelieu. The story included Acadians hiding out in the swamps up west and a family deported to Louisiana. We were all there for the performance, myself and Robbie, Melissa, Brucie, Dunbar and Fergie. Bailey, his work on the election over, was back in Rastafarian mode, his tam on his head, his smile on his face and his posture once again supple. There was a party afterwards where I drank, but only in moderation, and I didn't smoke any pot.

Afterwards, on the porch, I talked to Wallace, who adopted a tone I had never heard him use before: all seriousness. "I just want to do what I want," he said. "And not because it's me who wants it, either. It's just, people should."

"And what *do* you want, exactly?" I said.

"Fucked if I know. And if I did, I sure don't know what I might want a year from now. Or a week from now, for that matter. But I know that having this house gives me more choices to do whatever that is. That's what they're trying to take away from us, always. Freedom. What does it say about that in that Bill of Rights of yours, Christian?"

I couldn't help but notice that he used my real name.

Brucie came out from the kitchen. "I wrote a p-p-poem."

"Let's hear it," said Wallace.

Brucie straightened up and declaimed:

"Don't wanna go to England
Don't wanna go to France
Don't wanna go to Scotland
Where the people wear no pants.
Don't want to go to Charlottetown
To Rome or to Tangier
Don't wanna go
Nowhere, so
Guess I'll stay right here."

"Not bad," said Wallace. "What's this about no pants in

Scotland, though?"

"K-k-kilts."

"Ah."

***

I worked at the park for the rest of the summer, and continued to add to my beach report. I stayed out of Rattray's way, and he out of mine. My supervisor, Andrew Solomon, never showed up, though I found out that he was the one who had been responsible for the well-executed drawings in that pamphlet, which meant Claire had drawn the awful ones. I don't know why, but when I heard this, something readjusted inside me and I realized that I no longer pained for her. The knowledge diminished her, though not in any destructive way. It made her more human, and the woman I had fallen for was a fantasy. I had been like that Welsh wizard who created a wife out of flowers. At any rate, when I thought of her again, I realized I was no longer in love, or in thrall, or whatever it was that I had been in. As intense as my feelings had been for her, they had obviously been stitched together with nothing stronger than gossamer. My heart had not been broken, just bruised, like my face, and like my face, my heart healed. My hair grew back too, keeping pace with Bailey's, who stayed until Labour Day and then went back home.

The job came to an end. I finished the report and sent it to Project Ecology where it was promptly filed. I saved a copy and re-read it recently, just before I wrote the book you are reading now.

I went back to university that fall, took it more seriously, and graduated in three years. Somewhere in there I fell in love again, bruised my heart again, and it healed again, though more slowly this time.

I finished my studies and started my working life. When people ask me what I do, I always say, "The government pays me to lie around on beaches." It's not as easy as I make it sound, but try telling people that when you work for the government. My job description is Marine Biologist for Eastern Regions, and the geographical area which is my bailiwick is roughly the Gulf of St Lawrence. It's not all sand and surf. There are rock beaches on the Great Northern Peninsula and outside of Stephenville that roll great granite bowling balls under your feet, and ledges of Appalachian rock by Forillon, as well as Precambrian shelves along the Lower North Shore and up the Labrador Coast. I love them all. My *Littoral Environments On Canada's East Coast* is, I think, a respected work, albeit in a narrow field.

Of the people I worked with, some were good and some were bad, although it is probably truer to say that they were all just people, each with both good and bad in them. But of everybody I have come into contact with in the course of what is now a quite long life, nobody has ever seemed quite as vivid as who I met that summer.

Claire married. Actually she married a lot. I recently heard she is on her fifth. And apparently she's still smoking.

Smooth Lennie disappeared for good, no one knew where, and Robert Logan Head never got into power again. He also never shook off his new nickname. When he died, years later, a writer at *The Guardian* started his obituary with "The Island mourns the passing of Robert 'Dick' Head," and narrowly avoided being fired for the mistake.

Bailey, back in the States, was arrested for possession of marijuana. I believe that the drugs were planted, because at the time of his arrest he was helping organize an independent candidate who was starting to do quite well, and he never smoked pot when he was in campaign mode. He got seven years, but never served them. Two weeks into his sentence he hanged himself in his cell.

Wallace lived in the MacAkern home until his death. His last words were "Tell them that I...Ah, fuck it...See ya!" He was buried out on the point, as softening shades of evening fell, but no pipers were hired to perform that piece, which I think is a pity.

Brucie doesn't stammer anymore, and I visit him whenever I'm in the area. Usually during the course of the evenings we spend with each other we sing the one song we know together.

Robbie and Melissa continued to live with each other and eventually married. More surprisingly, so did Rattray and Toe, apparently happily, so how can you not believe in some sort of benevolent God?

I myself became religious, though not, I think, in any flashy way. I don't even go to church, because Jesus said not to. My scientific friends wonder about this spiritual side of me, but the older we get, the less we argue about it. My position is that God is the sum total of all good things, and if that's true (so go my prayers) those who don't have the knowledge of what Good is, let them be informed (that is, bless them). And those who do have that knowledge, bless them for having it. So, God bless everybody.

I went back to Barrisway last summer for the first time in years. The beach where I had set up my camp has disappeared, washed away in the tidal surge of two winters ago, which picked up all the sand, sucked it out, and in the next tide, moved it around the point where a new sandbar has appeared, a spit the shape of a billhook.

MacAkerns' house, now the Interpretation Centre, is being

slowly buried by the dune behind it, Things of God once again winning against the Things of Man. Picking of mushrooms or berries is not allowed anymore in the park, but some vegetable stands around the Island still work on the honour system.

I once knew a beach, shaped by the waves in front of the dunes that were shaped in turn by the wind. The marram grass held the sand with its roots, and in the swale behind, beach-pea grew over a jumble of driftwood. Behind that grew wild carrot and thyme and still further back, out from the floor of the spruce forest, briefly and magically the chanterelles sprang up, but if you weren't fast, you'd miss them. There was always something growing, though, each in its season, growing then dying to make room for new growth. The moon and the tides, the shape of the shore, the cry of the seabirds rising and falling. The bite of cold ocean, the taste of salt air, the tightness of sunburn, the lap of the waves, at times the memories almost overwhelm me.